The Cherokee Trail
Bent's Old Fort to Fort Bridger

The Cherokee Trail
Bent's Old Fort to Fort Bridger

Lee Whiteley

On the cover: The Cherokee Trail North Branch northwest of Saratoga, Wyoming. Looking east to the North Platte River and the Medicine Bow Mountains.

Copyright © 1999 by Lee Whiteley. All rights reserved. Cover design by Jim Krebs, photo by Lee Whiteley. Printed in the United States of America by Johnson Printing, Boulder, Colorado.

ISBN: 0-9671351-1-7

Foreword

Cherokee Indian gold seekers 150 years ago pioneered what was then--and now--Colorado's busiest highway. Travelers have long thronged this road along the eastern base of the Rocky Mountains. Starting at Bent's Fort on the Arkansas River, the Cherokee Trail runs west to Pueblo, then north along the Front Range into wild and wooly Wyoming. Some 600 miles from Bent's Fort it ends at Fort Bridger on Blacks Fork of the Green River. At Fort Bridger, Cherokee and other California-bound travelers switched to the Oregon-California Trail.

Nowadays, the Cherokee Trail has been replaced by U. S. 50, Interstate 25, and Interstate 80. On today's paved, high-speed highways, motorists travel in a day what once took nearly a month. But whether traveling now at 75 m.p.h. or then at three miles an hour, the Cherokee Trail has been a congested, colorful and cursed artery.

Named for Cherokee trailblazers, this highway is now jammed with Jeep Cherokees. So many travelers know the route that historians have taken it for granted. Oddly enough, neither the Cherokee Trail, U. S. 50, I-80 nor I-25 have attracted thorough biographers. Lee Whiteley is the right man, as you will find in these pages. His great-grandparents, John Gasper and Lucy Belle Rhudy, settled along the Cherokee Trail in Elbert County, Colorado, in 1884. The family owned the ranch until Lee's Uncle John Carroll Rhudy died in 1997.

Lee, a former Stapleton Airport computer programmer-analyst, now devotes full time to historical research and writing. He has been working on this book since 1992. Lee has been blessed with a wife who more than humors his obsession. Jane Whiteley teaches Colorado history to 4th graders in Aurora. Those nine and ten year olds hear and see a good deal of this route through Colorado's past, present and future. Some of the kids Jane teaches may live to see a median strip of light rail unclog the artery congested ever since the California Gold Rush.

In almost a decade of research, Lee and Jane have pursued the paper trail--and the real thing--from its birth at Bent's Old Fort in southeastern Colorado to its end at Fort Bridger in southwestern Wyoming. Lee, nearly always with Jane, has probed every mile of the trail--public and private--that could be inspected without inviting prosecution or bullets.

I will never forget standing with them on a remote prairie hilltop near the Virginia Dale Stage Stop. Lee pointed out the trail--with some of the tracks still faintly visible--as it squiggled out of the southern horizon and disappeared into Wyoming. His knowledge and clear language bring the trail back vividly. I bet that he has asked more questions, read more books, diaries and journals, given more talks, and thought longer and harder than any other Cherokee Trail devotee.

With this path-breaking research in hand, celebrate with Lee Whiteley the 150th anniversaries of the Cherokee Trail and the California Gold Rush, as well as the approaching millennium. Savor this readable definitive time travel on a historical mainstream of the Rockies.

Happy Trails!   **--Thomas J. Noel, Denver, 12/25/98**

Acknowledgments

As the journals and diaries of early travelers bring yesterday's trail alive, it is the people along the trail today who give meaning and excitement to the modern trail traveler. These individuals include ranchers, landowners, historians, and others who are willing to share their interests.

Moving from south to north along the trail in Colorado, thanks go to: Richard and May Ann Gehling of Colorado Springs, historians of the Garden of the Gods and the Jimmy Camp area; Jim and Ruth Ann Steele, and John and Mary Welty, ranchers on the Arkansas-Platte Divide, whose conservation efforts will insure protection of trail sites in the Black Forest; Carl Guy and Harold Zion for help in locating trail landmarks; Jack Linkul and Dave Olson of Russellville, who showed me sites in that area of the trail; Clyde Jones of Parker, whose preservation efforts will save much of the history of fast growing Douglas County; Johanna Harden, of the Douglas County Library District, a new trail enthusiast, who is collecting and preserving regional history; Loyd Glasier of Parker, for having me along on some of his many outings along the Cherry Creek Valley; Clarice Crowle of Foxfield, for her help and support in research of the Smoky Hill Trail; Jim Jones of Aurora, railroad historian, whose area of interest parallel many of my own; Les and Louise Erb of Littleton, for sharing their knowledge and enthusiasm for the Cherokee and Overland trails in Wyoming; Lee A. Erb of Niwot and Doug Boone of Parker for the interesting airplane flights over the trail; Eleanor Gehres and the entire staff of the Western History Department of the Denver Public Library, who helped find pertinent trail literature and maps from the extensive material at that facility; Glenn Scott of Lakewood, for his help and for his set of wonderful trail maps of eastern Colorado; Andy Senti, of the Bureau of Land Management in Lakewood; Marty Schloo and Wayne Sundberg of Fort Collins, and Betty Larson of Livermore, for sharing their knowledge of the trail north of Fort Collins.

In Wyoming, thanks go to Marty Winemiller, retired from the Bureau of Land Management in Cheyenne; Pat Harnden of Tie Siding, for his help on the trail to North Park; Rod Laird of Encampment, for the trip along the trail southeast of Riverside; Mike and Joyce Evans of Saratoga, for their hospitality and helping with field trips; Ray Ring, Daniel Kinnaman and Rans Baker of Rawlins, for sharing their knowledge of the trails.

Special thanks to members of The Denver Posse of Westerners, who helped proof my manuscript and offered many suggestions: Ed and Nancy Bathke of Manitou Springs, Bob Larson and Thomas Noel of Denver. Thanks to Jim Krebs, for helping to take the mystery out of computers and the publishing field.

Finally, the three individuals who made the book possible. Jack and Patricia Fletcher of Sequim, Washington. I am proud to be associated with these fine trail scholars. We have shared many trail experiences along the trail and around the dining room table. And thanks to my wife Jane, who has shared all my trail experiences and who has allowed me to pursue my trail obsession.

Lee Whiteley

Table of Contents

I. The Cherokee Trail

- List of Maps xi
- List of Illustrations xii
- **Bent's Old Fort to Fort Bridger** - Early Trails, The Trappers Trail, Trading Post Era, Landmarks in Colorado, Landmarks in Wyoming, Military Users, Mormon Use, Francis Parkman, California Gold Rush: the Cherokee of 1849 and 1850, An 1856 Trip, The Cheyenne Campaign, Loring-Marcy Expedition, Colorado Gold Rush, The Overland Trail, The Trail Today . . 3
- **Time Line** - Events and Travelers, 1803 - 1882 27
- **Use of the word "Cherokee"** 30
- **East of Bent's Old Fort** - The Cherokee Route from Tahlequah . . 32
- **The Santa Fe Trail** - Southwest to Santa Fe 34
- **Trails of Eastern Colorado** 35
- **Bent's Old Fort** 36
- **"Trail"** - Definitions 38
- **A Trail of Many Names** - Various names for the Cherokee Trail . . 39

II. The Cherokee Trail in Colorado

- **Wood, Water & Grass** - The Waterways of Eastern Colorado. . . 42
- **Along the Arkansas River** - Bent's Old Fort, Milk Fort, "Potato Hills," Gantt's Fort, Mormontown, Pueblo 44
- **The Taos-Trappers Trail** - Pueblo to Taos 48
- **Along Fountain Creek** - Fountain City, Independence Camp, Chico Creek Cutoff, The Buttes 49
  - **Pikes Peak** - Major Landmark of the Cherokee Trail . . . 52
- **Across the Arkansas-Platte Divide** - Jimmy Camp, Black Squirrel Creek - "Brush Corral," Black Forest, Point of Rocks and Fagans Grave, "Blackfoot" Cave, Russellville 53
  - **Weather and the Divide** 58
  - **Eastonville** - Campsite, Sawmill, Railroad Town, Ghost Town . . 60
- **Along Cherry Creek** - 20 Mile House and Smoky Hill (South) Junction, 12 Mile House and Smoky Hill (Middle) Junction, Four Mile House 63
  - **Interstate 25 Through Parker and Franktown?** . . . 68
  - **The Smoky Hill Trail** - Shortest Route to the Colorado Goldfields . 69
  - **South Platte River - Cherry Creek** - Pre-1859 Travelers . . 70
  - **Riverside Cemetery** 72
- **Along the South Platte River** - Fort Lupton, Fort Jackson, Fort Vasquez, Fort St. Vrain, South Platte River Crossing (1849) . . . 74
- **Along the Cache la Poudre River** - South Platte River Crossing (1849), Laporte 78
- **The South Platte River Trail** - Connection to the Oregon Trail . . 81
- **The Trappers Trail** - North to Fort Laramie 82

    Along the Foothills - South Platte River Crossing (1850), Clear Creek and
        Ralston Creek, St. Vrain Creek, Namaqua and Big Thompson River,
        Laporte and the Cache la Poudre River . . . 83
    Across the Laramie Mountains - Steamboat Rock, Virginia Dale,
        Laramie Mountains 86
        First Transcontinental Railroad through Greeley? . . 90

III. The Cherokee Trail in Wyoming

    The Trail in Wyoming - The Route, North and South Branches . . 94
    The North Branch - Laramie Plains, Elk Mountain, North Platte River,
        Great Divide Basin, Green River, Bitter Creek 96
    Elk Mountain and Pass Creek 100
    Crossing of the North Platte River 102
    The Continental Divide - South Pass, Great Divide Basin, Bridger Pass,
        Twin Groves 104
    Trail to Interstate - Trails, Railroads, Highways 108
    Bitter Creek - Wyoming's "Transportation Corridor" 111
    The South Branch - Chimney Rock, Laramie River, North Park, North
        Platte River, Twin Groves and the Continental Divide, Little Snake
        River, Lower Powder Spring, Fort Crockett, Armstrong Grave,
        Green River, Henrys Fork, Fort Bridger 114
    Fort Bridger 119
    West of Fort Bridger - The Cherokee Route to the California Goldfields . 120

IV. The Cherokee Trail: Later Uses

    Stage Stations in Eastern Colorado 124
    Railroads - The Decline of the Cherokee Trail 126
    Settlements and Homesteads - "Taming of the West" . . . 127
    Decline of the Jimmy Camp Road - Roads through Colorado City . 128
    Post Offices along the Trail - Counties and County Seats . . 130
    Post Roads along the Trail - Mail on the Wagon Roads . . 131
    Later Transportation Systems - Railroads, "Auto Trails," Highways . 132
    Interstate 25 and the Cherokee Trail in Colorado . . . 134
    Interstate 80 and the Cherokee Trail in Wyoming . . . 136

V. References and Resources

    Land plats and surveyor notes 142
    Trail Terminology - Depressions, Swales and Ruts 144
    Along Today's Trail - Sites, Activities, Museums and Historical Societies . 146
    Bibliography - Journal and Diary Quotes 149
    Bibliography - Secondary Sources 153
    Index 155

Maps

The Cherokee Trail - Bent's Old Fort to Fort Bridger	2
Landmarks and Origin of Names in Eastern Colorado	7
Landmarks and Origin of Names in Wyoming	8
East of Bent's Old Fort	32
Trails of Eastern Colorado	35
A Trail of Many Names	39
William Franklin Map of the 1845 Kearny Expedition	40
Waterways along the Cherokee Trail in Eastern Colorado	43
Along the Arkansas River	45
Along Fountain Creek	50
Across the Arkansas-Platte Divide	55
Diagram of Weir's Mill in 1873	61
Along Cherry Creek	65
South Platte River-Cherry Creek Confluence	70
Along the South Platte River	76
Along the Cache la Poudre River	79
Along the Foothills	84
Across the Laramie Mountains	87
Charles Preuss Map of the 1843-1844 Frémont Expedition	92
Wyoming's Cherokee Trail North Branch	96
Elk Mountain-Pass Creek	100
Crossing of the North Platte River	102
The Continental Divide in Wyoming	106
Bitter Creek: "Trail to Interstate"	111
Wyoming's Cherokee Trail South Branch	114
West of Fort Bridger	120
U.S.G.S. Map of the Riverside-Encampment, Wyoming, area	122
Stage Stations along the Cherokee Trail	124
Post Offices along the Cherokee Trail	130
Post Roads along the Cherokee Trail	131
The Cherokee Trail and Interstate 25 in Colorado	134
The Cherokee Trail and Interstate 80 in Wyoming	136

Illustrations

Cherokee Trail Elementary School Sign	xiv
Cherokee Trail ranch sign	31
1924 General Land Office Land Plat	31
Cherokee Capitol Square in Tahlequah, Oklahoma	33
Santa Fe Trail marker at Running Turkey Creek, Kansas	33
Mule pack train on the Santa Fe Trail	34
Traders at Bent's Old Fort	36
Old automobile entrance to Bent's Old Fort	37
Bent's Old Fort - fur press in the plaza	37
Cherokee Trail ruts in Wyoming	38
"Potato Hills" west of Bent's Old Fort	46
Arkansas River near the mouth of Chico Creek	46
Mormontown Memorial in Pueblo	47
Excavation at the Pueblo trading post site	47
Badito, on the Huerfano River	48
Arkansas River-Fountain Creek confluence	51
"The Buttes" on Fountain Creek	51
Jimmy Camp, on Jimmy Camp Creek	54
Housing development near Jimmy Camp	56
Homestead on the Arkansas-Platte Divide	56
Point of Rocks, on West Kiowa Creek	57
Pikes Peak from the top of Point of Rocks	57
Winter day on the Arkansas-Platte Divide	59
Charles Michael Fagan's grave	59
Weir's Mill site on Black Squirrel Creek	62
Abandoned buildings at Eastonville	62
Russellville on "East Cherry Creek"	64
Sulphur Gulch stage barn	66
Pine Grove Post Office-Twenty Mile House	66
Wagons at Cherry Creek Reservoir State Park	67
Stagecoach at Four Mile House	67
"Bridge to Nowhere" at Castlewood Canyon State Park	68
Butterfield Overland Despatch trail marker	69
The South Platte River-Cherry Creek confluence	71
16th Street Viaduct over the South Platte River	71
John S. Jones Grave at Riverside Cemetery	73
Daniel C. Oakes Grave at Riverside Cemetery	73
Fort Lupton trading post site	75
Adobe walls of Fort Vasquez	77
Marker at the site of Fort St. Vrain	77
South Platte River	78
South Platte River-Cache la Poudre River Confluence	80
Cache la Poudre River at Laporte	80
Old Julesburg and Pony Express markers	81
Fort Laramie	82

"Gold Was Discovered" marker in Inspiration Point Park	85
Bridge piling at Namaqua on the Big Thompson River	85
Cherokee Trail near Bonner Springs and Owl Canyon	88
Trail ruts near Grayback Ridge	88
Steamboat Rock and Tug Rock	89
Laramie Plains from the summit of the Laramie Mountains	89
Virginia Dale sign	91
Trail marker at the Colorado-Wyoming State Line	91
Overland Trail marker west of Laramie	98
Carl Oscrosse Grave on Sage Creek	98
Point of Rocks Stage Station	99
Oregon Trail marker at the junction with the Cherokee Trail	99
Pass Creek canyon	101
Pass Creek and Elk Mountain	101
Pick Bridge on the North Platte River	103
Cherokee Trail ruts west of North Platte River	103
Lincoln Highway marker	107
Trail crossing at Twin Groves	107
Point of Rocks, Wyoming	111
Grave at Point of Rocks	113
Railroad Depot in Green River, Wyoming	113
Sportsman Lake in the Laramie Plains	116
Wyoming-Colorado Scenic Railroad at Kings Canyon	116
Five Buttes, northeast of Baggs, Wyoming	117
Cherokee Rim and the Little Snake River	117
Lower Powder Spring, also known as "Sulphur Spring"	118
Malinda Armstrong Grave	118
Excavation at Fort Bridger	119
Echo Canyon, Utah, and the Union Pacific Railroad	121
Donner Spring and Pilot Peak	121
Cherokee Stage Station and Steamboat Rock	125
Virginia Dale Stage Station	125
Homestead on the Cherokee Trail	127
Colorado City	129
Palmer Lake, on the Arkansas-Platte Divide	129
Pikes Peak and interpretive sign	135
Gas station and Longs Peak	135
Rock Creek - Arlington	138
Wagonhound Rest Area	138
Red Desert Cafe	139
Union Pacific Train along Bitter Creek	139
Cherokee Trail "Depression"	144
Cherokee Trail "Swale"	144
Overland Trail "Ruts"	145
Cherokee Trail "Parallel Traces"	145
Cherokee Trail marker at the Wagonhound Rest Area	154

Sign for the Cherokee Trail Elementary School in Parker, Colorado.

The Cherokee Trail
Bent's Old Fort to Fort Bridger

The Cherokee Trail
Bent's Old Fort to Fort Bridger

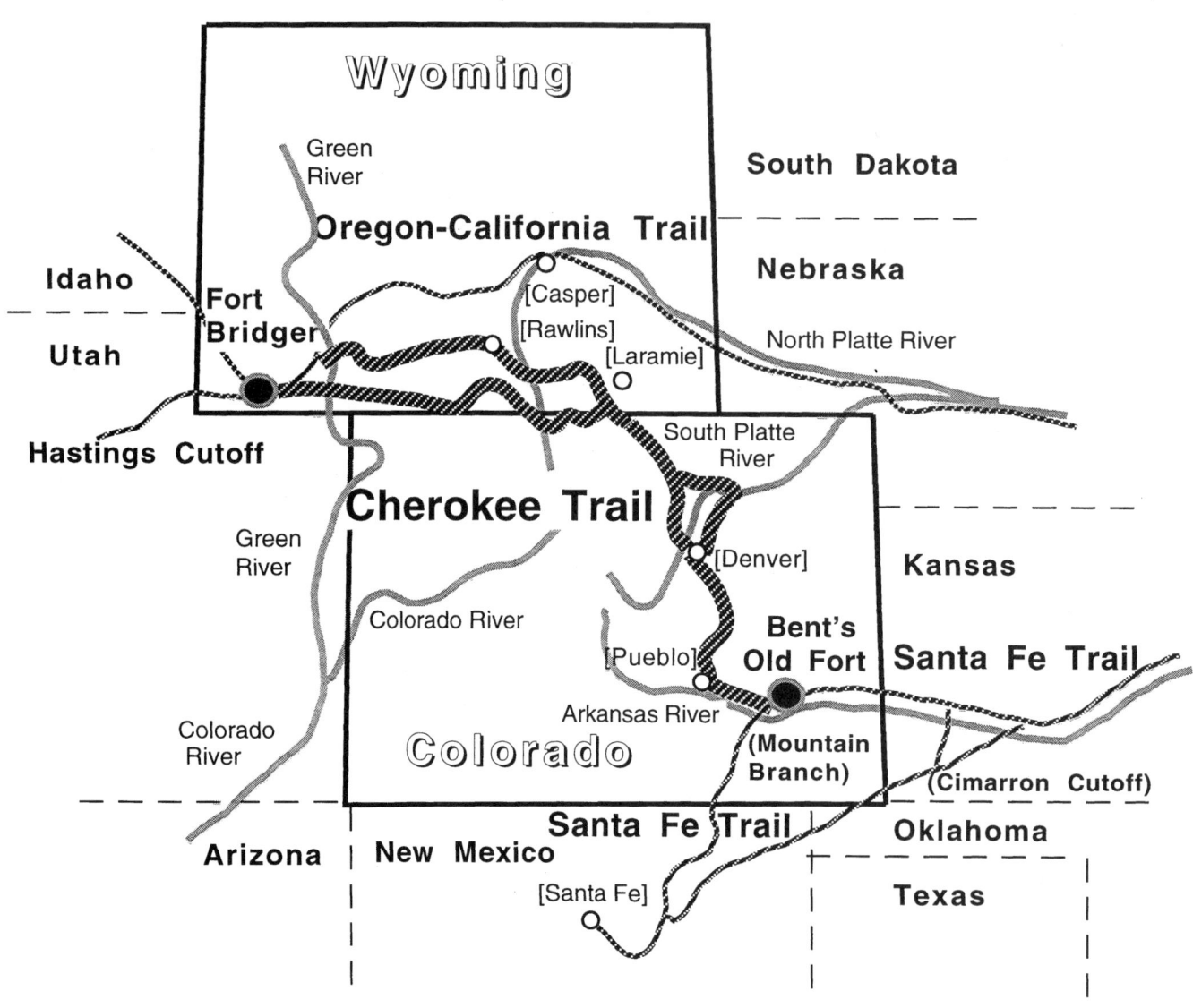

The Cherokee Trail
Bent's Old Fort to Fort Bridger

The Cherokee Trail. We have all heard of it. But there is little information and a lot of misinformation about the trail. Entering "Cherokee Trail" into the Denver Public Library's CARL computer catalog system results in 24 entries. Enter "Santa Fe Trail" and you get 229 hits; "Oregon Trail," 283. True, you don't expect as much on the Cherokee Trail, but of the 24 entries, 20 refer to the "Trail of Tears," the forced removal of the Cherokee Indians from Georgia, North Carolina, Tennessee and Alabama to Oklahoma in 1838. This is not the Cherokee Trail. Two references are to the fictional book by Louis L'Amour, *The Cherokee Trail*. His map shows 'Cherokee Trail' and in parenthesis 'Overland Stage Route.' The last entry, an 1859 map drawn by Randolph B. Marcy, points us to part of the trail in Colorado.

The Cherokee Trail was named for groups of Cherokee Indians who traveled from northeastern Oklahoma to the goldfields of California in 1849 and 1850. They were members of several wagon trains which traveled north to the established Santa Fe Trail eight miles east of McPherson, Kansas. They then followed west along the Santa Fe Trail Mountain Branch past Bent's Old Fort in Colorado. The Cherokee then left the Santa Fe Trail and traveled northwest to Fort Bridger, Wyoming. Here they joined the established Hastings Cutoff Trail through Utah, and finally followed various branches of the established California Trail to the goldfields. The Cherokee had gold mining experience in their native land of northwestern Georgia in the 1830s. This gold discovery had a role in the forced removal of the Cherokee from the east. The Cherokee routes to Oklahoma were called the "Trail of Tears," because of the hardships encountered on their winter trip. Some Cherokee would continue west to the goldfields of California.

The Cherokee Trail is the portion of the trail traveled by the 1849 and 1850 Cherokee between Bent's Old Fort and Fort Bridger. It connected the Santa Fe Trail with the Oregon-California and Hastings Cutoff Trails. But parts of this north-south connector trail evolved from other earlier trail segments, used for many purposes by many users, and each trail segment carried a variety of names. Other parts of the trail were pioneered by the Cherokee. Some segments of the 1849 and 1850 routes were subsequently used for other purposes and carried other names.

Early "Trails"

Before 1833, most long distance trails bypassed present-day Colorado. The Rocky Mountains were too much of an obstacle for wagons. The Santa Fe Trail Cimarron Branch, primarily a commercial trade route, was pioneered by William Becknell in 1822. This trail cut across the extreme southeastern corner of Colorado. The Oregon Trail, which first saw wagons in 1830, was the primary emigrant trail to the west coast. The trail passed north of Colorado, it ascended the North Platte River and crossed the Continental Divide at South Pass in Wyoming.

The few early travelers in eastern Colorado followed the waterways, for they provided game, water and wood. **Zebulon Pike** in 1806 and **Jacob Fowler** in 1821 ascended the Arkansas River to the Rocky Mountains. **Stephen H. Long** in 1820 and **Col. Henry Dodge** in 1835 ascended the South Platte River to the Rocky Mountains. Long and Dodge then turned south to the Arkansas River, which they then descended. **William Ashley**, fur trader, in the winter of 1824-1825 traveled up the South Platte River and Cache la Poudre River before turning north into Wyoming. Parts of these trails would evolve into the Cherokee Trail.

The Trappers Trail

The Trappers Trail is but one name for the multi-use trail which linked Fort Laramie, Wyoming and Taos, New Mexico. This north-south trail followed east of the Front Range of the Rocky Mountains, thereby avoiding the mountains to the west and the "Great American Desert" to the east. The trail connected trading settlements of the Rio Grande, Arkansas, South Platte and North Platte rivers. **Taos** was the northernmost major settlement in Mexico during the 1830s and 1840s, and was a favorite gathering place for trappers and mountain men. **Fort Laramie** was the headquarters for the American Fur Company.

From Taos, the Trappers Trail ran north through the San Luis Valley and across Sangre de Cristo Pass, west of present-day Walsenburg. The trail then crossed the Arkansas River at Pueblo. This section of the trail was also known as the **Taos Trail**. From Pueblo, the Trappers Trail followed up the east bank of Fountain Creek to present-day Fountain, at the mouth of Jimmy Camp Creek.

From the mouth of Jimmy Camp Creek, **two trails led over the Arkansas-South Platte Divide** to the South Platte River. The more westerly trail kept closer to the mountains, and was strictly a "pack trail" (no wagons) until the Colorado gold rush of 1859. This **west,** or **Monument-Plum Creek branch,** continued up Fountain Creek to Monument Creek at present-day Colorado Springs. The trail ascended Monument Creek to the Arkansas-Platte Divide at present-day Palmer Lake. The trail then descended either West or East Plum Creek, the two merging at present-day Sedalia. The trail then descended Plum Creek to the South Platte River, at present-day Chatfield Reservoir. The trail then followed down the east bank of the South Platte River.

The **east branch**, which would develop into the major wagon road across the Arkansas-Platte Divide, was also known as the **Jimmy Camp Trail**. This branch left Fountain Creek after crossing Jimmy Camp Creek and continued north to the popular campsite of Jimmy Camp, eight miles east of downtown Colorado Springs. The trail continued north and entered the Black Forest, the forested area of the Arkansas-Platte Divide. After crossing Black Squirrel Creek, the trail crossed the **Arkansas-South Platte Divide** at an elevation of 7,400 feet. The trail then passed Point of Rocks, a landmark and campsite on West Kiowa Creek. After crossing Running Creek, the trail descended Russellville Gulch to Cherry Creek, one mile south of present-day Franktown. The trail followed the east bank of Cherry Creek to its confluence with the South Platte River at present-day Denver. Here the east or Jimmy Camp branch of the Trappers Trail merged with the west or Monument-Plum Creek branch.

The Trappers Trail descended the east bank of the South Platte River to the mouth of the Cache la Poudre River east of present-day Greeley.

From Pueblo to the Cache la Poudre, the Trappers Trail via Jimmy Camp coincided with what would become known as the **Cherokee Trail**. The Trappers Trail but not the Cherokee Trail then continued north along Crow Creek into Wyoming.

Trading Post Era

The establishment of trading posts in the mid 1830s brought wagons to eastern Colorado and transformed many "trails" into "roads."

Bent's Old Fort was built in the fall of 1833. The fort increased traffic up the Arkansas River and firmly established the Mountain Branch of the Santa Fe Trail. The Mountain Branch ascended the Arkansas River to present-day La Junta, seven miles west of Bent's Old Fort, crossed the Arkansas River, and headed southwest over Raton Pass into New Mexico.

Four forts were then built on the South Platte River north of present-day Denver:
- Fort Vasquez, established by Louis Vasquez and Andrew Sublette, 1835.
- Fort Lupton, established by Lancaster Lupton, 1836.
- Fort Jackson, established by Peter Sarpy and Henry Fraeb, 1837.
- Fort St. Vrain, established by The Bent and St. Vrain Company, 1837.

To supply these forts, freight wagons traveled west along the Santa Fe Trail Mountain Branch past Bent's Old Fort, continued up the Arkansas River to Pueblo, then north along the Trappers Trail to the forts, the same route the Cherokee of 1849 were to take.

E. Willard Smith, a civil engineer and architect, traveled from Independence, Missouri to Fort Vasquez via the Santa Fe-Cherokee Trail in 1839.

> Left Independence Aug 6th 1839. The party, at starting, consisted of 32 persons, under the command of Messrs. Vasques & Sublette. There were four wagons loaded with goods, to be used in the Indian trade, drawn by six mules each. . . .
>
> . . . There were also, with us, a Mr. Thompson who had a trading post on the Western side of the Mountains . . .
>
> 31st. . . . Mr. Lupton encamped with us today as well as last night. He is trying to keep up with us, but probably will not succeed, as our mules can travel much faster than his oxen. . . .
>
> 7th. [September] . . . We ate our dinner at a creek called *Fontaine Quibouille, boiling Spring* . . . This is a famous resort in the winter for the Arapahoos and Shian Indians. The traders have houses here for trading with them in the winter. . . .
>
> 13th. To-day about four o'clock, we passed Mr. Lupton's fort. A little after five we reached the fort of Messrs. Sublette & Vasquez, the place of our destination. Our arrival caused considerable stir among the inmates. A great many free trappers are here at present.

On September 16th, Smith left Fort Vasquez and traveled with pack animals to Fort Crockett in Browns Hole, northwestern Colorado, arriving October 1st. His route took him over much of the trail used by the 1850 Cherokee in southern Wyoming and northwestern Colorado. His journal mentions:

> Cache-la-Poudre . . . hills piled on hills [Laramie Mountains] . . . Laramie's Fork . . . a very large valley, called the Park [North Park] . . . 'The Divide' . . . Snake river . . . some Sulphur Springs . . . a stream called the 'Vermillion.'

All of Smith's "landmarks" were mentioned in diaries of the Cherokee parties of 1850. Also in 1839, German physician **Frederick Wislizenus** traveled this "pack trail" from Fort Crockett to the forts on the South Platte. He stated:

> On September 3rd we came quite unexpectedly to the left bank of the South Fork and crossed the river. On the right bank there are here three forts, only some miles apart. Penn's [Bent's] and St. Vrain's fort, Vasquez and Sublett's and Lobdon's fort. . . . The evening before our departure, several owners of the forts arrived, bringing a new cargo of goods from the United States. Goods are usually transported to this place in great ox teams, and the same road is taken which we are about to follow to the boundary of Missouri.
> . . . We went up the South Fork for only half a day. . . . On the fourth day we crossed the divide between the waters of the South Fork and of the Arkansas. . . . reached in two days the left bank of the Arkansas . . . We went down the left bank of the river about sixty miles to Penn's [Bent's] Fort.

Rufus B. Sage traveled west in 1842, ascending the South Platte River and continuing south to Pueblo via the Cherokee Trail. He noted the forts and traders along his route:

> Twelve miles below Fort Lancaster we passed Fort George, a large trading post kept up by Bent and St. Vrain. . . .
> Six miles further on, we came to a recently deserted post [Fort Vasquez], which had been occupied the previous winter and summer by Messrs Lock and Randolph. . . .
> Between this point and Fort Lancaster, I noticed the ruins of another trading post [Jackson], much dilapidated in appearance, and nearly leveled with the ground. . . .
> Some twelve or fifteen Mexicans were at this time present at the Fort [Lancaster]. They constituted a trading party from Taos, escorting a caravan of pack-horses and mules, laden with flour, corn, bread, beans, onions, dried pumpkin, salt and pepper, to barter for robes, skins, furs, meat, moccasins, bows and arrows, ammunition, guns, coffee, calico,

The Cherokee Trail in Eastern Colorado

Landmarks (Origin of Names)

Scale: 0 — 25 — 50 Miles

Wyoming | Nebraska

- **Laramie Mountains** (Jacques LaRamie, trader)
- **Virginia Dale** (Virginia Slade, wife of Jack Slade)
- **Steamboat Rock** (shape of the rock formation)
- **Laporte** (French: the portage)
- **Cache la Poudre River** (French: Powder cache, hiding place)
- **Fort Collins** (Lt. Col. William O. Collins)
- **Big Thompson River** (Philip Thompson, trader)
- **Namaqua** (Namequa, daughter of Sauk Indian Chief Black Hawk)
- **Greeley** (Horace Greeley, newspaperman)
- **Longs Peak** (Stephen H. Long, explorer)
- **Fort St. Vrain** (Ceran St. Vrain, trader, aka Fort George, for George Bent, builder of the fort)
- **Fort Vasquez** (Louis Vasquez, trader)
- **Fort Jackson** (?)
- **St. Vrain Creek** (Ceran St. Vrain, trader)
- **Fort Lupton** (Lancaster Lupton, trader, aka Fort Lancaster)
- **Ralston Creek** (Louis Ralston, goldseeker)
- **South Platte River** (French: flat, level)
- **Clear Creek** (aka Vasquez Fork, for Louis Vasquez)
- **Denver** (James William Denver, Gov. of Kansas Territory)
- **Four Mile House** (four miles from Denver)
- **12 Mile House** (12 miles from Denver)
- **17 Mile House** (17 miles from Denver)
- **Cherry Creek** (chokecherry bushes)
- **20 Mile House** (20 miles from Denver)
- **Franktown** (James Frank Gardner, early resident, aka California Ranch, Frankstown)
- **Russellville** (William Green Russell)
- **Blackfoot Cave** (Blackfoot Indians, named by Rufus Sage)
- **Point of Rocks** (rock formation)
- **Fagans Grave** (Charles Michael Fagan)
- **Black Forest** (dense Ponderosa Pines, aka Pineries)
- **Black Squirrel Creek** (residents of the area)
- **Pikes Peak** (Zebulon Pike, explorer)
- **Jimmy Camp** (Jimmy Daugherty, trader)
- **Jimmy Camp Creek** (Jimmy Daugherty, trader)
- **The Buttes** (Sand hill formations)
- **Independence Camp** (Voorhees camp of July 4th, 1858)
- **Fountain Creek** (French: Fontaine qui Bouille, Fountain that Boils)
- **Pueblo** (Spanish: Town)
- **Chico Creek** (greasewood, a shrub; Spanish: little)
- **Arkansas River**
- **Gantt's Fort** (John Gantt, trader, aka Fort Cass)
- **Mormontown** (Mormon winter quarters, 1846 - 47)
- **Milk Fort** (goat milk supplier)
- **Spanish Peaks** (Aka Huajtolla or Wah-To-Yah, Indian: Breasts of the world)
- **La Junta** (Spanish: The Junction)
- **Bent's Old Fort** (Bent Brothers, traders, aka Fort William for William Bent)

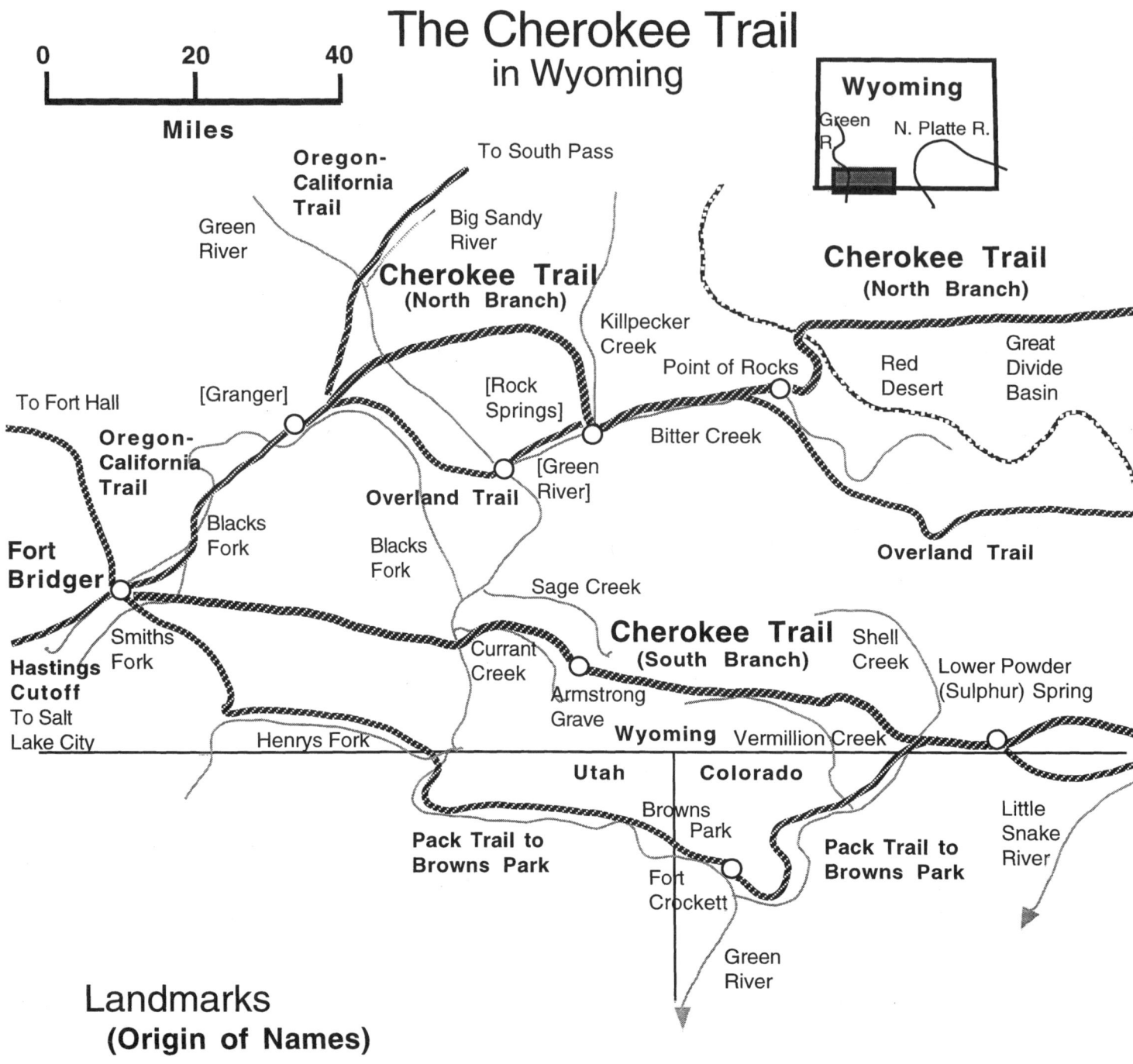

Landmarks
(Origin of Names)

Armstrong Grave (Malinda Armstrong, 1834-1852)
Bitter Creek (Alkali taste)
Blacks Fork (Daniel Black, member of the Ashley party)
Browns Park (Baptiste Brown, trapper)
Fort Crockett (Davy Crockett, frontiersman)
Fort Bridger (Jim Bridger, trader and guide)
Granger (Gen. Gordon Granger)
Green River (color of rock banks?; associate of Ashley?)
Henrys Fork (Major Andrew Henry, partner of Ashley)
Rock Springs (water source)
Sulphur Spring (taste of water)
Point of Rocks (ridge above Bitter Creek)
Smiths Fork (Jedediah Smith, trapper and frontiersman)
Vermillion Creek (red earth in the area)

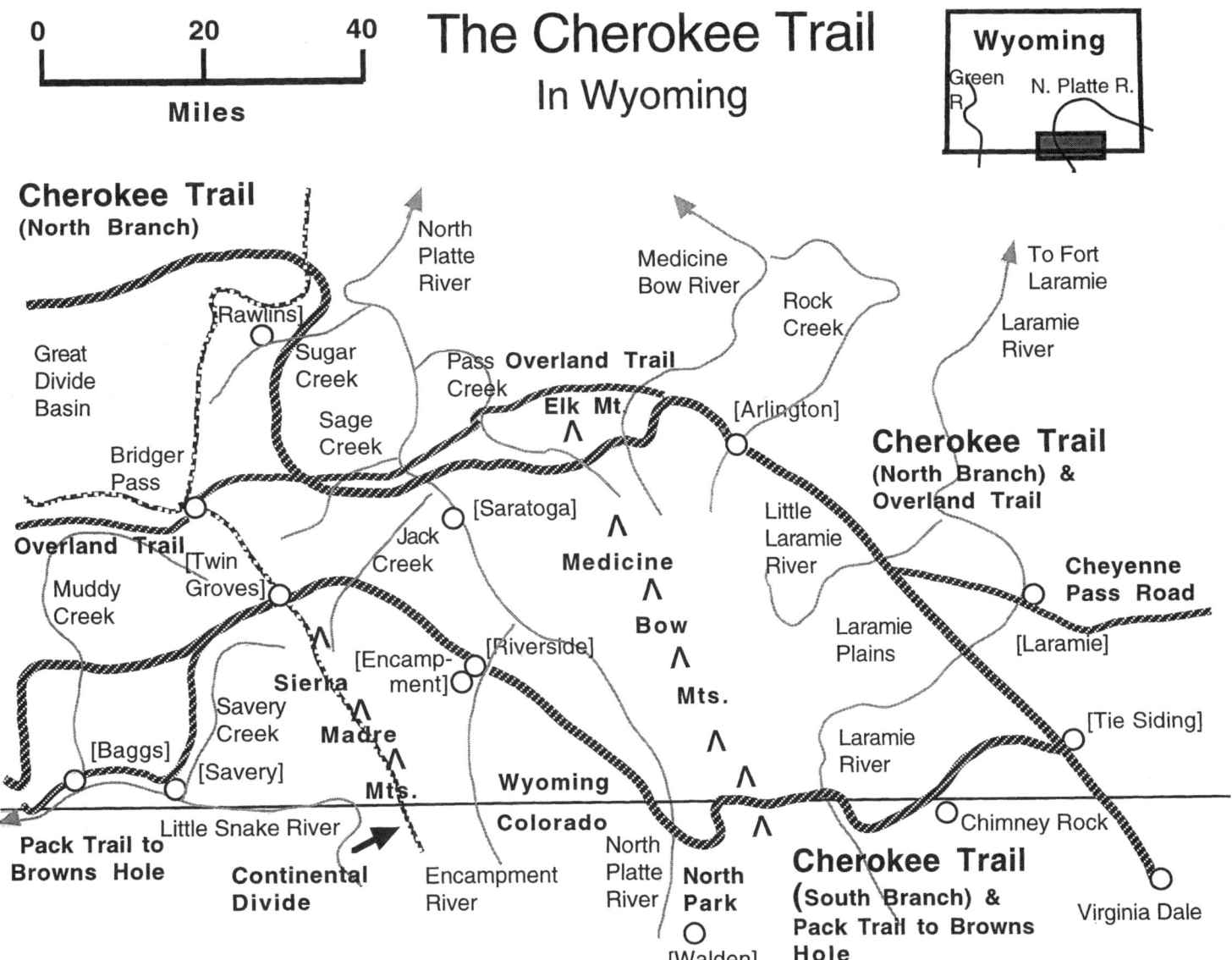

Landmarks
(Origin of Names)

Arlington (aka Rockdale, on Rock Creek)
Baggs (George & Maggie Baggs, area ranchers)
Chimney Rock (shape of rock formation)
Elk Mountain (animal?; Sioux Chief Standing Elk?;
 aka Medicine Bow Butte)
Encampment (rendezvous camp)
Jack Creek (Jack Watkins, local resident)
Laramie (Jacques La Ramie, trapper)
Little Snake River (many bends and turns;
 aka Bear River)

North Platte River (French: flat, level)
Pass Creek (pass between Elk and Coad Mts)
Rawlins (General John Rawlins, with railroad survey)
Riverside (located on Encampment River)
Savery (Savery?, trapper)
Sierra Madre Mts. (Spanish: Mother range;
 aka New Park Mountains)
Twin Groves (two groves of Aspen trees)
Tie Siding (railroad ties moved to this location)

cloth, tobacco, and old clothes, which were to compose their return freight. . . .

    Sept. 10th. . . . Following the trail leading from the Platte to the Arkansas, or *Rio Napeste*, we continued our way some thirty-five miles, and halted with a camp of free traders and hunters, on Cherry creek. . . .

    Sept. 14th. . . . Our place of stay was in a sweet little valley enclosed by piney ridges . . .

    The creek derives its names from [Jimmy] Daugherty, a trader who was murdered upon it several years since. At the time he was on his way to the Arkansas with a quantity of goods, accompanied by a Mexican. The latter, anxious to procure a few yards of calico that constituted a part of the freight, shot him in cold blood, and hastened to Taos with his ill-gotten gains, where he unblushingly boasted of his inhuman achievement. . . .

    At the delta, formed by the junction of the Fontaine qui Bouit [Fountain Creek] with the Arkansas, a trading fort, called the Pueblo, was built during the summer of 1842. This post is owned by a company of independent traders, on the common property system; and, from its situation, can command a profitable trade with both Mexicans and Indians. Its occupants number ten or twelve Americans, most of whom are married to Mexican women

Military Users, 1842-1845

In 1842, **John C. Frémont** ascended the South Platte River to Fort St. Vrain. He traveled no farther south but noted:

    The piney region of the mountains to the south was enveloped in smoke, and I was informed had been on fire for several months. Pike's peak is said to be visible from this place, about one hundred miles to the southward; but the smoky state of the atmosphere prevented my seeing it.

Frémont then traveled north to Fort Laramie and the Oregon-California Trail via the Trappers Trail. He returned to Fort St. Vrain in 1843, his **second expedition** west:

    About noon, on the 4th of July, we arrived at the fort, where Mr. St. Vrain received us with his customary kindness . . .

    Our animals were very much worn out, and our stock of provisions entirely exhausted when we arrived at the fort . . .

    I had been informed that a large number of mules had recently arrived at Taos, from Upper California; and as our friend, Mr. Maxwell, was about to continue his journey to that place, where a portion of his family resided, I engaged him to purchase for me 10 or 12 mules, with the understanding that he should pack them with provisions and other necessaries, and meet me at the mouth of *Fontaine qui bouit*, on the Arkansas river, to which point I would be led in the course of the survey.

. . . recommenced our journey up the Platte . . . Passing on the way the remains of two abandoned forts, (one of which, however, was still in good condition,) we reached, in 10 miles, Fort Lancaster, the trading establishment of Mr. Lupton. His post was beginning to assume the appearance of a comfortable farm: stock, hogs, and cattle, were ranging about on the prairie; there were different kinds of poultry; and there was a wreck of a promising garden, in which a considerable variety of vegetables had been in a flourishing condition, but it had been almost entirely ruined by the recent high waters.

Frémont continued up the South Platte River to Plum Creek, then up East Plum Creek to present-day Castle Rock. Here he traveled east to Bijou Creek, near present-day Fondis. He crossed the Cherokee Trail near present-day Russellville, noting it as "the road which runs from St. Vrain's fort to the Arkansas." Frémont camped at the head of West Bijou Creek, near the butte known today as Fremonts Fort. The next day Frémont rejoined the Cherokee Trail:

July 11. . . Turning the next day to the southwest, we reached, in the course of the morning, the wagon road to the settlements on the Arkansas river, and encamped in the afternoon on the *Fontaine-qui-bouit* (or Boiling Spring) river . . .

July 13 . . . Continuing down the river, we encamped at noon on the 14th at its mouth, on the Arkansas river, A short distance above our encampment, on the left bank of the Arkansas, is a *pueblo*, (as the Mexicans call their civilized Indian villages,) where a number of mountaineers, who have married Spanish women in the valley of Taos, had collected together, and occupied themselves in farming, carrying on at the same time the desultory Indian trade.

Frémont returned north to the South Platte River via the Monument-East Plum Creek branch of the Trappers Trail. Frémont called Monument Creek "the eastern fork of the *Fontaine-qui-bouit* river." On East Plum Creek, he noted present-day Castle Rock, calling it "Poundcake rock."

Frémont, with Kit Carson as guide, then traveled northwest from Fort St. Vrain, through the Laramie Plains to present-day Rawlins area, following the basic route which would be used by the Cherokee of 1849. While the Cherokee Trail would turn west at Rawlins, Frémont proceeded north to rejoin the Oregon-California Trail west of Devil's Gate, Wyoming.

In **1844**, on his return trip east, **Frémont** traveled much of what would become the 1850 Cherokee Trail South Branch:

On the 7th . . . we descended to '*Brown's hole*.' This is a place well known to trappers in the country, where the canons through which the

Colorado runs expand into a narrow but pretty valley. . . .

. . . our encampment, which was opposite to the remains of an old fort [Fort Crockett] . . .

. . . From the lower end of Brown's hole we issued by a remarkable dry canon . . . The Vermillion creek afforded us brackish water and indifferent grass for the night. [June 9]

. . . At night [June 10] we encamped in a fine grove of cottonwoods, on the bank of the Elk Head river [Little Snake River], the principal fork of the Yampah river, commonly called by the trappers the Bear river. . . .

On the 11th we continued up the river, which is a considerable stream . . . we encamped a little below a branch of the river, called St. Vrains fork [Savery Creek]. A few miles above was the fort at which Frapp's [Fraeb's] party had been defeated two years since . . . Leaving the river the next morning, we took our way across the hills . . .

[June 13] . . . Leaving St. Vrain's fork, we took our way directly towards the summit of the dividing ridge. . . . reached the summit towards midday, at an elevation of 8,000 feet. . . .

. . . we saw spread out before us the valley of the Platte, with the pass of the Medicine Butte beyond . . .

We were now about two degrees south of the South Pass, and our course home would have been eastwardly; but that would have taken us over ground already examined, and therefore without the interest which would excite curiosity. Southwardly there were objects worthy to be explored, to wit: the approximation of the head waters of three different rivers - the Platte, the Arkansas, and the Grand River fork of the Rio Colorado of the Gulf of California; the Passes at the heads of these rivers; and the three remarkable mountain coves, called Parks, in which they took their rise. . . . the locality of the THREE PARKS, were all objects of interest, and, although well known to hunters and trappers, were unknown to science and history. We therefore changed our course, and turned up the valley of the Platte instead of going down it. . . .

The valley narrowed as we ascended, and presently degenerated into a gorge, through which the river passed as though thru a gate. We entered into it, and found ourselves in the New Park [North Park] - a beautiful circular valley of thirty miles diameter . . . We halted for the night just inside the gate.

The Fort Crockett to North Park route was the same route used by Smith in 1839. Frémont continued south through Middle and South Parks, then descended the Arkansas River, passing Pueblo and Bent's Old Fort.

Lt. William B. Franklin kept a journal of his march with Stephen Watts Kearny to South Pass in 1845. While traveling from Fort Laramie to Bent's Old Fort, Franklin stated:

> We turned off from Crow Creek about 11 miles from our mornings camp, and struck the Cache creek near its mouth. . . . Our march to-day was along the Platte . . . We very soon struck a road which has been made by the waggons from Bents Fort, and followed this road with but little variation from it until we reached the Fort.
>
> About 6 miles from camp we passed St. Vrains Fort and 6 miles further another old one of the Bent's. A few miles brought us to Luptons Fort and we passed two others during the day. These are all deserted now, the trade having become too small to support them . . .
>
> . . . Cherry C. . . . stream which is I believe the Kioway . . . The point at which we struck the last Creek is called Jimmie's camp . . . Fontaine qui bouil.

Philip St. George Cooke was also a member of the 1845 Kearny expedition. He commented on the desert-like conditions of the trail:

> July 16th. . . . We have but three wants, - so remote in civilization, which counts them by the thousand, - water, grass, and fuel, and wonderfully little and various in kind of the last; and we find the Earth a '*step*-mother,' for she seldom grants us more than two of them, and when in an ill-humor, denies us all three.
>
> July 21st. - We marched south, following the river [South Platte] . . . We were on a hard, level road, over prairies, and river-bottom too, of great barrenness; the effect being heightened by ruins of several adobe trading forts: I only wondered that man could be tempted to tarry here, where animals come not even for security. . . .
>
> . . . Some say this country has a soil, but that the difficulty lies in the dry climate: all effects have some cause; it is certainly a barren, desolate country: we come hundreds of miles, and see scarcely an Indian, or an animal; it is in fact a desert. . . .
>
> July 29th. . . . We have found it about four hundred miles from Fort Laramie, and the route we have followed is the best natural road we have yet seen. There is nothing to prevent a light carriage from passing it, twelve miles to the hour; and this so near the mountains, and in view of perpetual snow.

Mormon Use, 1846-1847

Detachments of Mormon emigrants to the Salt Lake Valley used the Trappers-Cherokee Trail in 1846-1847. **John Brown** was a member of the "Mississippi Saints," 43 Mormon converts from Monroe County, Mississippi. They were ascending the North Platte in July, 1846, hoping to join Brigham Young and the main party of emigrants. He stated:

A few miles below Laramie, we met with Mr. John Reshaw [Richard]. He had some robes to trade and was camped in Goshen Hole. He said he heard the Mormons were going up the South Fork of the Platte. We held a council and concluded to go no further west but find a place for the company to winter on the east side of the mountains. Mr. Reshaw said that the head of Arkansas River was the best place, as there was some corn growing there and it was near the Spanish country where the company could get supplies. He was going to Pueblo in a few days with two ox teams, there being no road and as he was acquainted with the route, we concluded to stop and go with him. . . .

. . . we moved to the South Fork of the Platte. We searched in vain for the trail of the Mormons, not knowing anything of their moves. We crossed the South Fork the 27th of July, a few miles below St. Vrains Fort. Here, we struck a wagon road that led to Pueblo, made by the traders. We reached Pueblo on the 7th of August. . . . News had reached this place that the Mormons had stopped at the Missouri River and 500 of them had joined the army and were on their way to New Mexico.

We counseled the brethren to prepare for winter to build them some cabins in the form of a fort.

After spending the winter near Pueblo, the Mormons continued on their journey to the Salt Lake Valley, again crossing the Arkansas-Platte Divide via the Cherokee Trail. **John Steele** noted:

After bidding adieu to our long camp at Pueblo, we crossed the Arkansas River. The first day we made 8 miles, the next 23 miles, and camped James Camp him that James's Peak was named for. Next day we made 30 miles over a beautiful prairie, thence to point of rocks to Cherry Creek, 18 miles. . . . Camped on the south fork of the Platte, eight days out from Winter Quarters we came on to Cache La Poudre, or where the powder had been cached. . . . we passed four trading houses and found a six pound cannon there.

Steele's James's Peak is today's Pikes Peak. The peak was named James Peak by the Stephen Long expedition in 1820 to honor Edwin James, expedition geologist and botanist, and the first known white to climb the peak.

Francis Parkman, 1846

Francis Parkman traveled the Trappers-Cherokee Trail from Fort Laramie to Pueblo two weeks after the Mississippi Saints. Following are a few excerpts of his trip to Pueblo, from his widely read book, *The Oregon Trail*, in a chapter titled "The Lonely Journey."

We forded the South Fork of the Platte. . . . At noon we rested under the walls of a large fort, built in these solitudes some years since by M. St. Vrain. It was now abandoned and fast falling into ruin. The walls of unbaked bricks were cracked from top to bottom. Our horses recoiled in terror from the neglected entrance, where the heavy gates were torn from their hinges and flung down. The area within was overgrown with weeds, and the long ranges of apartments once occupied by the motley concourse of traders, Canadians, and squaws, were now miserably dilapidated. Twelve miles farther on, near the spot where we encamped, were the remains of another fort, standing in melancholy desertion and neglect.

. . . reached Cherry Creek. Here was a great abundance of wild cherries, plums, gooseberries, and currants. The stream, however, like most of the others which we passed, was dried up from the heat, and we had to dig in the sand to find water for ourselves and our horses. Two days after, we left the banks of the creek, which we had been following for some time, and began to cross the high dividing ridge which separates the waters of the Platte from those of the Arkansas. . . .

We pushed through an extensive tract of pine woods. Large black-squirrels were leaping among the branches. From the farther edge of this forest we saw the prairie again, hollowed out before us into a vast basin.

Through the afternoon and the next morning we were passing down the banks of the stream, called 'Boiling Spring Creek,' from the boiling spring whose waters flow into it. . . .

We approached the gate of the Pueblo. It was a wretched species of fort, of most primitive construction, being nothing more than a large square enclosure, surrounded by a wall of mud, miserable cracked and dilapidated. . . . as we rode up to the gate, a light active little figure came out to meet us. It was our old friend Richard. He had come from Fort Laramie on a trading expedition to Taos; but finding when he reached the Pueblo that the war would prevent his going farther, he was quietly waiting till the conquest of the country should allow him to proceed.

California Gold Rush, 1849 Cherokee

John Rankin Pyeatt traveled from Arkansas to California with the California-bound Lewis Evans Cherokee Party in 1849. He described the trail and the crossing of the South Platte River below the mouth of the Cache la Poudre River east of present-day Greeley.

From Pueblo to St. Vrain on the south fork of the Platte, a distance of 140 miles, we had a good road and down the Platte to the mouth of another stream that runs in on the other side of the Platte 17 miles, we had a old trail. We had to go below the mouth of this stream to avoid having to ferry it and the Platte both being swiming. We made a ferry boat

> . . . This boat was large enough to carry the largest of our wagons without unloading them. When we were done crossing we drew the boat out on the north side of the river and left it for the benefit of the men that should come along this road. This took four days. We sout out from this place without road, trail or guide through the plains and hills.

Five weeks later, Pyeatt reported:

> This Bridgers Fort is 48 miles from Green River and 440 miles from the South Fork of the Platte. 36 miles of this distance we had a road and the balance we had to make our own road, without trail or guide through mountains and plains. Thus you will see why we have bin so long gittin hear

The 1849 Cherokee party did not have a guide but they probably had a copy of Lt. John C. Frémont's map and/or journal, for they closely followed his 1843 route from the Cache la Poudre River to the Rawlins, Wyoming area. Diary reference is made to a "Fremont's Camp" near Elk Mountain, Wyoming. The 1849 Cherokee route traveled up the Cache la Poudre River past present-day Laporte, then closely followed today's U. S. Highway 287 across the Laramie Mountains into the Laramie Plains of Wyoming. The Laramie Mountains were often referred to as the "Black Hills." Much of this route was closely followed by the later Overland Stage Line.

Capt. Howard Stansbury, returning east after his Great Salt Lake survey expedition recorded in his journal September 23, 1850:

> we arrived at the bank of a small stream putting out of the pass between Medicine Bow Butte & the main range South thro which Fremont passed in 18 [blank] & afterward Evans team of 47 wagons. As Fremont had represented this pass as very rough & Bridger declared it extremely difficult for wagons, I determined to examine the route farther north. We nooned upon the banks of this little stream which we gave the name of Pass Creek.

Stansbury, with guide Jim Bridger, then passed north of Elk Mountain, his "Medicine Bow Butte," as did the Overland Trail in the 1860s. Elk Mountain is south of Interstate 80, midway between Laramie and Rawlins.

Albert Carrington, with the Stansbury expedition, mentioned the Evans trail while traveling in the area east of Bridgers Pass:

> start for the gap south of Medicine Butte & in about 2 miles strike Evans' road on our left & soon leave it on our right, of course from this point to Evans' Fork of the Bitter, the Evans' road must have passed across the plateau of table country & divide north of our track, & Bridger says it is very poorly grassed & watered.

The 1849 Cherokee crossed Wyoming's Red Desert, well north of Bridger Pass, the route taken by Howard Stansbury and the Overland Trail of the 1860s. After crossing the Red Desert, the Cherokee Trail hit Bitter Creek and rejoined the Stansbury-Overland route at Point of Rocks, 25 miles east of Rock Springs. **Lt. John Gunnison**, also on the Stansbury expedition, commented on the Evans road while traveling along Bitter Creek at Point of Rocks:

> At the 'Bend' S. we leave the Evans track altogether which takes a more Northerly & worse route - Up a branch.

The 1849 Cherokee joined the established Oregon-California Trail northeast of Granger, Wyoming, and followed it to Fort Bridger.

California Gold Rush, 1850 Cherokee

In 1850, other Cherokee parties traveled the trail to the California goldfields. In Colorado, the trail coincided with the 1849 Cherokee route until they reached the South Platte at present-day Denver. One exception was the 1850 Cherokee party which took what was to become known as the Chico Creek Cutoff. This trail left the Arkansas River at the mouth of Chico Creek, 12 miles east of Pueblo, and rejoined the main trail on Fountain Creek, 14 miles north of Pueblo.

The Cherokee crossed the South Platte River just below the mouth of Cherry Creek. **John Lowery Brown**, a Cherokee, said:

> Came to the South fork of Platt River. Made a raft & commenced crossing the waggons . . . Left the Platt and traveled 6 miles to Creek . . . we called this Ralstons Creek because a man of that name found gold here.
> June 22: Lay Bye. Gold found.

The 1850 Cherokee were the first to take wagons along what is today U. S. Highway 287. They crossed St. Vrain Creek at present-day Longmont, crossed Big Thompson River at Namaqua Park in present-day Loveland, then crossed the Cache la Poudre River at present-day Laporte. Here the 1850 route merged with the 1849 trail. In the Laramie Plains of southern Wyoming, the 1850 route again split off from the 1849 trail. **James Mitchell**, traveling with a Cherokee party:

> got over the hills into the Larame plains . . . we pased a waggon trail Supposed to be Evans trail made last year our gide would not travel it far because he thought he could go a nearer way

The guide was Ben Simon, a veteran mountain man. He led the 1850 Cherokee ox train over a route through southern Wyoming which became known as the Cherokee Trail [South Branch]. This route had been used by others, including E. Willard Smith's pack train of 1839, to travel from the South Platte River to the Browns

Park area of Colorado and Utah.

While the 1849 Cherokee route [North Branch] rounded the north end of the Medicine Bow Range (but south of Elk Mountain), the 1850 Cherokee route cut west upon entering the Laramie Plains, and crossed the Medicine Bow Range near the Colorado-Wyoming border. The trail then reentered Colorado and cut across the north edge of North Park.

Reference to the Cherokee Trail in this area was made by **Ferdinand V. Hayden**. In August, 1868 he made a tour of North Park with a party of Army officers. He stated:

> Our course along the Cherokee Trail was about southwest from the Big Laramie River, over ridge after ridge, and after traveling twenty-five miles we entered the North Park.

The 1850 Cherokee route then traveled northwest to cross the Continental Divide at the north end of the Sierra Madre mountain range, at Twin Groves.

The trail continued west, over the largely unpopulated and undeveloped landscape of southern Wyoming. **John Lowery Brown** stated on July 13, 1850:

> Traveled until sometime in the night when we came to Sulphur Springs. Not fit for man or beast to drink.

W.A. Richards, on the south boundary survey of Wyoming in 1873 said:

> Camped at 223rd M. C. on small sulphur spring . . . An old road runs west about 20 chains north of this camp. . . . Suppose it to be the old Cherokee Trail . . . it runs nearly west and we must follow it to get through the country.

This "sulphur spring" is known today as Lower Powder Spring and is located west of present-day Baggs, Wyoming. The Cherokee of 1850 continued west to Fort Bridger and the Oregon-California Trail.

An 1856 Trip

The amount of traffic on the Cherokee Trail before the Colorado gold rush is noted by **Ellen Hundley**, who was traveling west to east in 1856.

> June 29 . . . met 3 trains from Arkansas. Going to California with sheep and cattle   we came on 30 miles and camped in the black hills
> July 2 . . . camped on a small creek . . . there was a cherokee train camped just below us
> July 5 . . . lying bye on the Platte . . . met 2 arkansas trains
> July 7 . . . met 2 arkansas trains with about 1000 head of cattle . . . camped on cherry creek

> July 8 . . . traveled 15 miles and camped at the head of cherry creek   passed a mexican camp on C C
>
> July 10 . . . met 3 arkansas trains with more than 1000 head of cattle   we came on and nooned on the fountain Cabuoba

The Cherokee Trail, as with most trails, was a two way trail, much traffic flowed from west to east, although more journals and diaries were kept while traveling west.

The Cheyenne Campaign, 1857

Military expeditions returned to the Cherokee Trail in 1857, when Col. Edwin Sumner led a campaign against the Cheyenne Indians. At Fort Leavenworth, he divided his command, sending Maj. John Sedgwick west along the Santa Fe Trail-Cherokee Trail to the mouth of the Cache la Poudre River. Sumner proceeded west along the Oregon-California Trail to Fort Laramie, then south on the Trappers Trail to the Cache la Poudre River.

Robert M. Peck was a member of the Sedgwick command of the Sumner expedition, and while traveling the southern route, noted:

> Shortly after passing Bent's Fort, following the California trail up the river, we got our first sight of the snow-covered summit of Pike's Peak, resting on the western horizon like a small white cloud, which many of us thought it really was; but day after day, as we marched towards it, the white cloud grew larger, higher, and plainer, other mountains on each side of it coming into view, till in a few days it seemed like we were running up against the whole Rocky Mountain range.
>
> Near the mouth of a creek called Fountain que Bouille, we turned off from the Arkansas and struck over the divide for the head of Cherry Creek, passing through some fine bodies of fine timber. At a point shortly before leaving the Arkansas, a small collection of 'dobe shanties on the opposite bank of the river had been pointed out to me as Pueblo, then a small settlement of Mexicans and trappers. . . .
>
> The California trail, which we had been following, crosses the South Platte here, just below (north of) the mouth of Cherry Creek, and seems to take through the mountains, while we leave it and follow down the right bank of the river on a dim wagon-trail that did not appear to be used much.
>
> This part of Kansas Territory was literally a 'howling wilderness,' with little indications of its having been occupied or traversed by white men, except the old wagon-road we have been traveling, with here and there a stump and a few chips by the roadside, as the mark of some California emigrant. . . .
>
> On the Second day's march down the South Platte, after leaving the mouth of Cherry Creek, we passed the ruins of three old abandoned trading posts, a few miles apart, which I was told were formerly called

respectively: Forts Lupton, Lancaster and St. Vrain, after their several owners. They seemed to have been abandoned several years, nothing remained but the crumbling 'dobe walls.

Loring-Marcy Expedition, 1858

Col. William W. Loring and Capt. Randolph B. Marcy were moving mules and supplies from Fort Union, New Mexico to the Fort Bridger, Wyoming, area. This expedition was part of the Mormon campaign of 1857-1858. They followed the Cherokee Trail north from Pueblo, taking the 1850 branch north of Denver. **Col. Loring** mentioned the snowstorm which took the life of Charles Michael Fagan.

> Point of Rocks - Crossed Squirrel creek thirteen miles, and six or seven miles to camp to-day; this camp is on the dividing ridge between the Arkansas and the South Fork of the Platte river; a snow storm commenced to-day at 5 p. m. and continued unremittingly until the 2nd of May . . . a civilian teamster in the quartermaster's employ froze to death, and several hundred sheep perished in the storm . . .
>
> . . . duty and inclination required me to confer with Captain Marcy . . . the road he had selected leading in the direction of Bridger's Pass was continued, but in consequence of the guide, who knew the route, having left the command, a large portion being without a road, it was thought safest to take the route known as 'Evans' trail;' this with several cut-offs, proved the best and nearest for the season we were marching

Capt. Marcy weathered the snowstorm on Black Squirrel Creek:

> On the 29th of April we again set forward and proceeded as far as the ridge dividing the waters of the Arkansas from those of the Platte. . . . about dark a snow storm set in . . . We immediately set to work making 'corrals' for the animals. . . .
>
> We were detained at this camp until the 5th of May, when we again resumed the march down Cherry Creek to its confluence with the South Platte, which we found so deep and rapid as to make it necessary for us to halt and build a ferry-boat. This, with the time consumed in crossing, delayed us four days.
>
> From hence we continued on upon the 'Cherokee California trail,' skirting the eastern base of the Rocky mountains, and crossing small tributaries of the South Platte until we reached the 'Cache la Poudre' creek.

The Loring-Marcy expedition continued north and west on the Cherokee Trail North Branch, crossing the Laramie Plains and passing south of Elk Mountain to the North Platte River. They followed the trail to present-day Rawlins, where they turned west across the Great Divide Basin. The Cherokee of 1849 passed north of Rawlins

Peak and Cherokee Peak. Excerpts from **Marcy's** journal:

> This route strikes the Platte upon the Cherokee trail about two miles above Bryan's crossing [Johnson Island], and is decidedly preferable for the season; that the bluffs upon the east side are much lower and the approach march much more shallow at the Cherokee crossing....
>
> From thence [North Platte crossing] we continued on the Cherokee trail for thirty-eight miles to a small creek which runs into the Platte [Sugar Creek at Rawlins] ...
>
> ... our train leaves the emigrant road at this place and bears to the left around the mountains ... Our next days march was over fine ground but without water until we arrived at camp ... We again intersected Evans' trail at this point. It makes a very great bend to the north around the mountains ... From hence we followed Evans' road

Colorado Gold Rush, 1859

Robert Peck's 1857 "howling wilderness" and "dim wagon trail" was to change drastically a year later. With the discovery of gold in 1858 and the resulting rush in 1859, the South Platte-Cherry Creek confluence region became a <u>destination</u>: Denver, gateway to the Colorado mining district to the west. Many of these gold seekers had previously passed through the area, via the Cherokee Trail, on their way to the California goldfields.

Augustus Voorhees, member of the 1858 Lawrence, Kansas, party noted on July 4th while on Fountain Creek:

> Struck the road from Taos to Fort Bridger.
> [July] 8. ... We left the Cherokee trail to the right, and followed the creek to the foot of the mountain [Pikes Peak].
> [July] 10. ... The mountain was covered with hail. We got to the top at 3 o'clock, but it was so cloudy we could not see the country beyond.
> [July] 12. We broke up camp and struck east for the old road. We got to what is called Jims Camp. There is a fine spring and lots of pine wood there. It is on the Cherokee trail, to Calaforny.

Luke Tierney, in his *History of the Gold Discoveries on the South Platte*, stated on June 21, 1858:

> We passed a perpendicular rock, five hundred feet high, at the base of which was a tomb of recent origin, occupied by some unfortunate itinerant. At its head stood a wooden cross, bearing the inscription, 'Charles Michael Fagan - 1858'

Fagan was the civilian teamster with the Loring-Marcy military expedition, and froze to death in a snowstorm May 2, 1858.

With the discovery of gold in Colorado in 1858 and the rush of 1859, the Cherokee Trail segment along the Arkansas River and across the Arkansas-Platte Divide was heavily used. The South Platte River-Cherry Creek confluence area became a destination, not just a site for people passing through.

Luke Tierney continues, June 24th, 1858:

> One of the towns located, is worthy of special notice. It is called AURARIA. It is situated on the junction of Cherry Creek and South Platte river, on the great military road leading from the territories of New Mexico and southern Kansas, to Salt Lake City, Fort Laramie, and all the northwestern forts. . . . continued our march, reaching our destination - RALSTON'S CREEK, about six o'clock P.M. Here, according to the statements of the returned Californians, we were in the immediate vicinity of the gold mines.

William Parsons published his *The New Gold Mines of Western Kansas* guide book in 1859, one of several which appeared as the result of the Colorado gold discoveries. Concerning the routes he stated:

> Routes: Of these there are three: first, by way of the Santa Fe road to the point where it crosses the Arkansas river: thence up the Arkansas, by way of Bent's Fort, Fontaine qui Bouille, and Jim's Camp, to Cherry Creek, and known as the 'southern' or 'Santa Fe' route.
> Second . . . by way of Fort Kearny to the crossing of the Platte, and up said river to Cherry Creek, and known as the northern route.
> Third . . . up the Smoky Hill Fork, across to the head-waters of the tributaries of the Platte, to Cherry creek, and known as the 'middle' or 'Smoky Hill' route.

The Smoky Hill Trail crossed the high plains of Eastern Colorado. The early branch of the trail was called the Middle or "Starvation" branch, for it lacked water and game. In Arapahoe County, it followed down both today's Smoky Hill Road and Piney Creek, and struck Cherry Creek and the Cherokee Trail within Cherry Creek Reservoir State Park. It then followed the Cherokee Trail into Denver. The South Platte Route coincided with the 1849 Cherokee route from the mouth of the Cache la Poudre upstream to Denver. Thus virtually all travel to the Colorado goldfields followed at least a portion of the Cherokee Trail.

George Willing, a geologist and M. D. from St. Louis, traveled the southern route to the goldfields in 1859.

> June 1st . . . The road we have traveled is the great Cherokee trail to California, over which all travel from the Southern States must cross the continent . . .

> June 4th. . . . Just ahead of us and in sight there is a drove of about a thousand head of loose stock, from Texas and Arkansas, destined for California. . . .
>
> June 6th . . . reach Pueblo, a miserable village of about thirty log huts . . . The men at present are in the mines . . .
>
> June 7 . . . Fall into the Fort Union and Laramie trail . . . Met a train of Mexican carts returning from Auraria, whither they had gone with flour.
>
> June 9 . . . leave the Fountain river . . . strike across the hills for the head of Cherry Creek. . . . At Jim's Spring, fifty miles south of Auraria, on Thursday, June 9th, we deposited in their last resting place, the remains of Thomas Alexander . . .
>
> June 10 . . . Pass the grave of a man named Fagan . . . Pass a large flock of sheep destined for Auraria. Met a trader returning to New Mexico. Had taken flour to the mines . . . In camp at last on head waters of the long sought, anxiously looked for Cherry Creek . . . All about us is another grand pine forest, and in the midst of it is a new town called Russellville. Here there is a steam sawmill in operation . . .
>
> June 12 . . . Camp at 6 P. M., in the midst of a thunder storm, at the forks of the Smoky Hill route, and 12 miles from Denver
>
> June 13 . . . at noon reached Denver City, the goal toward which we had so long been wending a weary way.

Russellville is situated on Russellville Gulch, a tributary of Cherry Creek. But the 1866 General Land Office surveyor notes listed the waterway as "East Cherry Creek." Thus the mention of "head of Cherry Creek" puts the traveler in the Russellville area.

Even though Denver was now a destination, travelers were still continuing west from Denver. **Horace Greeley**, editor of the New York Tribune, mentioned in his 1859 overland journey:

> I left Denver at 3 p. m. . . . there are two roads thence to this point: that usually preferred follows down the east fork of the South Platte some forty miles, crossing that river near St. Vrain's Fort . . . learned that the South Platte was entirely too high to be forded near St. Vrains Fort, or anywhere else . . . had no choice but to take the upper or mountain route. So we crossed the Platte directly at Denver . . . we pushed on 10 miles and camped . . . Four or five men who, having taken a look at the gold region, had decided to push on for California, most of them, I believe, through what is known as the Cherokee Trail, which forms a part of the shortest practical route from Denver to Salt Lake.

The Overland Trail, 1862-1868

In 1860, the Central Overland California & Pikes Peak Express Company received the contract to carry the United States mail from Missouri to Salt Lake City. The route followed the North Platte River-South Pass, Wyoming, route to Fort Bridger.

In 1862, Ben Holladay purchased the line and renamed it the Overland Stage Line.

Also in 1862, the route was moved south because of Indian troubles. The main route followed up Lodgepole Creek. Denver was on a branch line from Julesburg, running up the South Platte. **Frank Root**, mail agent for the Holladay lines tells of the next change:

> The Overland stage route changed its route from Lodge Pole creek, opposite Julesburg, to near the site of Cherokee City post-office - [now] Latham - . . . The new crossing of the south fork of the Platte was a short distance below the mouth of the Cache la Poudre. . . . After the change to the new route the stages forded the South Platte at Latham station and followed up the Cherokee trail along the Cache la Poudre to LaPorte.

The Overland Stage now followed the 1849 Cherokee route up the Cache la Poudre River and into the Laramie Plains. A branch line still ran to Denver down the South Platte. In Wyoming, the new route passed north of Elk Mountain, then crossed the North Platte River at Johnson Island, five miles below the Cherokee Trail North Branch crossing. The Overland Trail crossed the Continental Divide via Bridger Pass, then continues west to Bitter Creek, passing south of the Great Divide Basin.

In 1864 the main line Overland Stage route in Colorado was moved again, to pass through Denver. The route followed the Fort Morgan Cutoff, leaving the South Platte River near Fort Morgan and traveled overland to enter Denver from the east. The route then crossed the South Platte River at Denver and followed the 1850 Cherokee route north through Laporte.

The Trail's Decline

The coming of the railroads cut into the usage of the Cherokee Trail as a long distance trail. The Union Pacific completed its transcontinental line across Wyoming in 1869. It closely followed the 1849 Cherokee route from Rawlins west to Fort Bridger. Denver's first railroad, the Denver Pacific, linked the city with Cheyenne on the Union Pacific. This line followed the 1849 Cherokee route from Platteville to Denver. The Denver and Rio Grande completed its Denver to Pueblo line in 1872, reducing the importance and usage of the Cherokee Trail south of Denver.

The Cherokee Trail Today, Colorado

Traveling west from Bent's Old Fort, the Santa Fe Trail Mountain Branch closely follows Colorado Highway 194 to North La Junta. Here, the Santa Fe Trail crossed the Arkansas River and headed southwest. The Cherokee Trail continued west, following along the north bank of the Arkansas River. Few landmarks were recorded in this area, most of the attention was directed to the wonderful views of the Rocky Mountains to the west. Colorado Highway 96 closely follows the Cherokee Trail from Olney Springs west to Pueblo.

In Pueblo, the site of the 1842 trading post is on the grounds of the El Pueblo Museum at 324 W. 1st Street. Foundations and artifacts are being uncovered during an on again-off again archaeological dig conducted by the University of Southern Colorado.

At Pueblo, the Cherokee Trail left the Arkansas River and followed up the east bank of Fountain Creek to the town of Fountain. Overton Road, north out of Pueblo, and Old Pueblo Road, south out of Fountain, closely follow the trail. This "back road" is a scenic alternative to Interstate 25, which runs west of Fountain Creek.

After crossing Jimmy Camp Creek, the Cherokee Trail left Fountain Creek. Eight miles east of downtown Colorado Springs, the trail reached Jimmy Camp.

Jimmy Camp was part of the large Banning-Lewis Ranch. Colorado Springs has title to some land here; hopefully part of this scenic area will be left open space.

The Cherokee Trail continued north, closely following Meridian Road north of Falcon. The trail entered the Black Forest, known as the "Pineries" in trail days. After crossing the Arkansas-Platte Divide, elevation 7,500 feet, the Cherokee Trail passed "Point of Rocks," a famous landmark and camping site. At the base of Point of Rocks is Fagan's grave.

The trail continued northwest, crossing the southwestern corner of Elbert County, and continued to Russellville. Local groups are pursuing National Historic District status for the Russellville area.

The Cherokee Trail followed Cherry Creek from Franktown to its confluence with the South Platte River in Denver. The town of Parker developed around the 20 Mile House, where the South Branch of the Smoky Hill Trail merged with the Cherokee Trail. The last stage stop on the combined Smoky Hill-Cherokee Trail was Four Mile House, the oldest standing house in Denver.

The 1849 Cherokee Trail followed the South Platte River north out of the Denver area, following Brighton Blvd. and Old Brighton Road. This 1849 route passed the four forts of the 1830s and early 1840s.

The South Platte Valley Historical Society has plans to reconstruct Fort Lupton, which is 1/2 mile northwest of downtown Fort Lupton. The exact site of Fort Jackson is unknown. Fort Vasquez sits between traffic lanes of U. S. Highway 85 a mile south of Platteville. The walls of Fort Vasquez were rebuilt in the 1930s as a Work Projects Administration project and today the Colorado Historical Society has a small museum here. A marker sits on the site of Fort St. Vrain, four miles due west of Gilcrest.

The 1850 Cherokee crossed the South Platte River below the mouth of Cherry Creek. It crossed Clear Creek below the mouth of Ralston Creek. The Arvada Historical Society has been successful in getting the Ralston gold discovery site listed on the State Register of Historic Sites.

The Cherokee Trail, 1850 Branch, closely followed today's U. S. Highway 287 through the towns of Longmont and Loveland. At Laporte, the 1850 Cherokee crossed the Cache la Poudre River and merged with the 1849 route. Three miles northwest of Laporte, at Teds Place, the trail left the Cache la Poudre and headed north, still following closely U. S. Highway 287. The trail then crossed the Laramie Mountains into Wyoming.

The Cherokee Trail Today, Wyoming

The combined 1849 and 1850 Cherokee Trail entered Wyoming one mile east of U. S. Highway 287. At Tie Siding, 16 miles south of Laramie, the trail split.

The 1849 Lewis Evans Cherokee expedition continued northwest across the Laramie Plains to pass south of Elk Mountain, at the north end of the Medicine Bow mountain range. This "North Branch" of the Cherokee Trail was subsequently used in part by the Overland Trail in the 1860s, both passing 11 miles west of Laramie. The trail crossed the North Platte River 1/2 mile north of Pick Bridge, eight miles northwest of Saratoga. This is five miles upstream from the Overland Trail crossing at Johnson Island. The trail continued northwest to Rawlins; then west across the Red Desert. The Union Pacific Railroad, the first transcontinental railroad; the Lincoln Highway, first transcontinental auto road, and Interstate Highway 80 all follow closely the Cherokee Trail North Branch west to Fort Bridger.

The 1850 Cherokee "South Branch" turned west at Tie Siding and traveled the southern edge of the Laramie Plains. The Laramie River crossing was a mile and a half north of the Colorado-Wyoming border, six miles south of Woods Landing. West of the river the trail entered the Medicine Bow Range, following closely the Forest Service road #526 between the historic Boswell Ranch and the Wyocolo-Mountain Home area on Wyoming Highway 230. This crossing of the Medicine Bow Range is the highest elevation on the Cherokee Trail, 8,870 feet. The Cherokee Trail South Branch crossed the extreme northern end of North Park, then turned northwest to the Encampment-Riverside area in Wyoming.

The Cherokee Trail South Branch crossed the Continental Divide at the north end of the Sierra Madre Mountain Range, at a point called Twin Groves, elevation 8,100 feet, 20 miles west southwest of Saratoga. Twin Groves is 18 miles southeast of Bridger Pass, where the Overland Trail crossed the Continental Divide.

The trail continued west, over the largely unpopulated and undeveloped landscape of southern Wyoming. The trail crossed Wyoming Highway 789 and Muddy Creek 14 miles due north of Baggs, Wyoming.

The Cherokee Trail South Branch crossed the Green River just below the mouth of Currant Creek, north of Buckboard Crossing in the Flaming Gorge National Recreation Area.

The Cherokee Trail then arrived at Fort Bridger. Here the trail hit the Oregon-California and Hastings Cutoff trails. Fort Bridger today is a State Historic Site. Excavations have revealed the site of the original trading post, which has been reconstructed nearby. Some of the buildings constructed during the Army occupation of 1858 to 1890 have been preserved.

Fort Bridger is the end of the trail segment called the Cherokee Trail, but the Cherokee of 1849-1850 had another 1,000 miles to travel to reach the California goldfields.

The Cherokee Trail Time Line

Some of the major **events** that affected travel on the Cherokee Trail and **travelers** and **expeditions** that followed sections of the trail.

1803 **Louisiana Purchase** expands U. S. territory west to the Continental Divide.

1806 **Zebulon Pike** expedition ascends the Arkansas River and attempts to climb Pikes Peak. The expedition's official mission was to find the source of the Red River, the approximate south boundary of the Louisiana Purchase.

1820 **Stephen H. Long** expedition travels up the South Platte River, Dr. Edwin James climbs Pikes Peak. Expedition descends the Arkansas River to the Rocky Ford area, where the expedition split.

1821 **William Becknell** packs trade goods to Santa Fe. This was the year that Mexico achieved independence from Spain.

Jacob Fowler ascends the Arkansas River, camps at present-day Pueblo. In January, 1822, he travels southwest to cross Sangre de Cristo Pass to the San Luis Valley and Taos.

1822 **William Becknell** first to take wagons over the Santa Fe Trail, Cimarron Branch.

1825 **William Ashley** ascends the South Platte River and Cache la Poudre River, then crosses the Laramie Mountains and Laramie Plains on his way to the first mountain man rendezvous on Henrys Fork in southwestern Wyoming.

1833 **Bent's Old Fort** constructed by the Bent & St. Vrain Company, increasing the use of the Santa Fe Trail Mountain Branch.

1835 **Henry Dodge** and the Dragoons travel west to demonstrate to the Indians the military force of the United States. They travel up the South Platte River, cross the Arkansas-Platte Divide, descend Fountain Creek and the Arkansas River. Journals kept by Lt. Gaines Kingsley and Hugh Evans.

1835 **Fort Vasquez** built by Louis Vasquez and Andrew Sublette.

1836 **Fort Lancaster** built by Lancaster Lupton.

Fort Crockett established in Browns Hole.

1837 **Fort St. Vrain** built by the Bent & St. Vrain Company.

Fort Jackson built by Peter Sarpy and Henry Fraeb.

1839 **E. Willard Smith** travels the Santa Fe Trail and Cherokee Trail to Fort Vasquez with a supply train led by Louis Vasquez. Smith then continues west to Fort Crockett in Browns Hole, via North Park and Twin Groves.

Robert Shortess and **Thomas Farnham** visit Fort Crockett.

Frederick Wislizenus, German Physician, travels west to east from Fort Hall to Fort Crockett, Fort St. Vrain and Bent's Old Fort.

1842 **John C. Frémont** travels up the South Platte River to Fort St. Vrain, then north on the Trappers Trail to Fort Laramie.

Rufus B. Sage travels much of the trail in Colorado and Wyoming.

Pueblo trading post established by independent traders.

1843	**John C. Frémont** travels sections of the Cherokee Trail, on this his second expedition. **Fort Bridger** built by Jim Bridger and Louis Vasquez to cater to the Oregon-California Trail traveler.
1844	**John C. Frémont** travels from Fort Crockett east through North Park; descends the Arkansas River.
1845	**Col. Stephen W. Kearny** expedition travels from Fort Laramie on the North Platte River to Bent's Old Fort on the Arkansas River. Journals kept by William B. Franklin and Philip St. George Cooke.
1846	**Francis Parkman**, his "tour of curiosity and amusement to the Rocky Mountains" includes travel from Fort Laramie to Bent's Old Fort. **John Brown** and the Mormon "Mississippi Saints" travel from Fort Laramie to "Winter Quarters" at Pueblo. **Hastings Cutoff** established west of Fort Bridger. Used by the ill-fated Donner Party.
1847	**John Steele** and the Mormon "Mississippi Saints" travel north from Pueblo to Fort Laramie. **Mormons** emigrate to the Salt Lake Valley.
1849	**California Gold Rush** **Lewis Evans** and Cherokee gold seekers first to take wagons north and west from the Cache la Poudre River to the Oregon-California Trail. John Rankin Pyeatt letters. **Bent's Old Fort** abandoned.
1850	**Howard Stansbury** survey expedition travel sections of the Cherokee Trail in Wyoming. Led by guide Jim Bridger, Stansbury is looking for a shorter route from Fort Bridger to Fort Kearny, Nebraska. Journals kept by Stansbury, Albert Carrington and John Gunnison. **John Lowery Brown**, William Quesenbury, James Mitchell, and the Cherokee first to take wagons over the Cherokee Trail South Branch in Wyoming.
1852	**Malinda Armstrong** dies on the trail in Wyoming. Her family was returning east from California.
1853	**Railroad surveys** along the 38th and 39th Parallel travel sections of the Cherokee and Taos-Trappers trails. Journal kept by E. G. Beckwith. **Bent's New Fort** established.
1854	**William H. Engels** drives cattle from Fort Smith, Arkansas, to California. **Pueblo** trading post residents massacred by Ute Indians.
1855	**Fort Bridger** purchased by the Mormon Church.
1856	**Ellen Hundley** travels from Utah to Texas. **Francis T. Bryan** military expedition from Leavenworth to Bridger Pass. Notes the Cherokee "Evans" party south of Elk Mountain, Wyoming, and at the North Platte River crossing.
1857	**Maj. John Sedgwick,** part of the Col. Edwin Sumner campaign against the Cheyenne, travels part of the Cherokee Trail. Journal kept by R. M. Peck.

1858 **Capt. Randolph B. Marcy** and **Col. William W. Loring** military expedition travels from Fort Union, New Mexico to Utah.
Francis T. Bryan military expedition crosses Bridger Pass, then continues west to Fort Bridger.
Colorado Gold Seekers William Green Russell, Luke Tierney, William Parsons, Augustus Voorhees, and others travel the Arkansas River and "Divide" sections of the Cherokee Trail.

1859 **Colorado Gold Rush.** Gold seekers include George Willing, Charles Post, A. M. Gass and E. H. Patterson.
Smoky Hill Trail Middle (Starvation) Branch used by gold seekers.
Leavenworth & Pikes Peak Express Company (L&PPX) established: first stagecoach arrives Denver May 7.
Horace Greeley & Henry Villard travel the Smoky Hill Trail and sections of the Cherokee Trail.
Colorado City established. Much of the traffic south of Denver travels through Colorado City, lessening the travel on the Cherokee-"Jimmy Camp" Trail.
Albert D. Richardson travels sections of the Taos-Trappers and Cherokee trails.
Fort Bridger becomes a U. S. Army post.

1861 **Colorado Territory** established, William Gilpin, governor.

1862 **Ben Holladay** moves his Overland Stage Line from the South Pass route to the Cache la Poudre River-Bridger Pass route. This route follows much of the Cherokee Trail North Branch.
Edward Bliss and **Jeff Durley** travel Overland Stage route from Denver to Fort Bridger.

1864 **Overland Stage Line** route changed to include Denver. Route includes the Fort Morgan Cutoff and the Cherokee Trail 1850 Branch north of Denver.

1865 **David Butterfield** establishes his Butterfield Overland Despatch (BOD) on the Smoky Hill Trail South Branch. The route merged with the Cherokee Trail at present-day Parker, Colorado.

1866 **Ben Holladay** buys BOD, moves the route to the Smoky Hill Trail North Branch. He then sells to **Wells Fargo**.
Grenville M. Dodge and **Silas Seymour** travel sections of the Cherokee Trail searching for a route for the Union Pacific Railroad.

1868 **Union Pacific Railroad** completed west to Evanston, Wyoming. Sections of the route follow the Cherokee Trail North Branch.
Ferdinand Hayden surveys sections of the Cherokee Trail.

1870 **Denver Pacific Railroad** completed from Cheyenne to Denver, eliminating need for long-distance stage travel.

1872 **Denver & Rio Grande Railroad** completed from Denver to Pueblo.

1873 **William A. Richards** survey of the south boundary of Wyoming notes the Cherokee Trail.

1876 **Colorado** becomes the 38th state.

1882 **Denver & New Orleans Railroad** completed from Denver to Pueblo.

Use of the word "Cherokee"

> *struck into the emigrant road along the foot of the Medicine-Bon. This road we suppose to coincide with the trail followed by Captain Stansbury. The road today is very good, having occasional ascents and descents, and over a fine, hard gravel*
> Lt. Francis T. Bryan, August 5, 1856

> *To-day marched along the Cherokee road. This road is over the return route of Captain Stansbury, and is very good, with occasional ascents and descents, and over a fine hard gravel*
> Lt. Francis T. Bryan, June 28, 1858

Two items of interest in Bryan's 1858 report:
  First, he plagiarized his 1856 report.
  Second, he used the word "**Cherokee**."

The year 1858 is the earliest the author has found for the use of the word "Cherokee" in describing the trail taken by California-bound Cherokee Indian gold seekers of 1849 and 1850.

Capt. Randolph B. Marcy also used the term in his 1858 report of his expedition from Fort Union, New Mexico, to Utah. His book, *The Prairie Traveler*, published in 1859, contained a map with the trail along Colorado's Front Range labeled "Cherokee Trail."

Most early references to the trail included the trail's final destination: California.
  "**Cherokee California trail**" - Randolph B. Marcy, 1858.
  "**the Cherokee Trail, to Calaforny**" - Augustus Voorhees, 1858.
  "**the great Cherokee trail to California**" - George M. Willing, 1859.

General Land Office surveyors conducting the first land surveys in Colorado and Wyoming mentioned the Cherokee Trail by name. Two townships southeast of Denver, along Cherry Creek, labeled the road "old Cherokee Trail" in 1862. Sixteen township land plats in southern Wyoming label the road "Cherokee Trail."

Parker, Colorado, has a Cherokee Trail Elementary School.
Many natural and man-made features in Wyoming carry the name "Cherokee." All are on or near one of the two branches of the Cherokee Trail.
  > Cherokee Creek and Cherokee Trail Reservoir east and southeast of Encampment and Riverside.
  > Cherokee Creek southwest of Saratoga.
  > Cherokee Creek, Cherokee Rim, Cherokee Draw, Cherokee Basin and Cherokee Trail Road west of Baggs.
  > Cherokee Creek, Cherokee Spring and Cherokee Mountain immediately west of Rawlins.
  > Cherokee Hill and Cherokee railroad siding on the Union Pacific Railroad near Creston Junction, west of Rawlins.

The word "Cherokee" has been applied to a variety of natural features, such as creeks and mountains, and man-made features such as ranches and schools.

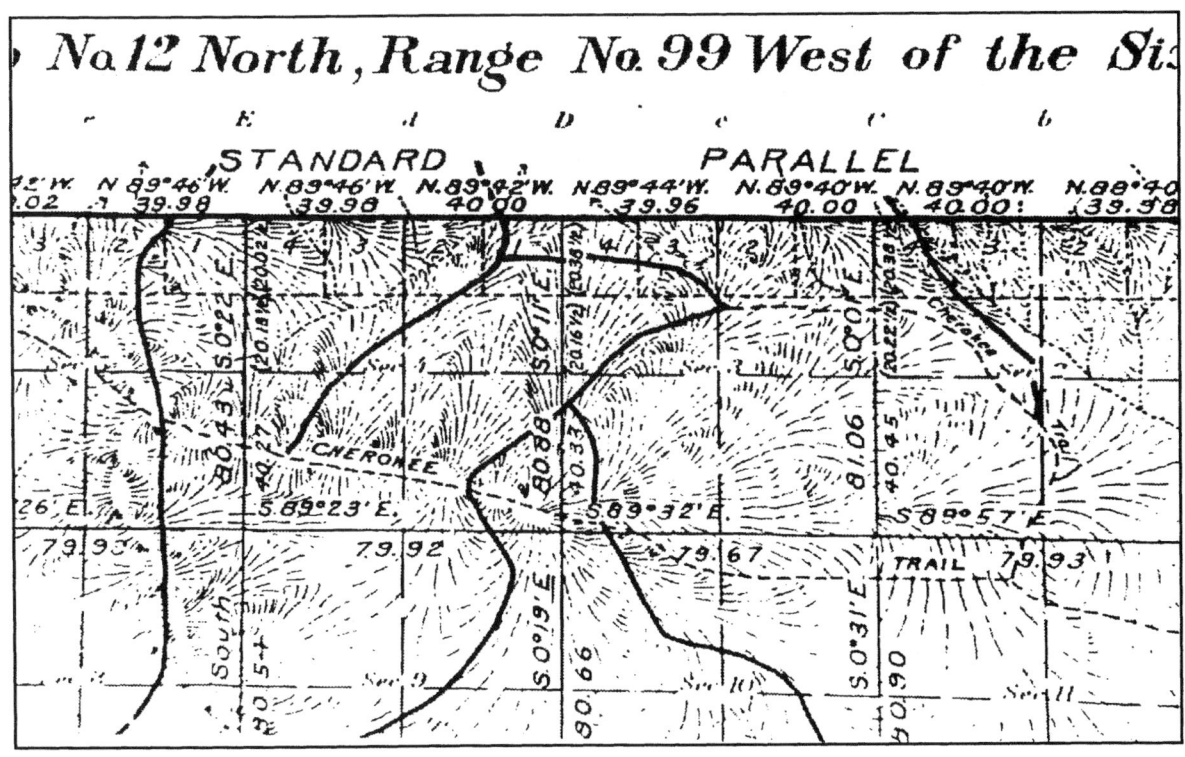

The townships along the trail at the Colorado-Wyoming border were originally surveyed in the early 1880s. This 1924 resurvey still notes the Cherokee Trail.

East Of Bent's Old Fort

Members of the California-bound Cherokee gold seeker parties of 1849 and 1850 were primarily from northeastern Oklahoma, northwestern Arkansas and southwestern Missouri. They traveled into Kansas on a trail which became known as "Evans Road," named for Lewis Evans, captain of the 1849 Cherokee party. Early land plats also label this trail "Cherokee Trail" and "California Trail."

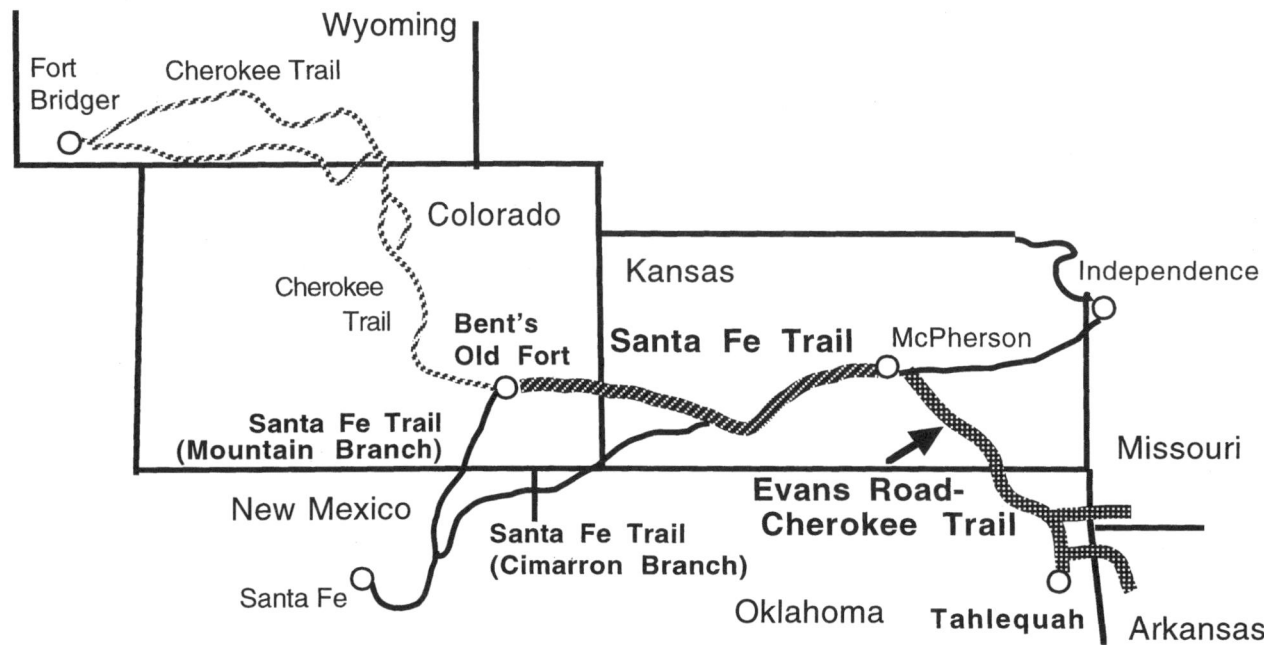

The trail ran northwest from Tahlequah, Oklahoma, to "Grand Saline," the salt springs at Salina. This was the site of Auguste Pierre Choteau's trading post, established in 1821. Trails from northwestern Arkansas merged with the trail from Tahlequah here. The combined trail crossed the Neosho (also called the Grand) River west of Salina. The trail crossed the Verdigris River north of the mouth of Salt Creek, southeast of present-day Nowata, and south of the trail landmark of Coody's Bluff. Here also, a trail from southwestern Missouri joined the Evans Road. The trail then closely followed the ridge between the Verdigris and Caney rivers. The trail entered present-day Kansas east of Caney. Turning more to the northwest, the trail crossed Walnut River just south of El Dorado. The Evans Road merged with the established Santa Fe Trail at Running Turkey Creek, eight miles east-southeast of McPherson, Kansas. The Santa Fe Trail ran from Independence, Missouri, and the Missouri River to Santa Fe, New Mexico. The Cherokee parties followed the Santa Fe Trail Mountain Branch west to Bent's Old Fort, in present-day Colorado. Seven miles west of the fort, the Santa Fe Trail crossed the Arkansas River and ran southwest to Santa Fe. The Cherokee Trail continued west up the Arkansas River.

Tahlequah, Oklahoma, Capital of the Cherokee Nation, was the end of the "Trail of Tears" and the starting point for many California-bound gold seekers.

The trail from Tahlequah joined the established Santa Fe Trail at Fuller's Ranch, on Running Turkey Creek, eight miles east of McPherson, Kansas.

The Santa Fe Trail

The Santa Fe Trail was originally a commercial route from the Missouri River to Santa Fe in Mexican Territory. In 1821, Mexico received its independence from Spain, and the territory was opened for trade. In 1822, William Becknell took the first freight wagons over the trail, using what would be known as the Cimarron Cutoff.

The Santa Fe Trail followed up the Arkansas River from Great Bend, Kansas. Between Cimarron and Lakin, Kansas, several branches of the Cimarron Cutoff forded the river and led southwest to the Cimarron River. This trail cut across the extreme southeastern corner of Colorado, following the north bank of the Cimarron River.

With the establishment of Bent's Old Fort in 1833, travel increased on what became known as the Mountain Branch of the Santa Fe Trail. The branch of the trail continued up the Arkansas River from western Kansas to a point seven miles west of Bent's Old Fort at present-day La Junta. Here the Mountain Branch crossed the Arkansas River and ran southwest to Trinidad and Raton Pass.

With the California gold rush of 1849, gold seekers traveled the Santa Fe Trail Mountain Branch to La Junta, then continued west along the Arkansas River on the Cherokee Trail.

The importance of the Santa Fe Trail decreased with the coming of the railroad. In 1870, the Kansas Pacific Railroad had reached Kit Carson, Colorado, on the Smoky Hill Trail. Here wagons would proceed southwest to join the Mountain Branch east of Bent's Old Fort. In 1880, the Atchison, Topeka & Santa Fe Railroad reached Santa Fe.

A U.S. Forest Service pack train follows the Santa Fe Trail Mountain Branch southwest of La Junta. Note the trail marker near the trailing mule.

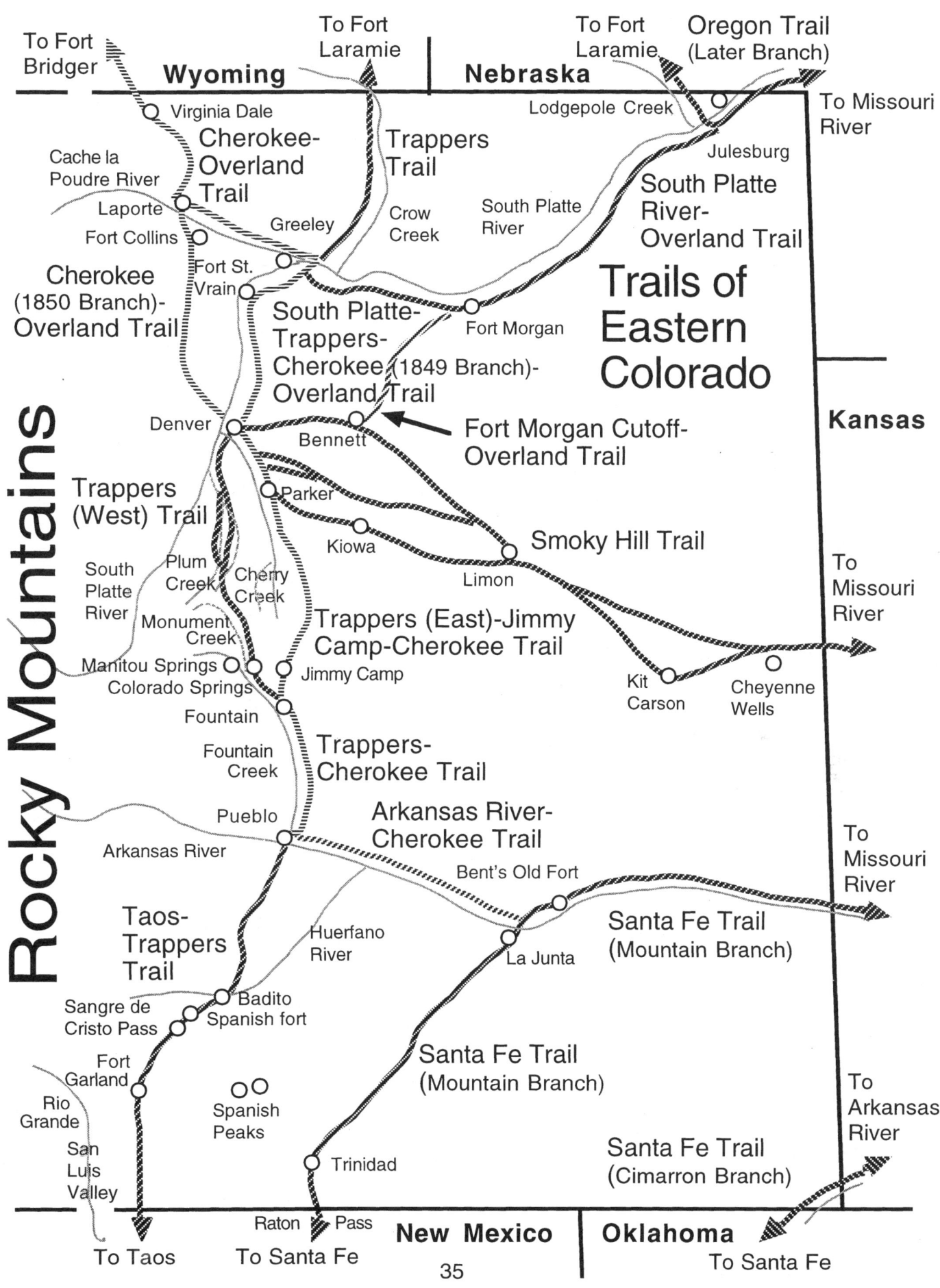

Bent's Old Fort

Bent's Old Fort was built in 1833 by William and Charles Bent, and Ceran St. Vrain. The Bent, St. Vrain & Company, formed in 1831, was engaged in freighting supplies to Santa Fe and Taos, where they had established trading posts. The company could supply their new adobe post on the Arkansas River via the Santa Fe Trail Mountain Branch, then continue on to Santa Fe and Taos.

The fort carried on an active trade with Americans, Mexicans and Indians. But on August 21, 1849, William Bent removed valuables from the fort and burned it.

Lt. E. G. Beckwith, member of the 1853 John Gunnison railroad survey noted:

> Mr. Bent abandoned his fort about four years ago, but not until he had destroyed it. Its adobe walls still stand in part only, with here and there a tower and chimney. . . . It is of easy access from its central position, from the east, from Santa Fe, from Taos through the Sangre de Cristo Pass, and from Fort Laramie. It is on an emigrant road from southern Missouri and Arkansas, either by the North Park or Coochetopa Pass; and it is in the heart of the Indian country

Also in 1853, William Bent constructed a new fort, built of stone, 38 miles east. After the Colorado gold rush, the old fort was used as a stage station and post office.

Bent's Old Fort presents living history programs representing the 1846 trail era, the year Stephen Kearny's "Army of the West" visited the fort.

The stone arch served as an auto entrance to the site of Bent's Old Fort. The fort was reconstructed in 1976 and is now a National Historic Site.

The fort was a major supply post for Americans, Mexicans and Indians from 1833 to 1849. A fur press stands in the middle of the plaza.

Trail

trail, trāl, *v.t.* . . . **3**. to follow the track, trail or scent of; track. **4**. to follow along behind (another) in a race . . . **6**. to tread down or make a path through (grass or the like) . . . **12**. to follow as if drawn along . . . **14**. to go slowly, lazily or wearily along . . . **23**. a path or track made across a wild region over rough country, or the like, by the passage of people or animals . . .

The 23rd definition of trail in the Random House Unabridged Dictionary, second edition, 1993, accurately defines the Cherokee Trail.

Ralph Moody, in his book *The Old Trails West*, gives an oldtime cowhand's idea of a trail:

> Didn't ever you take note how the deepest buffalo and wild horse trails always leads by the easiest way to the nearest water, the best grass, and the lowest mountain passes? . . . Don't no man nor no wild critter wear a trail where he happens to go; only where he needs to go. Find where a trail changed course and you'll find where the need of them passing over it changed. It's all wrote down for them that can read, just like it is with a man. An old man's story is wrote in lines on his face; an old trail's story is wrote in lines on the face of the earth.

Over the Cherokee Trail passed trappers, traders, military expeditions, adventurers, gold seekers, immigrants and homesteaders.

The Cherokee Trail
A Trail of Many Names

GLO Land Plats:
- Laramie Road (1878)
- Laramie City Stage Road (1877)
- Old Denver and Cheyenne Road (1876)
- Old Laramie Road (1864)
- Road to Camp Collins (1866)
- Cherokee Trail (1862)
- Road to Denver (1865)
- Cherry Creek Road to Denver (1865)
- Denver Road (1865)
- Old Military Road (1866)
- Santa Fe Road (1869)
- Squirrel Creek Road (1866)
- Old Southern Road (1866)
- Road from Colorado [City] to Pueblo (1862)
- Road to Pueblo (1866)
- Pueblo and Fort Lyon Road (1865)
- Arkansas River Road (1866)

Trail Users:
- The Cherokee Trail (Marcy, map, 1858)
- Cherokee trail (Root, 1901)
- road which had been made by the waggons from Bents Fort (Franklin, 1845)
- a wagon trail that led to Pueblo, made by the traders (Brown, 1846)
- Cherokee Trail . . . shortest practical road from Denver to Salt Lake (Greeley, 1859)
- Cherokee California trail (Marcy, 1858)
- old trail from Santa Fe to Salt Lake (Richardson, 1859)
- old Taos road (Fitch, 1865)
- The Santa Fe tract (Villard, 1859)
- Road which runs from St. Vrains fort to the Arkansas (Frémont, 1843)
- Jimmy Camp Road (Easton P. O. App., 1872)
- divide road (Post, 1859)
- Cherokee Trail to Calefornay (Voorhees, 1858)
- Road from Taos to Fort Bridger (Voorhees, 1858)
- Wagon road to the settlements on the Arkansas (Frémont, 1843)
- "Arkansas Emigrant Trail" (Du Bois, 1859)
- New Mexico Laramie Fort Bridger and Salt Lake Road (Hartley, map, 1858)
- The Fort Union and Laramie Trail (Willing, 1859)
- Trail to Ft. St. Vrain (Berthoud, map, 1858)
- California trail (Peck, 1857)
- The great Cherokee trail to California (Willing, 1859)
- Southern, or Santa Fe route (Parsons, 1858)

Locations: [Fort Collins], [Greeley], [South Platte River], [Denver], [Franktown], [Colorado Springs], [Fountain], [Pueblo], [Arkansas River], [Bent's Old Fort]

Borders: Wyoming, Nebraska, Kansas, New Mexico, Oklahoma

The Cherokee Trail in eastern Colorado has been called many different names by users of the trail and by surveyors for the General Land Office (GLO)

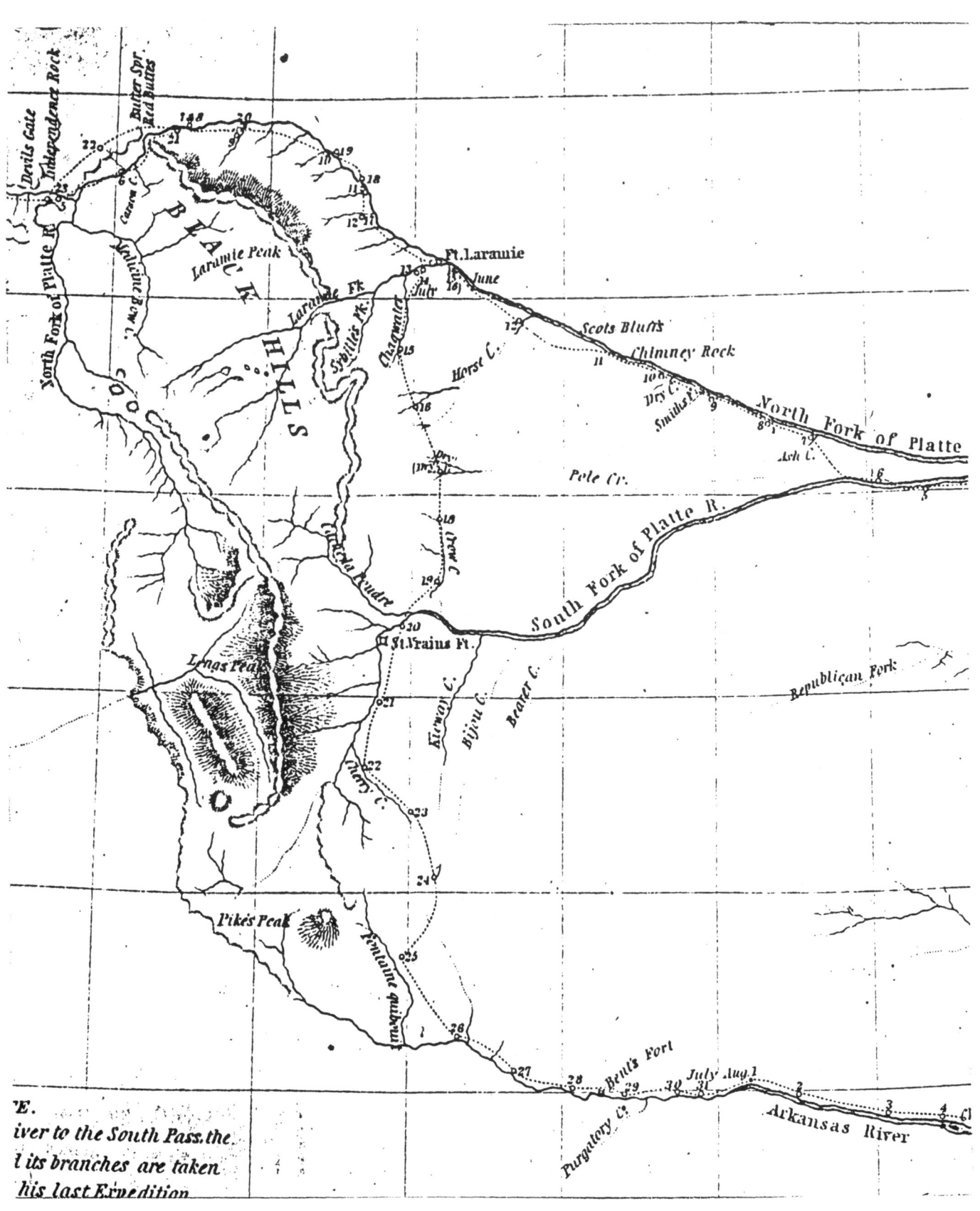

Map of the Stephen Watts Kearny expedition of 1845. Drawn by William B. Franklin, the map was printed in the 1845 U. S. Senate Public Documents, Serial set 470.

II.
The Cherokee Trail
In Colorado

The Cherokee Trail and Waterways of Eastern Colorado

"Wood, Water & Grass"

Trail travelers were dependent on these items for comfort and survival for themselves and their animals. **Waterways** provided for these needs.

The two major rivers of eastern Colorado, the Arkansas and South Platte, and their tributaries, enabled Cherokee Trail travelers to pass through Stephen Long's "Great American Desert."

The Santa Fe Trail Mountain Branch ascended the **Arkansas River** to a point seven miles west of Bent's Old Fort. Here it crossed the river and headed southwest for Raton Pass and Santa Fe. The Cherokee Trail continued up the Arkansas River to the mouth of Fountain Creek at Pueblo.

The Cherokee Trail then left the Arkansas River and traveled up the east bank of **Fountain Creek**, the largest tributary of the Arkansas River in Colorado.

At Fountain, the Cherokee Trail left Fountain Creek and continued north to cross the **Arkansas-Platte Divide** or "Palmer Divide," the divide between the Arkansas and South Platte River drainages. Good water and campsites were usually to be had at Jimmy Camp Creek and Black Squirrel Creek (Arkansas River drainage), and West Kiowa Creek, Running Creek and Russellville Gulch (South Platte River drainage).

At Franktown, the Cherokee Trail hit **Cherry Creek** and followed the east bank to its confluence with the South Platte River at Denver.

The 1849 branch of the Cherokee Trail then continued down the **South Platte River** to the mouth of the Cache la Poudre River, east of Greeley. After crossing the South Platte, the trail followed up the north bank of the **Cache la Poudre River** to Laporte, northwest of Fort Collins.

The 1850 branch of the Cherokee Trail crossed the South Platte River at Denver and followed along the east base of the **foothills** of the Rocky Mountains to the Cache la Poudre River at Laporte. Water and good campsites were available at Clear Creek, Boulder Creek, St. Vrain Creek, Little Thompson River and Big Thompson River.

After crossing the Cache la Poudre River, the 1850 Branch merged with the 1849 Branch and the combined trail crossed the **Laramie Mountains** (often called the "Black Hills" by early travelers), the divide between the drainages of the South Platte and North Platte rivers. Water and campsites were available at Owl Creek, Stonewall Creek and Dale Creek (South Platte River drainage), and Willow Creek in Wyoming (North Platte River drainage).

We have but three wants, - so remote in civilization, which counts them by the thousand, - water, grass, and fuel, and wonderfully little and various in kind of the last; and we find the Earth a '*step*-mother,' for she seldom grants us more than two of them, and when in an ill-humor, denies us all three.

Philip St. George Cooke, July 16, 1845

The Cherokee Trail in Eastern Colorado

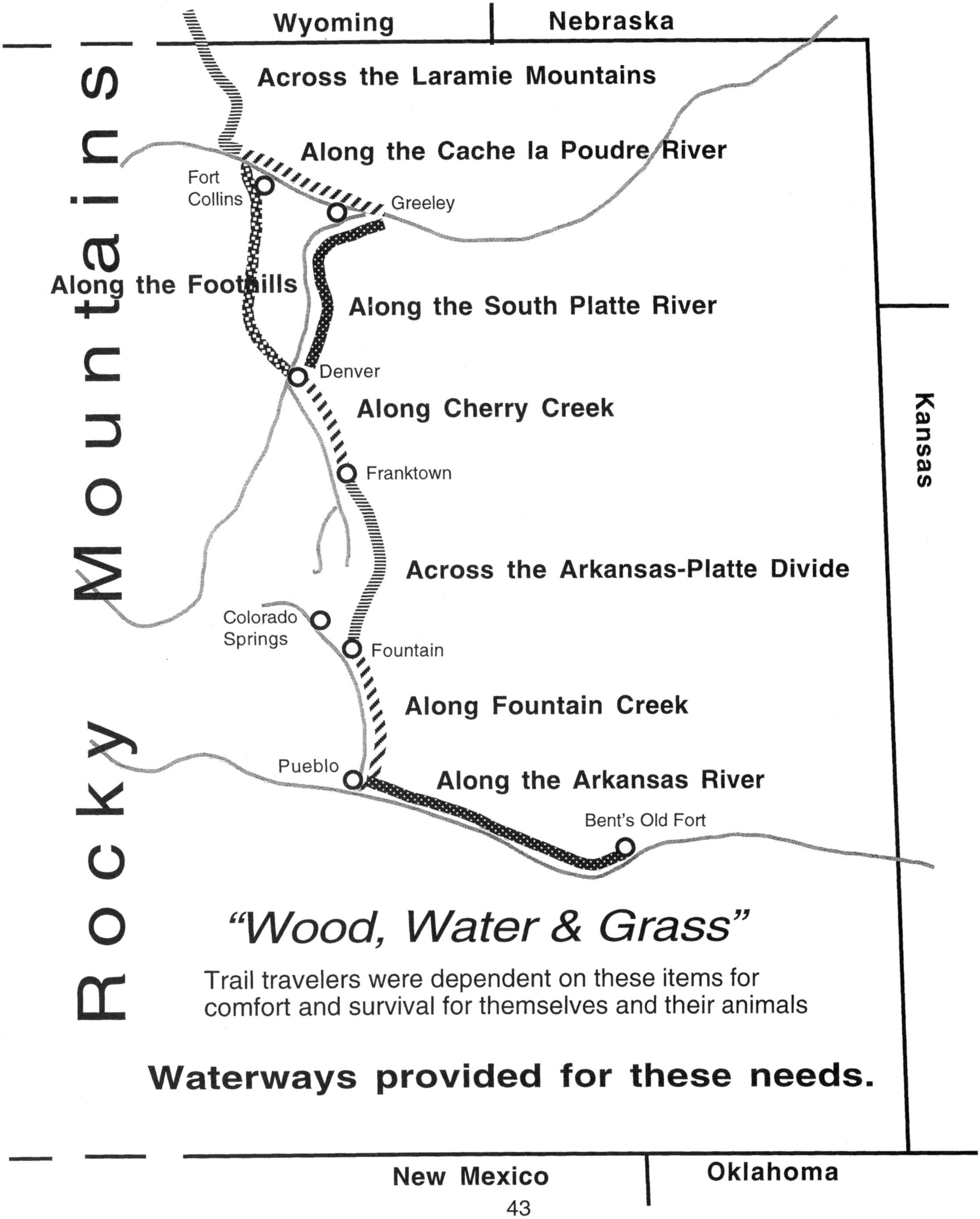

Wyoming | Nebraska

Across the Laramie Mountains

Along the Cache la Poudre River

Fort Collins — Greeley

Along the Foothills

Along the South Platte River

Denver

Along Cherry Creek

Franktown

Across the Arkansas-Platte Divide

Colorado Springs — Fountain

Along Fountain Creek

Pueblo — Along the Arkansas River

Bent's Old Fort

Rocky Mountains

Kansas

"Wood, Water & Grass"

Trail travelers were dependent on these items for comfort and survival for themselves and their animals

Waterways provided for these needs.

New Mexico | Oklahoma

The Cherokee Trail Along the Arkansas River

Shortly after passing Bent's Fort, following the California trail up the river, we got our first sight of Pike's Peak, resting on the western horizon like a small white cloud, which many of us thought it really was; but day after day, as we marched toward it, the white cloud grew larger, higher, and plainer, other mountains on each side of it coming into view, till in a few days it seemed we were running up against the whole Rocky Mountain Range.   Robert M. Peck, 1857

The **Arkansas River** has its headwaters in the Rocky Mountains northeast of Leadville. The river then flows onto the plains, passing Pueblo and Bent's Old Fort before entering Kansas.

From Kansas, the Santa Fe Trail Mountain Branch ascended the Arkansas River to present-day La Junta, where the trail crossed the river and headed southwest to Raton Pass and Santa Fe, New Mexico. The Cherokee Trail continued west, up the Arkansas River to Fountain Creek and Pueblo. Most early-day trail traffic followed the north bank of the river, for until 1848, the south side of the river was Mexican Territory.

Bent's Old Fort, built in 1833 by the Bent & St. Vrain Company, was a major stop and landmark on the Mountain Branch of the Santa Fe Trail. William Bent abandoned the fort in 1849, but the ruins were still a major curiosity, and later were revived as a stage stop.

Approximately four miles west of Bent's Old Fort was **Milk Fort**. Nothing remains of this small post, established to service Bent's Old Fort and possibly a home for individuals not really welcomed at Bent's.

Near Milk Fort, some travelers noted the hills or bluffs near present-day North La Junta. Referred to as "**potato hills**," these relatively low formations were noticed by travelers traveling the flat plains along the Arkansas River.

Proceeding west, few landmarks were passed and most of the attention was directed to the Rocky Mountains: **Pikes Peak** to the northwest and the **Spanish Peaks** to the southwest.

Twelve miles east of Pueblo, the Cherokee Trail crossed **Chico Creek**. Here many travelers left the Arkansas River and followed up Chico Creek. This "**Chico Creek Cutoff**" rejoined the main Cherokee Trail on Fountain Creek, 15 miles north of Pueblo.

Near present-day Baxter, six miles east of Pueblo, was the site of short-lived **Gantt's Fort**. This trading post was built by John Gantt in 1832. Gantt was a member of the Henry Dodge Dragoon Expedition, which passed the abandoned fort in 1835.

On the south side of the Arkansas River, opposite the mouth of Fountain Creek, was **Mormontown**. This was 1846-1847 winter quarters for a party of Mormon emigrants, and three sick detachments of the Mormon Battalion of General Stephen Watts Kearny's Army of the West.

The trading post of **Pueblo**, built in 1842, was on the west side of Fountain Creek. Here a trail, called the Taos or Trappers Trail, led southwest over Sangre de Cristo Pass to the San Luis Valley and Taos. The Cherokee Trail turned north to follow the east side of Fountain Creek.

Ⓕ Pueblo

"At the delta, formed by the junction of Fontaine qui Bouit with the Arkansas, a trading fort, called the Pueblo, was built during the summer of 1842. The post is owned by a company of independent traders, on the common property system . . . profitable trade with both Mexicans and Indians" Sage, 1842

"reached Pueblo on the 7th of August. We found some six or eight mountaineers in the fort with their families. They had Indian and Spanish women for wives." Brown, 1846

"We approached the gates of Pueblo. It is a wretched species of a fort, of most primitive construction." Parkman, 1846

"found the remains of an old settlement called 'El Pueblo,' all the inhabitants of which had been murdered in one night by the Indians." Du Bois, 1858

Ⓓ Gantt's Fort

"passed an old trading establishment formerally occupied by Capt. Gant." Evans, 1835

"Some six miles below the mouth of Fontaine qui Bouit are the ruins of an old fort, occupied several years since by one Capt. Grant as a trading post." Sage, 1842

The Cherokee Trail
Along the Arkansas River

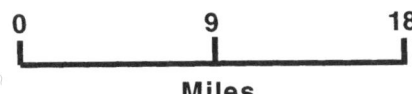

Ⓐ Bent's Old Fort

"Messrs. Bent and St. Vrain have a large trading establishment at this place, and carry on an extensive trade with the Indians." Kingsbury, 1835

"pass Bent's Old Fort, built chiefly of adobes: having been abandoned more than five years, it is fast falling into ruins. The Arkansas almost washes its base." Willing, 1859

"crossed the Arkansas at Bent's old fort, now used as a stage station and post office. The stages from Santa Fe and Denver meet here" Allyn, 1863

"This is a grand rambling old frontier trading post; with tremendously thick adobe walls; bastions, and all the necessary defenses against Indian assault. The stage company have made it a very complete and comfortable station." Rocky Mountain News, 1866

Ⓒ "Potato Hills"

"We had the finest scenery yet, being a succession of round Potato hills some two hundred feet above bottom lands. . . . Dr. Rose, while out on Potato hills, first saw Pike's Peak." Post, 1859

"We see many things new to our eyes, too tedious to mention. These hilly patches of broken country put me in mind of a large sweet potato patch that hasn't been set in slips. They are hills of pure sand." Powell, 1860

Ⓔ Mormontown

"a party of Mormons . . . were now preparing to spend the winter at a spot about half a mile from the Pueblo . . We crossed the river . . . log huts rising along the edge of the woods" Parkman, 1846

"came to Pueblo, our intended winter quarters . . . We soon put 18 or 20 houses up, also a blacksmith shop, and a large corral." Steele, 1846

"Fandango at Mormontown." Barclay, 1846

Ⓑ Milk Fort

"Five miles above Fort William, we came to Fort El Puebla. It is constructed of adobies, and consists of a series of one-story houses built around a quadrangle . . It belongs to a company of American and Mexican trappers, who, wearied with the service, have retired to this spot to spend the remainder of their days in raising grain, vegetables, horses, mules &c., for the various trading establishments in these regions." Farnham, 1839

"*Pueblo de Leche* The Milk People are a community residing in a mud fort on the Arkansas . . . there cannot exist in any nook or corner of the wide universe a wilder, stranger, more remarkable collection of human beings for a civilized eye to look upon . . . Milk Fort is so termed from the number of goats possessed by its tenants" Field, 1840

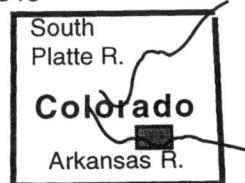

45

The sand hills west of Bent's Old Fort were known as the "Potato Hills." The west-bound traveler was now within sight of the Rocky Mountains.

Beaver activity along the Arkansas River near the mouth of Chico Creek. Here the "Chico Creek Cutoff" left the river and ran northwest to Fountain Creek.

The Mormontown marker at Runyon Field in Pueblo. Across the river from Pueblo, a detachment of Mormon emigrants spent the winter of 1846-1847.

Excavation of the Pueblo trading post, built in 1842 by independent traders. Ute Indians massacred residents of the fort on December 25, 1854.

The Taos-Trappers Trail

The Taos-Trappers Trail ran from Taos, New Mexico, north to Fort Laramie, Wyoming. The trail connected settlements and trading posts on the Rio Grande, Arkansas, South Platte and North Platte rivers. The section of the trail from Taos to Pueblo was known primarily as the Taos Trail.

From Taos, the trail ran north to Sangre de Cristo Creek in the San Luis Valley. The trail ascended the creek to Sangre de Cristo Pass, the divide between the Rio Grande and the Arkansas River watersheds. After descending Oak Creek, the trail crossed the Huerfano River at present-day Badito. The trail rounded the southern end of the Wet Mountains and crossed the Arkansas River to Pueblo. Here the Taos Trail merged with the Cherokee Trail.

Jacob Fowler traveled the Taos Trail from Pueblo to Taos in January of 1822. He noted an abandoned fort below the east summit of Sangre de Cristo Pass. This was a fort built by the Spanish in 1819 to ward off foreign invaders. Land south of the Arkansas River was Mexican Territory until 1848.

The trail was heavily used by Mexican and American traders, supplying Pueblo, the forts on the South Platte River and Fort Laramie.

Sections of the Taos Trail were used by the 38th and 39th Parallel railroad survey expeditions in 1853. The Edward Beale and John Gunnison survey parties ascended the Huerfano River to the Taos Trail at Badito. They then crossed Sangre de Cristo Pass to the San Luis Valley.

Site of Badito, at the confluence of the Huerfano River and Oak Creek. Here the Taos Trail crossed the Huerfano River.

The Cherokee Trail Along Fountain Creek

Fontaine qui Bouit, or the Boiling Fountain, is the name bestowed upon a considerable stream that heads under Pikes Peak . . . and pursues a southerly course till it unites with the Arkansas.
Rufus Sage, 1842

Fountain Creek, the largest tributary of the Arkansas River in Colorado, has its headwaters on the north side of Pikes Peak, near Woodland Park. It flows southeast out of the mountains to pass Manitou Springs, from which the creek derives its name. After passing through Colorado Springs, the creek turns due south to empty into the Arkansas River at Pueblo.

After following up the Arkansas River, the Cherokee Trail turned north at Pueblo to follow up the east side of Fountain Creek. Interstate 25 follows the west side of Fountain Creek. A more leisurely drive is to follow Jerry Murphy Road north from Pueblo, on the east side of Fountain Creek. This single road to Fountain, which closely follows the Cherokee Trail, has several name changes: Overton Road, Meridian Road, Hanover Road and finally Old Pueblo Road.

Pueblo, the 1842 trading post, was situated west of Fountain Creek. Here also, the Taos-Trappers Trail from Taos, New Mexico, joined the Cherokee Trail.

Near Runyon Field stands a monument:

THE MORMON BATTALION IN THE MEXICAN WAR SPENT THE WINTER OF 1846-1847 NEAR THIS SITE. WITH THEIR FAMILIES AND MORMON IMMIGRANTS FROM MISSISSIPPI THEY FORMED A SETTLEMENT OF 275 PERSONS. THEY ERECTED A CHURCH AND ROWS OF DWELLINGS OF COTTONWOOD LOGS. HERE WERE BORN THE FIRST WHITE CHILDREN IN COLORADO.

A small settlement called **Fountain City** was established on the east side of Fountain Creek. A Colorado Historical Society marker at the intersection of Joplin Ave. and Damson St. reads:

THE HILL ONE BLOCK EAST IS **JACOB FOWLERS LOOKOUT** LATER CALLED SUGAR LOAF HILL. NEAR IT IN A LOG HOUSE FOWLER AND HIS TRAPPERS LIVED IN JAN. 1822. **FOUNTAIN CITY** PREDECESSOR OF PUEBLO AND FOUNDED IN THE FALL OF 1858, RAN WEST FROM THE HILL TO THE FOUNTAIN RIVER. MEN WHO CAME AS GOLDSEEKERS REMAINED TO FARM, TRADE AND FOUND A CITY.

Fifteen miles north of Pueblo, the **Chico Creek Cutoff** branch of the Cherokee Trail merged with the Fountain Creek branch. The campsite at this junction became known as **Independence Camp**. On the 4th of July, 1858, a party of gold seekers camped at this site. Although Pikes Peak and the Rocky Mountains dominated the landscape to the west of the trail, **The Buttes**, a series of natural sand hills six miles south of Fountain, stand to the east of the trail.

At present-day Fountain, The Cherokee Trail crossed **Jimmy Camp Creek**, then left Fountain Creek to head north-northeast to cross the Arkansas-Platte Divide. A trail also continued up Fountain Creek to Manitou Springs.

The Cherokee Trail
Along Fountain Creek

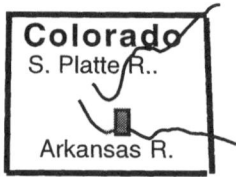

"Fontaine qui Bouit, or the Boiling Fountain, is the name bestowed upon a considerable stream that heads under Pikes Peak . . . and pursues a southerly course till it unites with the Arkansas."   Sage, 1842

"We resumed our journey very early down the river, following an extremely good lodge trail."   Frémont, 1843

Ⓒ The Buttes

"to the northeast, we viewed four or five remarkable piles, reminding the student of history of the ruins of the ancient edifices of Greece and Rome. They appeared to be comprised of a species of sand, with here and there a green tree dotting their surfaces."   Tierney, 1858

Ⓑ Independence Camp - Chico Creek Cutoff

"Left the river this morning. Crossed the bluffs [on the Chico Creek Cutoff] and struck the creek fifteen miles above the old town [Pueblo] and camped. Struck the road from Taos to Fort Bridger."   Voorhees, July 4, 1858

"the road continues up the river [Arkansas] . . and then leaves it, bearing to the right [Chico Creek Cutoff]. . . it strikes the Fontaine qui Bouille creek, at a beautiful grove of cottonwoods called Independence Camp."   Parsons, 1858

"Fall into the Fort Union and Laramie Trail . . Met a train of Mexican carts, returning from Auraria, whither they had gone with flour."   Willing, 1859

Ⓐ Fountain City

"Traveled six miles to Fountain City. Here the road leaves the Arkansas and follows the Fountain Qui Bourat."   Post, 1859

"we got to Fountain city, which consisted of forty or fifty log and mud cabins, inhabited by Americans and Mexicans; or rather WERE; for most of them had gone to the diggings."   Gass, 1859

The clear waters of the Arkansas River (left) merge with the muddy waters of Fountain Creek. Photo taken in 1995, an exceptionally high runoff season.

Sand hills, known as The Buttes, northeast of the Pinon Truck Stop. The hills can be seen from Interstate 25, which follows the west side of Fountain Creek.

Pikes Peak

Thus far no gold had been discovered within sixty miles of Pike's Peak; but the first reports located the diggings near that mountain, and 'Pike's Peak' - one of those happy alliterations which stick like burs in the public memory - was now the general name for the whole region.
Albert D. Richardson, 1859

Pikes Peak was named for **Zebulon Pike**, who, in 1806, visited the area but was not able to climb the peak because of snow. He stated, on November 27th:

The summit of the Grand Peak, which was entirely bare of vegetation, and covered with snow, now appeared at a distance of fifteen or sixteen miles from us, and as high again as that we had ascended . . . I believe no human being could have ascended to its summit

The peak was climbed 14 years later by Dr. Edwin James, a member of the Stephen H. Long Expedition.

Dr. James & party returned from the mountains, the Dr. with two of the men having visited the summit of the Peake . . . the commanding officer [Stephen Long] announced the following compliments, by naming the high Peake, 'James Peak' believing him to be the first American that ever ascended to its summit.
John R. Bell, July, 1820

The peak was referred to as Pikes Peak by subsequent travelers and the "James Peak" name did not stick. Dr. James did get a peak named for him, on the Continental Divide northeast of Berthoud Pass. Pikes Peak was the major landmark on the Cherokee Trail in eastern Colorado. Mentioned in almost every journal, the peak was visible from as far east as Bent's Old Fort. Its sight lifted the spirits of the westward bound traveler, for the Rocky Mountains had been their goal during the long march along the Arkansas River. Pikes Peak was also visible from the Cherokee Trail as far north as Fort Collins and Greeley.

The piney region of the mountains to the south was enveloped in smoke, and I was informed had been on fire for several months. Pike's Peak is said to be visible from this place [Fort St. Vrain], about one hundred miles to the southward; but the smoky state of the atmosphere prevented my seeing it.
John C. Frémont, July 11, 1842

The Colorado gold rush of 1858-1859 was often referred to as the "Pike's Peak" gold rush. "Pike's Peak or Bust" was a well-used phrase. Pikes Peak was one of the few known place names in what was then western Kansas Territory.

'Pike's Peak Hotel,' 'Pike's Peak Ranch,' 'Pike's Peak Lunch,' 'Pike's Peak Outfits,' 'Pike's Peak Line,' the shortest, cheapest and most reliable route, and Pike's Peak almost everything, greets you upon either hand, and Leavenworth is realizing glorious profits out of the general excitement.
Libeus Barney, May, 1859

The Cherokee Trail Across the Arkansas-Platte Divide

the route led over a rough country, interspersed with high piney ridges and beautiful valleys, sustaining a luxuriant growth of vegetation, which is known as the Divide. This romantic region gives rise to several large tributaries both of the Platte and Arkansas
Rufus Sage, September, 1842

The **Arkansas-Platte Divide**, north and northeast of Colorado Springs, is a high plateau running east of the Rocky Mountains. It is the headwaters of Monument, Black Squirrel, Big Sandy and other creeks running south into the Arkansas River; and Plum, Cherry, Running, Kiowa and other creeks running north into the South Platte River. The Ponderosa Pine-covered land of the "Divide" is called the Black Forest, often called the "Pineries" in trail days.

Today's modern trail, Interstate 25, crosses the Arkansas-Platte Divide, also called the Palmer Divide, at Monument Hill, 15 miles west of the Cherokee Trail.

After crossing Jimmy Camp Creek, the Cherokee Trail left Fountain Creek and headed north to cross the Arkansas-Platte Divide. North of Fountain, the trail closely follows present-day Fountain Mesa Drive, keeping to the high, dry land between Fountain Creek to the west and Jimmy Camp Creek to the east. The trail passed by Big Johnson Reservoir, then is crossed by the east runway of the Colorado Springs Municipal Airport.

The Cherokee Trail hit Jimmy Camp Creek again at **Jimmy Camp**, eight miles east of downtown Colorado Springs. The site, named for Jimmy Daugherty, mountain man and trader, was a well used and well documented campsite.

Near the intersection of Constitution Ave. and U. S. Highway 24 <u>was</u> an historical marker:

ONE MILE SOUTHEAST ARE THE SPRING AND SITE OF JIMMY'S CAMP, NAMED FOR JIMMY (LAST NAME UNDETERMINED), AN EARLY TRAPPER WHO WAS MURDERED THERE. A FAMOUS CAMP SITE ON THE TRAIL CONNECTING THE ARKANSAS AND PLATTE RIVERS, AND VARIOUSLY KNOWN AS "TRAPPERS TRAIL," "CHEROKEE TRAIL," AND "JIMMY'S CAMP TRAIL." SITE VISITED BY RUFUS SAGE (1842), FRANCIS PARKMAN (1846), MORMONS (1847) AND BY MANY GOLD SEEKERS OF 1858-59.

After leaving Jimmy Camp, the Cherokee Trail continued north and entered the **Black Forest** one mile before reaching **Black Squirrel Creek**. Here Capt. Randolph B. Marcy built corrals to protect his stock in the spring of 1858. The location was thereafter often called "**Brush Corral**."

Here also was built an early Colorado sawmill called Weir's Mill. This mill became the Easton Post Office in 1872. Later the post office was renamed Eastonville and moved to a new site on the Denver & New Orleans (later the Colorado & Southern) Railroad four miles to the northeast.

The trail continued north through the Black Forest, closely following Meridian Road. After crossing the Arkansas-Platte Divide, the Cherokee Trail reached **Point of Rocks**, well known landmark and campsite on West Kiowa Creek. Here also is **Fagan's Grave**. Charles Michael Fagan, a civilian teamster with the Col. William Loring and Capt. Randolph Marcy military expedition, froze to death in a snowstorm May 2, 1858.

Continuing north-northwest, the Cherokee Trail crossed Running Creek, then followed over the plateau east of East Cherry Creek. West of the trail, overlooking East Cherry Creek was "**Blackfoot Cave**," visited and named by Rufus Sage in 1842.

The Cherokee Trail hit Russellville Gulch at **Russellville**. The 1866 General Land Office survey of the Russellville area labeled present-day Russellville Gulch "East Cherry Creek." Many trail travelers referred to the gulch as "Head of Cherry Creek."

The town was named for William Green Russell, who found small amounts of gold here in 1858. This and other small discoveries led to the Colorado gold rush of 1859. Recent archaeological work in the Russellville area indicate that the area may have been a Confederate recruitment and training area.

The Cherokee Trail continued down Russellville Gulch, striking Cherry Creek one mile south of Franktown. The trail then continued down Cherry Creek to its confluence with the South Platte River at Denver.

Foundations of a cabin at Jimmy Camp. To the upper right, one of the springs on the west bank of Jimmy Camp Creek.

The Cherokee Trail
Across the Arkansas-Platte Divide

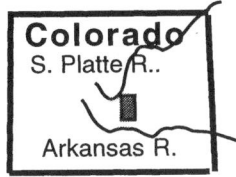

F Russellville

"In camp at last on head waters of the long sought, anxiously looked for Cherry Creek . . . All about us is another grand pine forest, and in the midst of it is a new town called Russellville."   Willing, 1859

"Tonight we are camped on the far famed Cherry creek . . . Several cabins have been built, and forty or fifty more commenced and left unfinished; and nearly all have left here and gone to Clear creek diggings"   Gass, 1859

E "Blackfoot" Cave

"night finds us at Blackfoot-camp, snugly chambered in a spacious cave"   Sage, 1842

"found Blackfoot Spring & went into camp."   Du Bois, 1858

"Pass a large flock of sheep destined for Auraria. Met a trader returning to New Mexico. Had taken flour to the mines"   Willing, 1859

"made 30 miles over a most beautiful prairie, thence to point of rocks to Cherry Creek, 18 miles"   Steele, 1847

D Point of Rock & Fagan's Grave

"camped on prairie branch . . . Leaving Stony Point we have rolling prairie road"   Engels, 1854

"We passed a perpendicular rock, five hundred feet high, at the base of which was a tomb of recent origin, occupied by some unfortunate itinerant, at its head stood a wooden cross, bearing the inscription 'Charles Michael Fagan 1858'"
   Tierney, 1858

C Black Forest

"We pushed through an extensive tract of pine woods. Large black squirrels were leaping among the branches"   Parkman, 1846

"The people of Auraria which is forty miles distant drew their supply of venison from this neighborhood last winter"   Willing, 1859

B Black Squirrel Creek - "Brush Corral"

"This creek is near the crest of the high divide between the Arkansas and Platte Rivers. It is a small creek, but always affords good water."   Marcy, 1858

"a snow storm set in . . . and continued without cessation for sixty hours. We immediately set to work making "corrals" for the animals"   Marcy, 1858

"we move forward over a high but level road to Squirrel Creek, where there is a large pine forest extending some thirty miles east and west."   Post, 1859

A Jimmy Camp

"we reached an affluent of the Fontaine qui Bouit, called Daugherty's creek . . . Our place of stay is a sweet little valley enclosed by piney ridges . . . the creek derives its name from Daugherty, a trader who was murdered upon it several years ago"   Sage, 1842

"We got to what is called Jims Camp. There is a fine spring and lots of pine wood here. It is on the Cherokee trail, to Calaforny."   Voorhees, 1858

"At Jim's Spring, fifty miles south of Auraria, on Thursday, June 9th, we deposited in their final resting place, the remains of Thomas Alexander, from Montgomery County, Missouri"   Willing, June, 1859

"We nooned today, at a spring of the coldest and best water that I have seen on the route. It is Jimmy's spring, or Alexander's grave"   Gass, June 11, 1859

"met 3 arkansas trains with more than 1000 head of cattle we came on and nooned on fountain Cabuoba"   Hundley, 1856

Housing developments in Colorado Springs are encroaching on the Jimmy Camp area. Pikes Peak, the major trail landmark is in the background.

Homestead on the Arkansas-Platte Divide. Permanent residents, settlements and sawmills developed as the result of the 1859 gold rush.

Point of Rocks, at the trail crossing of West Kiowa Creek. The creek, on the north side of the Arkansas-Platte Divide, runs north to the South Platte River.

From the top of Point of Rocks, traces of the trail can be seen crossing the pasture. Pikes Peak in the background.

Weather and the "Divide"

This is a locality which is very subject to severe storms, and it is here that I encountered the most severe snow-storm that I have ever known, on the first day of May, 1858. I would advise travelers to hasten past this spot as rapidly as possible during the winter and spring months, as a storm might prove very serious here.
Capt. Randolph B. Marcy, 1858

Bad weather conditions were a real problem for trail travelers. Although most of the travel through eastern Colorado was during the spring and summer months, violent storms could occur at any time.

The country hereabouts . . . is much subject to storms of rain, hail, snow, and wind, - and it is rarely a person can pass through it without being caught by a storm of some kind.
Rufus Sage, September 13, 1842

One particularly bad storm in 1858 caught the Col. W. W. Loring and Capt. Randolph B. Marcy military expedition by surprise. They were moving supplies and animals from Fort Union, New Mexico, to the Fort Bridger area. On April 29, 1858, they were on the Arkansas-Platte Divide: Capt. Marcy at Black Squirrel Creek and Col. Loring at Point of Rocks, seven miles to the north.

It was a mild and pleasant spring day, with no appearance of bad weather, but as night approached it became cloudy, and about dark a snow storm set in accompanied by a violent gale of wind from the north, which increased until it became a perfect tempest, and continued without cessation for sixty hours. We immediately set to work making "corrals" for the animals, but before all were secured one herd of three hundred mules and horses stampeded and broke away in spite of the headmen, and ran directly with the wind for fifty miles.
Capt. Randolph B. Marcy, 1858

Charles Michael Fagan, civilian teamster for the expedition, froze to death in the snowstorm and is buried at the base of Point of Rocks.
Mrs. A. C. Hunt recorded the following on June 25, 1859:

traveled 15 miles to a pine forest - very beautiful but sad from a number of graves here - 8 are in view of persons who have frozen to death, one as late as June third, '59. The changes are so sudden even in the summer that from being very warm it will be so cold as to benumb the body before fire can be made to warm it.

Monument Hill, today's Interstate 25 "trail" across the Arkansas-Platte Divide, is well known for its frequent adverse traveling conditions.

Trail travelers often mentioned the adverse weather conditions on the "Divide," as do many travelers on Monument Hill, today's Interstate 25 crossing.

Charles Michael Fagan froze to death in a snowstorm on May 2, 1858. He was a civilian teamster for the William Loring-Randolph Marcy military expedition.

Eastonville
Campsite, Sawmill, Railroad Town, Ghost Town

Eastonville today is a ghost town on the abandoned Colorado & Southern Railroad, ten miles north of Falcon. The town, still on many current road maps, has a few standing buildings and many stone foundations. It is home to one family.

The "town" started as a campsite on the Cherokee Trail, five miles to the southwest, on Black Squirrel Creek. On the south edge of the Black Forest, the creek had dependable water, and was ten miles north of Jimmy Camp, another popular campsite on the trail. Capt. Randolph B. Marcy's itinerary stated: "Black Squirrel creek always affords good water and grass."

It was here that Capt. Marcy was caught in a violent snowstorm in 1858:

> it became a perfect tempest, and continued without cessation for sixty hours. We immediately set to work making "corrals" for the animals

The Black Squirrel Creek site was thereafter often called the "Brush Corral."

After the discovery of gold, and the establishment of Denver and Colorado City, Weir's Mill was established on Black Squirrel Creek. The sawmill provided building material for towns along the front range. Later, the area provided railroad ties for the Kansas Pacific Railroad to the east. Joseph P. Harper, a resident of Weir's Mill stated:

> Came to Rocky Mts. 1870 (To Kit Carson, Colo. Apr 2d) assisted in bldg. KP. into Denver and in starting of the D&RG system in fall of '70 . . . Weirs Mill was at place where old Santa Fe trail crossed the head of Squirrel Creek. The Easton P.O. was later established in the office bldg. of the mill.

The Easton Post Office was established in 1872, Austin H. Weir, postmaster. The post office application stated that the office would service 110 people in the area, and that 12 families lived within two miles of the post office.

In 1882, the Denver & New Orleans Railroad was completed from Denver to Pueblo. The route passed east of Weir's Mill. The post office was moved from Black Squirrel Creek to the railroad, five miles to the northeast. The "trail town" became a "railroad town." The town was referred to as McConnelsville in early railroad publications. In 1883, the name Easton was changed to Eastonville to avoid similarity to the Eaton post office north of Greeley.

The new town of Eastonville prospered. The population reached 400 by 1910, and supported the many ranches and farms in the area. The town called itself the "Potato Capital of the World." But a potato blight hit the area in the 1920s, and the Eastonville Post Office closed in 1932. The school closed in 1954. The railroad was severely damaged in a flood in 1935, and was never rebuilt.

The following 1901 Joseph P. Harper statement is from the Carl Mathews manuscript collection at the Elbert County Historical Society Museum in Kiowa.

Statement of Joseph P. Harper 8-1-'01

Diagram of Weir's Mill, as in 1873

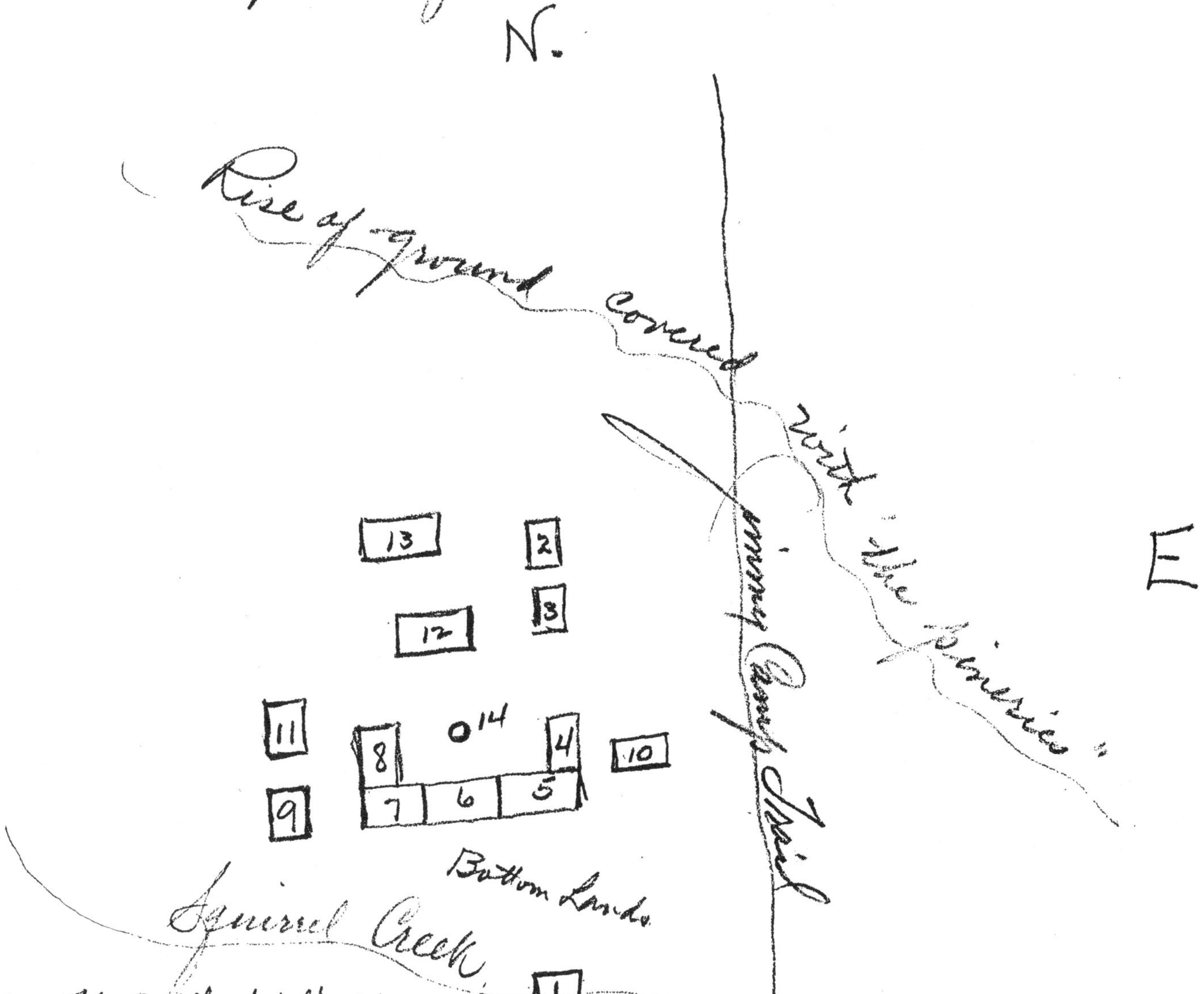

N.
E
Rise of Ground covered with "the Prairies".
Jimmy Camp Trail
13
2
3
12
11
014
8
4
10
7
6
5
9
Bottom Lands
Squirrel Creek
1

1 - The Mill - built of boards.
2 - Squares' House.
3 - Harper's "
4 - The Loggers' "
5 - Weir's "
6 - Dining Hall
7 - Bunk House
8 - House
9 - Mill Office (Later Easton P.O.)
10 - Frame House neatly built

11-13 - Stables
14 - Well.

(All bldgs were of one story, and (Except 1 and 10) were built of heavy saw logs.

Weir's Mill was located on Black Squirrel Creek, at the south edge of the Black Forest, the Ponderosa-timbered region of the Arkansas-Platte Divide.

Buildings, now gone, at Eastonville. The town moved from the Weir's sawmill site when the Denver & New Orleans Railroad arrived here in 1882.

The Cherokee Trail Along Cherry Creek

After striking the Santa Fe tract the road appears as well traveled as any country road in Ohio, and enables the different kind of vehicles to make good speed for the common point of destination.
                                                            Henry Villard, 1859

Cherry Creek has its headwaters on the Arkansas-Platte Divide and flows north and northwest to empty into the South Platte River at Denver. The Cherokee Trail hit Cherry Creek one mile south of present-day Franktown and followed down the east bank of the creek. Today, Colorado Highway 83, also known as Parker Road, closely follows the route: the trail running between Cherry Creek and the present highway.

Before the Colorado gold rush in 1859 and the establishment of Denver, travelers along Cherry Creek were "just passing through." Travelers followed down Cherry Creek to reach the South Platte River, then continued north. Or they traveled up the creek to reach the Arkansas-Platte Divide and then southward to the Arkansas River. But after 1858, the traffic led to or from the town of Denver, the gateway to the mining districts to the west.

The gold rush also resulted in the establishment of the **Smoky Hill Trail**, the shortest route to the goldfields from the Missouri River. The earliest branch, the Middle or "Starvation" branch, struck Cherry Creek and the Cherokee Trail either nine miles or 12 miles upstream from Denver, depending on whether the traveler followed Piney Creek or the high ridge to the north (today's Smoky Hill Road). In 1865, David Butterfield established his "Butterfield Overland Despatch" (BOD), a stagecoach and freighting company. He established the Smoky Hill Trail South Branch which hit Cherry Creek at present-day Parker, 20 miles from Denver. Stage stops or roadhouses were established along this combined Cherokee Trail-Smoky Hill Trail and were named for their distance from Denver: Four Mile House, Nine Mile House, 12 Mile House, 17 Mile House and 20 Mile House. A stop was also established at Franktown, on the Cherokee Trail. The historical marker at Franktown reads:

> NAMED FOR J. FRANK GARDNER, A PIONEER WHO SETTLED HERE IN 1859. FIRST KNOWN AS "CALIFORNIA RANCH," IT WAS A WAY STATION ON THE STAGE LINE BETWEEN DENVER AND SANTA FE. IN A STOCKADE BUILT HERE, NEIGHBORS FOUND REFUGE FROM INDIANS IN 1864. FRANKTOWN BECAME THE FIRST COUNTY SEAT OF DOUGLAS COUNTY IN 1861.

A mile north of Franktown, on the west side of Highway 83, is the Pikes Peak Grange. The old road, (the location of the Cherokee Trail) ran in front of, or west of the grange building. The Cherokee Trail merged with the Smoky Hill Trail South Branch at **20 Mile House**, present-day Parker, originally called Pine Grove. Some of the remains of the Pine Grove post office were incorporated in a house 1/8 mile west of Parker Road. The house was demolished in 1998, but the Pine Grove post office building was restored by the Parker Area Historical Society. Also on this site was the Sulphur Gulch stage barn, which originally sat 1/2 mile southeast, on the Smoky Hill Trail South Branch. The barn has been dismantled and will be reconstructed on another site. A marker 1/8 mile east of Parker Road reads:

DUE WEST 1/4 MILE STOOD THE **TWENTY MILE HOUSE** (TWENTY MILES FROM DENVER)   FIRST HOUSE BUILT IN PARKER, 1864. ON THE SMOKY HILL TRAIL, AN EMIGRANT ROUTE THAT WAS DOTTED WITH UNMARKED GRAVES OF PIONEERS. JUNCTION OF THE SMOKY HILL TRAIL AND SANTA FE STAGE LINES. A REFUGE OF EARLY SETTLERS AGAINST INDIAN ATTACKS. HOSTELRY IN TURN KEPT BY NELSON DOUD AND JAMES S. PARKER (FOR WHOM THE TOWN OF PARKER IS NAMED).

Continuing north, the Cherokee Trail passed through present-day Cherry Creek Reservoir State Park. Near the south end of the park was the site of the **12 Mile House**, a stage stop and hotel operated by John & Jane Melvin. The site of the Nine Mile House is underwater, north of the park's swim beach.

Four miles from the center of early-day Denver was **Four Mile House**, the final stage stop before entering Denver on the combined Cherokee-Smoky Hill Trail. The house is the oldest still-standing house in Denver, and is part of the Four Mile Historic Park. Cherry Creek empties into the **South Platte River** at present-day Denver. Denver was the end of the Smoky Hill Trail. The Cherokee Trail continued north. The 1849 Branch followed down the east side of the South Platte River, traveling north to the mouth of the Cache la Poudre River, east of Greeley. The 1850 Branch crossed the South Platte River at Denver and traveled north along the foothills of the Rocky Mountains.

The small settlement of Russellville was established in 1859. Russellville Gulch was called "East Cherry Creek" when first surveyed in 1866.

The Cherokee Trail
Along Cherry Creek

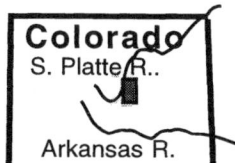

Cherokee Trail (1850 Branch)

South Platte River

[Denver]

Cherokee Trail (1849 Branch)

"reached Cherry Creek, here was a great abundance of wild cherries, plums, gooseberries and currants . . . The stream was dried up with the heat and we had to dig holes in the sand to find water"   Parkman, 1846

Ⓒ Four Mile House

"four miles from the town, we reached a neat little tavern . . . Here there were two or three ranches in the process of establishment. . . . Our next sign of life was the evidence of death, - the unfenced cemetery of Denver, on the top of a ridge."   Villard, 1859

Four Mile House Ⓒ

Cherry Creek

"After striking the Santa Fe tract the road appears as well traveled as any country road in Ohio, and enables the different kind of vehicles to make good speed for the common point of destination."   Villard, 1859

Smoky Hill Trail Middle Branch

South Platte River

"met 2 arkansas trains with about 1,000 head of cattle . . . camped on Cherry Creek"   Hundley, 1856

Ⓑ

Ⓑ 12 Mile House & Smoky Hill (Middle) Jct

"we had a three-room log house, but at once built an additional ten rooms that we might handle the transient trade on the Smoky Hill Road . . . Our house soon became known as the "Twelve Mile House" The stage stopped once each day"   Jane Melvin

"halted with a camp of free traders and hunters, on Cherry creek. This stream is an affluent of the Platte, from the southeast, heading in a broad ridge of pine hills and rocks, known as the 'Divide' . . . we passed a village of Arapahos on its way to the mountains, in pursuit of game."   Sage, 1842

[Parker] Ⓐ

Ⓐ 20 Mile House & Smoky Hill (South) Jct

"To-day we still followed up Cherry Creek, or its dry sands; but towards noon, it is running to meet us; and there were the patronymic cherries, - or rather the bushes; and of the sort called choke-cherries. We are again encamped on it; but the highlands is before us, and adorned, as the nearer hills, with pines."   Cooke, 1845

Smoky Hill Trail South Branch

"Cherry creek is a beautiful, clear and cold stream, narrow and swift. Its Bottoms are rich, and may be easily irrigated. . . But little timber along the creek, some cottonwoods and willow and a few wild cherry bushes"   Willing, 1859

"Wood, water, and grass abundant throughout the valley of Cherry creek"   Marcy, 1858

[Franktown]

The Sulphur Gulch stage barn in Parker was disassembled and saved in 1998. Here the Smoky Hill Trail South Branch merged with the Cherokee Trail.

The Parker Area Historical Society has restored the Pine Grove Post Office. The structure was part of the 20 Mile House.

The Cherokee Trail passed through present-day Cherry Creek Reservoir State Park. Here the Smoky Hill Trail Middle Branch merged with the Cherokee Trail.

Four Mile House, now part of the Four Mile House Historic Park, was the last stage stop before entering Denver on the combined Cherokee-Smoky Hill Trail.

It Almost Happened
Interstate 25 Through Parker and Franktown?

Colorado Highway 83, the Cherokee Trail route along Cherry Creek, was considered for the route of Interstate 25. *The Denver Post*, September 1, 1948:

State Builds Road that Goes Nowhere
The Colorado state highway department has built a sturdy new highway four miles south of Franktown, leading up to an almost $144,000 bridge now under construction across Cherry creek.

There's just one trouble about this highway and bridge.

They don't go anywhere.

Beyond the bridge, there's not even a cow path. Furthermore, the department has no definite plan to continue the road, no money allocated for one.

Original plans called for the Franktown-Black Forest route to be part of a straight, major interstate, and to be the replacement for the present 'ribbon of death' between Denver and Colorado Springs. . . .

. . . Highway Engineer Mark U. Watrous suddenly changed his mind and decided that the new interstate highway from Denver to Colorado Springs should be along the route of the present main highway - U. S. 85-87.

Colorado Highway 83 followed the Cherokee Trail through Russellville before the completion of the road south of "The Bridge to Nowhere."

The Smoky Hill Trail

Three primary travel routes to Denver emerged as the result of the 1859 gold rush. The heaviest traveled was the South Platte River route, which branched off the established Oregon-California Trail at North Platte, Nebraska. This route coincided with the Cherokee Trail 1849 Branch from the mouth of the Cache la Poudre River to Denver. The second route to Denver followed the Santa Fe Trail-Cherokee Trail up the Arkansas River to Pueblo, then over the Arkansas-Platte Divide via the Cherokee Trail.

The third route was the Smoky Hill Trail. This trail was the shortest route from the Missouri River, but it lacked water. The first of the three branches was thus known as the Starvation (or Middle) Branch. After passing through present-day Elbert County from the Limon area, the trail descended either present-day Smoky Hill Road or Piney Creek to merge with the Cherokee Trail within Cherry Creek Reservoir State Park. In 1865, David Butterfield (no relationship to John Butterfield of the earlier Southern Overland Mail) established his Butterfield Overland Despatch (BOD), a freighting and stagecoach enterprise. His route became known as the Smoky Hill Trail South Branch, which descended Hilltop Road to Parker and the Cherokee Trail. Butterfield sold to Ben Holladay in 1866, who in turn sold to Wells Fargo. The route was changed to what would be known as the Smoky Hill Trail North Branch. At Bennett, this trail merged with the Fort Morgan Cutoff, a branch of the Overland Trail which entered Denver from the east. The completion of the Kansas Pacific Railroad in 1870 ended most long-distance travel on the Smoky Hill Trail.

Howard Raynesford, in the mid 1960s, marked the route of the Butterfield Overland Despatch in western Kansas with 138 limestone posts.

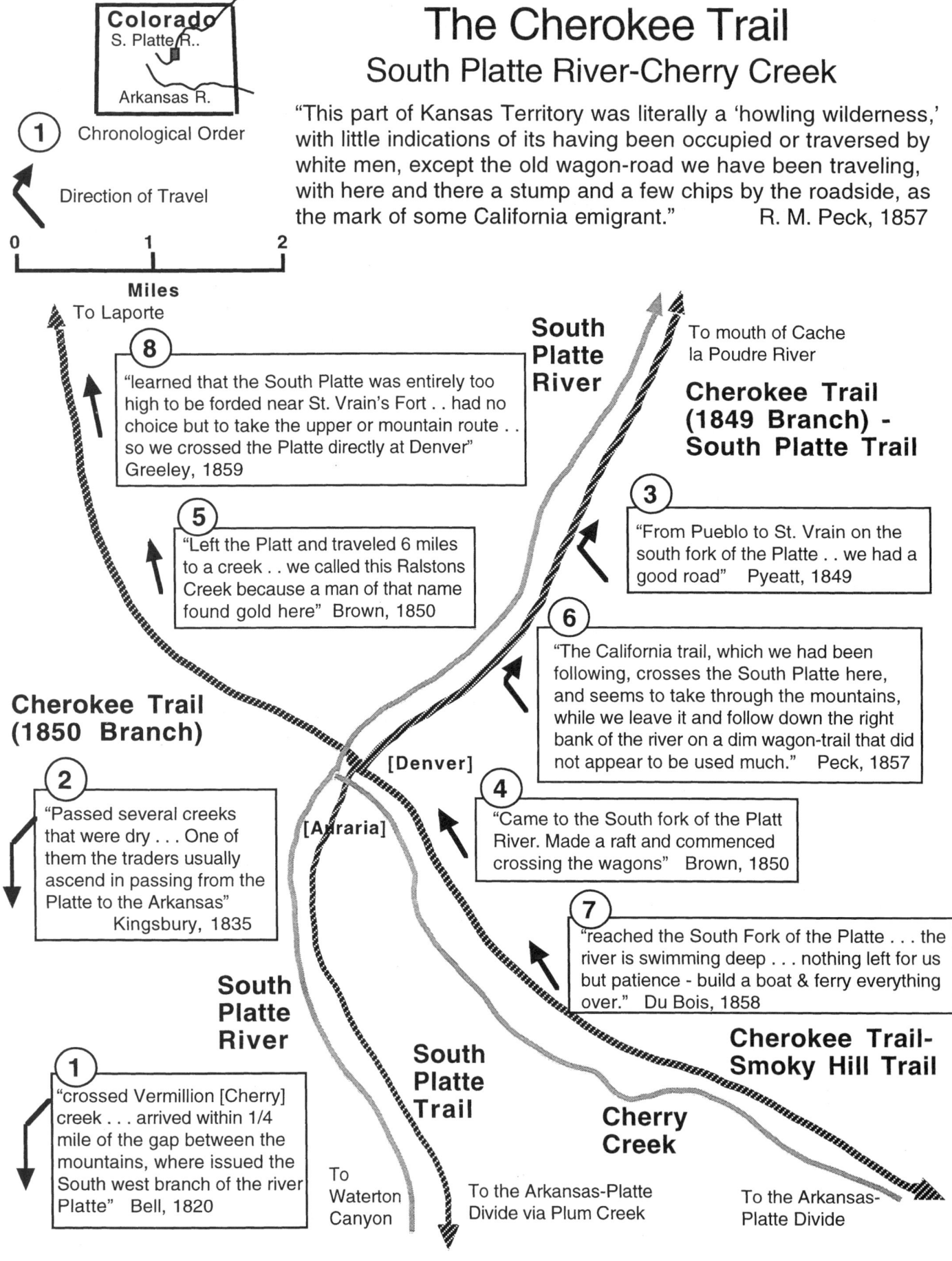

Cherry Creek empties into the South Platte River at Confluence Park in Denver. The Forney Transportation Museum has since moved to a new location.

A portion of the old 16th Street viaduct stands near the Cherokee Trail, 1850 Branch, crossing of the South Platte River.

Riverside Cemetery

Riverside Cemetery is located at 5201 Brighton Blvd., four miles north of downtown Denver. It is located on the South Platte River-Cherokee Trail 1849 Branch. It is open from 7 A. M. to sunset every day.

Started in 1876, it is the oldest operating cemetery in Denver.

Riverside Cemetery is the final resting place of the following trail and transportation pioneers.

Archer, Col. James. Instrumental in bringing the Kansas Pacific Railroad to Denver in 1870. Block 13.

Drake, Lester. Early gold seeker, his marker is a sandstone replica of his mining cabin. Block 4.

Elbert, Samuel. Sixth Territorial governor of Colorado. Elbert County and the state's highest mountain are named for him. Block 13.

Evans, John. Second territorial governor of Colorado. Built the Denver & New Orleans Railroad, which followed portions of the Cherokee Trail from Denver to Pueblo. Block 13.

Gomer, Philip. One of the first settlers on Running Creek in Elbert County. He ran several sawmills near the Cherokee Trail. Block 2.

Jones, John S. Co-founder of the Leavenworth & Pikes Peak Express Company, first stagecoach to Denver. Block 6.

Oakes, Daniel C. Produced a gold rush guidebook. General Land Office surveyor, some of his surveys included the Cherokee Trail in northwestern Colorado. Block 5.

Pierce, James H. 1858 gold seeker, arrived via the Santa Fe-Cherokee Trail route. Block 28.

Van Wormer, Isaac P. Traveled the Santa Fe-Cherokee Trail to Denver in 1859. His property in Elbert County was the site of the 1864 Hungate Massacre. Block 7.

Woodward, Benjamin F. Built the first telegraph into Denver in 1863. His "Overland Telegraph Company" ran from Julesburg to Denver via the Fort Morgan Cutoff. Block 7.

Riverside Cemetery is the final resting place of John S. Jones, co-founder of the Leavenworth & Pike's Peak Express, the first stagecoach line to Denver.

Daniel C. Oakes operated a sawmill south of Denver, surveyed portions of the Cherokee Trail, and authored various guidebooks.

The Cherokee Trail Along the South Platte River

Our march to-day was along the Platte which here runs nearly N, the distance was 27 miles and the direction of course nearly S. We very soon struck a road which had been made by the waggons from Bents Fort . . . passed St. Vrain's Fort . . . A few miles brought us to Luptons Fort and we passed two others during the day. These are all deserted now, the trade having become too small to support them . . . To-day Pike's Peak was first seen, at a great distance from us and bearing directly ahead.
William B. Franklin, 1845

The **South Platte River** has its headwaters in South Park and flows onto the plains, passing Denver and Greeley before leaving the state in the extreme northeast corner. The Cherokee Trail followed down Cherry Creek, hitting the South Platte River at Denver. Here the Cherokee Trail split into two branches. The Cherokee of 1849 followed <u>down</u> the South Platte River to the mouth of Cache la Poudre River east of Greeley. Here they crossed the South Platte River. The Cherokee of 1850 <u>crossed</u> the South Platte River at Denver and followed the foothills north.

The Cherokee Trail of 1849 followed down the east bank of the South Platte River. Its route approximates present-day Brighton Blvd.-Brighton Road, passing the Denver Stockyards and Riverside Cemetery. At the corner of Brighton Blvd. and York St. stands a marker:

COMMEMORATING THE ROUTE OF THE **PLATTE RIVER TRAIL**   PRINCIPAL ROUTE OF COLORADO PIONEERS; TRAIL OF MAJOR S. H. LONG IN 1820; TRAPPERS TRAIL 1830 AND 1840; THE 1858-9 ROUTE OF GOLD SEEKERS WITH PICK AND PAN; HOME-SEEKERS IN COVERED WAGONS; BULL WHACKERS WITH OX-TEAMS; STAGE COACHES WITH TREASURE AND MAIL - THE PATH THAT BECAME AN EMPIRE.

Between Brighton and Platteville, the trail closely follows U. S. Highway 85. **Fort Lupton** was located northwest of present-day Fort Lupton. A marker north of town reads:

DUE WEST 1/4 MILE IS THE SITE OF **FORT LUPTON**   ESTABLISHED IN 1836 BY LANCASTER P. LUPTON   A RENDEZVOUS OF THE EARLY FUR TRADERS VISITED BY FREMONT AND KIT CARSON IN 1843   FARMING BEGAN HERE IN THE EARLY FORTIES   OVERLAND STAGE STATION AND REFUGE FROM INDIANS IN THE SIXTIES

The site of **Fort Jackson** was approximately four miles south of Platteville.
One mile south of Platteville, between traffic lanes of U. S. Highway 85, are the reconstructed walls of **Fort Vasquez**, reconstructed in the 1930s by the Works Project Administration. The property is operated by the Colorado Historical Society.
A marker here reads:

FORT VASQUEZ ESTABLISHED IN 1837 BY LOUIS VASQUEZ AND ANDREW W. SUBLETTE MAINTAINED UNTIL 1842 AS A POST FOR TRADE IN BUFFALO ROBES AND BEAVER SKINS WITH THE ARAPAHOES AND CHEYENNES. RENDEZVOUS OF EARLY TRAPPERS. EMIGRANT STATION ON THE PLATTE RIVER TRAIL AFTER GOLD RUSH OF 1859.

At Platteville, The South Platte River and the Cherokee Trail make a westerly bend away from U. S. Highway 85, which makes a direct line to Greeley.

The **Fort St. Vrain** site is four miles west of Gilcrest. A marker at the fort site:

FORT ST. VRAIN BUILT ABOUT 1837 BY COL. CERAN ST. VRAIN GEN. FREMONT REORGANIZED HIS HISTORIC EXPLORING EXPEDITION HERE ON JULY 23, 1843. THIS FORT WAS ALSO VISITED BY FRANCIS PARKMAN AND KIT CARSON

The trail then crosses U. S. Highway 85 between La Salle and Evans, and crosses U. S. Highway 34 four miles southeast of downtown Greeley.

The Cherokee Trail 1849 Branch then crossed the South Platte River below the mouth of the **Cache la Poudre River**. The confluence is located in the Mitani-Tokuyasu State Wildlife Area five miles east of Greeley.

The Cherokee Trail 1849 Branch then followed up the north bank of the Cache la Poudre River, merging with the 1850 Branch at Laporte.

Site of Fort Lupton, established by Lancaster Lupton in 1836. The South Platte Valley Historical Society plans to reconstruct the fort.

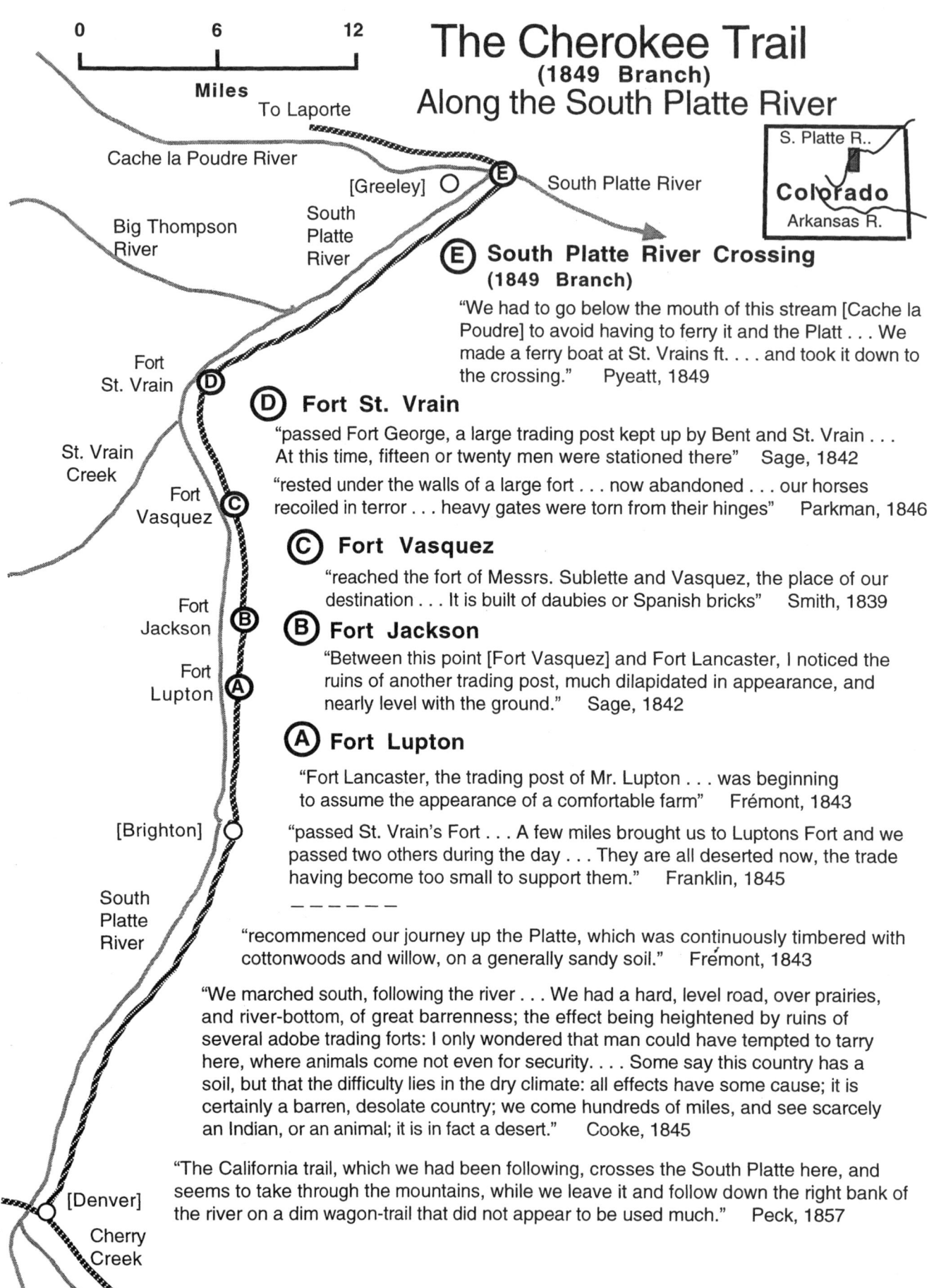

The adobe walls of Fort Vasquez were rebuilt in the 1930s. The original fort was opened in 1835 by Louis Vasquez and Andrew Sublette.

Marker at the site of Fort St. Vrain, established by the Bent & St. Vrain Company. The site overlooks the South Platte River, with Longs Peak in the background.

The Cherokee Trail Along the Cache la Poudre River

We had to go below the mouth of this stream to avoid having to ferry it and the Platte . . . . We sout out from this place without road, trail or guide through the plains and hills.   John Pyeatt, 1849

    The **Cache la Poudre River** has its headwaters in Rocky Mountain National Park, north of Trail Ridge Road. It flows out of the mountains and onto the plains, passing through Fort Collins and Greeley before emptying into the South Platte River five miles east of Greeley.

    The Cherokee Trail, 1849 Branch, followed down the South Platte River from Denver to the mouth of the Cache la Poudre River. After crossing the South Platte, the trail followed up the Cache la Poudre River, passing through present-day Windsor and Timnath, to Laporte, three miles northwest of Fort Collins. Here the trail merged with the Cherokee Trail, 1850 Branch. At present-day Teds Place, three miles northwest of Laporte, the combined trail left the Cache la Poudre to cross the Laramie Mountains.

    In 1862, Ben Holladay and his Overland Stage Line moved south from the Oregon Trail-South Pass route. The new route followed up the South Platte River to the Cache la Poudre, then followed the Cherokee Trail 1849 Branch up the Cache la Poudre, then over the Laramie Mountains to the Laramie Plains in Wyoming, still following the Cherokee Trail. Denver was served by a branch line from Latham, a stage station near the South Platte-Cache la Poudre confluence.

The Cherokee Trail 1849 Branch crossed the South Platte River below the mouth of the Cache la Poudre River, east of present-day Greeley.

The Cherokee Trail
(1849 Branch)
Along the Cache la Poudre River

Ⓑ Laporte & Cache la Poudre River

"came to a large Creek . . . Cache la poodra . . . Finished a raft . . . Early start. traveled up north Bank of the Cache la Poudra 3 miles when we left the River turned north into a pass through the hills."   Brown, 1850

"Lay by today at Cache La Poudrie . . . There is a temporary blacksmith shop here. Swapped some cattle."   Engles, 1854

"Cache-la-Poudre seems to be the center of the antelope country. There are no settlements, save a small beginning just at the ford, as yet hardly three months old, between Denver, seventy miles on one side, and Laramie, one hundred and thirty on the other. . . The Cherokee Trail plunges into the mountains on the north side of and very near to Cache-la-Poudre."   Greeley, 1859

"We found a good bridge across the stream at a little town called Colona. Charged us 50 cents per wagon. . . . There was quite a town built up here a year or two ago, but the most of the houses have been moved onto ranches on the creek below. . . . Followed the creek for three miles then our road turned north"   Durley, 1862

Ⓐ South Platte River Crossing
(1849 Branch)

We made a ferry boat at St. Vrain's ft. . . . and took it down to the crossing. This boat was large enough to carry the largest of our wagons without unloading them . . . We sout out from this place without road, trail or guide through the plains and hills."   Pyeatt, 1849

"The Overland stage route changed its route from Lodge Pole creek, opposite Julesburg, to near the Cherokee City post office - Latham . . . The new crossing of the south fork of the Platte was a short distance below the mouth of the Cache la Poudre. . . . After the change to the new route the stages forded the South Platte at Latham station and followed up the Cherokee trail along the Cache la Poudre to La Porte."   Root, 1901

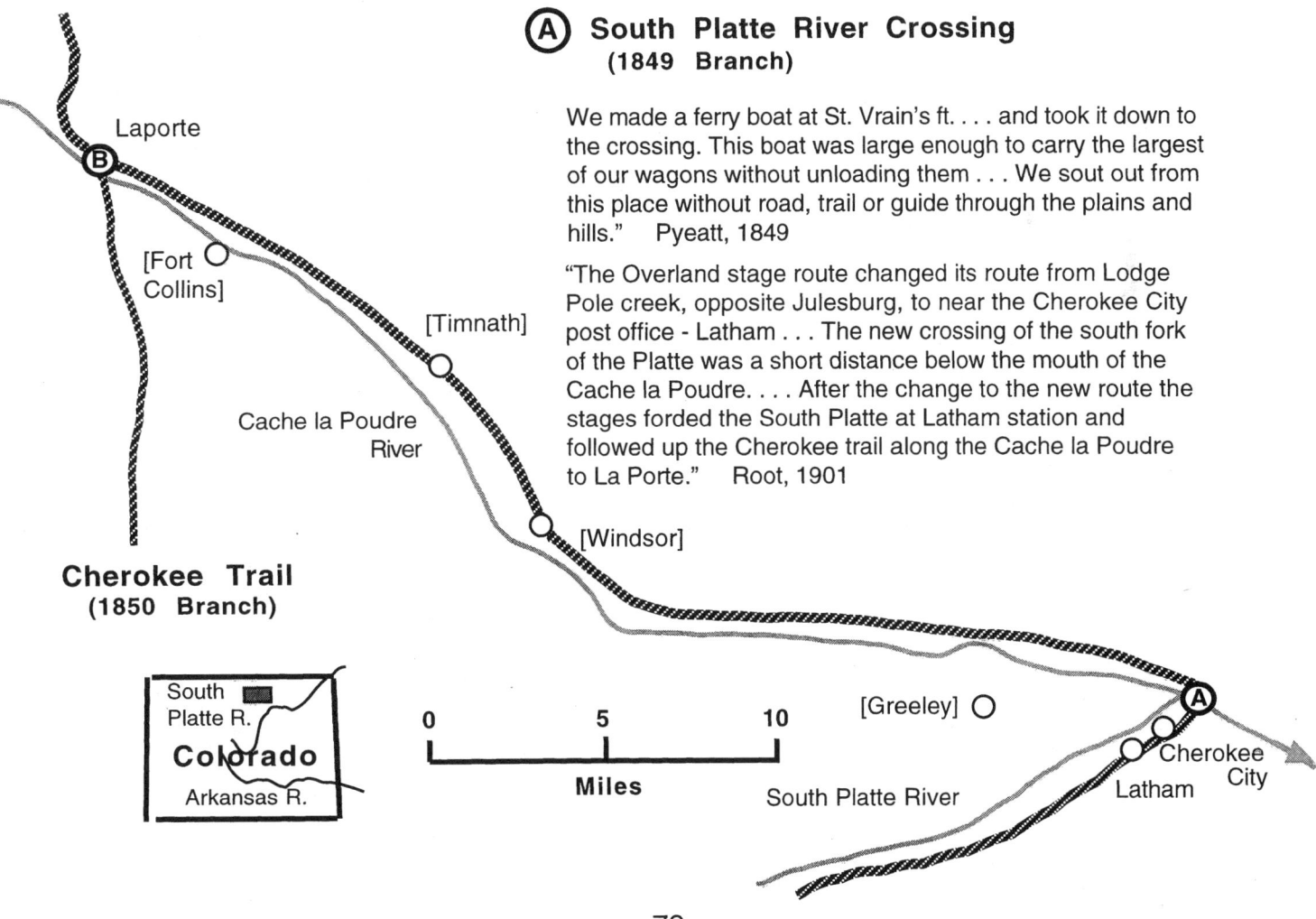

The Cache la Poudre River (right) empties into the South Platte River east of Greeley. Near here, the Cherokee Trail 1849 Branch crossed the South Platte.

The Cache la Poudre River at Laporte. Here the Cherokee Trail 1850 Branch crossed the river and merged with the 1849 Branch.

The South Platte River Trail

The Platte River and its north branch was the route of the Oregon-California Trail, the primary emigrant trail west. This route took advantage of the easy crossing of the Continental Divide at South Pass in Wyoming.

Early travelers and military expeditions did ascend the South Platte River to the east base of the Rocky Mountains, but would then turn north or south, seldom entering the mountains. Stephen Long in 1820 and Henry Dodge in 1835 ascended the South Platte River to the base of the mountains at present-day Waterton Canyon. Here both expeditions turned south to the Arkansas River.

With the discovery of gold in 1859, the Denver area became a destination, and the South Platte River Trail was the main travel route to the goldfields. After 1859, many California-bound travelers would ascend the South Platte River to the Ovid and Julesburg area in extreme northeastern Colorado, then turn north up Lodgepole Creek into Nebraska. This South Platte River-Lodgepole Creek route was used by the Pony Express in 1860-61, and the Union Pacific transcontinental railroad.

In 1862, Ben Holladay moved his Overland Stage Line south from the South Pass route to the South Platte River. He ascended the river to the Cache la Poudre River, which he ascended to Laporte (as did the Cherokee Trail 1849 Branch) before turning northwest into Wyoming. A branch line ran up the South Platte River to Denver until 1864, when the main Overland Stage Line left the South Platte River west of Fort Morgan and traveled to Denver on the Fort Morgan Cutoff.

Pony Express and Old Julesburg markers on the South Platte River west of Julesburg. A branch of the Oregon-California Trail crossed the river here.

The Trappers Trail

The Taos-Trappers Trail ran from Taos, New Mexico, to Fort Laramie, Wyoming. The trail from Taos to Pueblo was primarily known as the Taos Trail. From Pueblo, the trail crossed the Arkansas-Platte Divide, then descended the South Platte River to the mouth of the Cache la Poudre River, as did the Cherokee Trail 1849 Branch. The Cherokee Trail turned northwest up the Cache la Poudre River while the Trappers Trail ran north up Crow Creek.

The Trappers Trail left Crow Creek about six miles north of the Colorado-Wyoming border, where Crow Creek made a sharp bend to the west. The trail crossed Lodgepole Creek north of present-day Burns, 22 miles east of Cheyenne. Continuing north, the Trappers Trail crossed the South Platte-North Platte Divide. After crossing Horse Creek and Bear Creek, the trail reached the Goshen Hole Rim, a rugged escarpment at the southern end of Goshen Hole. The trail descended into Goshen Hole via Fox Creek Gap, at the west end of Castle Rocks, 13 miles northwest of present-day LaGrange. The trail crossed Goshen Hole to Fort Laramie, on the Oregon-California Trail and the North Platte River.

American and Mexican traders were the primary users of the Trappers Trail. Military users of the Trappers Trail included John C. Frémont in 1842, Stephen Watts Kearny in 1845, and Col. Edwin Sumner in 1857. A detachment of Mormons known as the "Mississippi Saints" used the trail to travel to and from their winter quarters in Pueblo in 1846-1847.

Fort Laramie. The large building is "Old Bedlam," the oldest standing military building in Wyoming. The model is of "Fort John," predecessor of Fort Laramie.

The Cherokee Trail Along the Foothills

There are two roads thence to this point [Denver]: that usually preferred follows down the east fork of the South Platte some forty miles . . . My guide had expected to take this route till the last moment, when he learned that the South Platte was entirely too high to be forded near St. Vrain's Fort, or anywhere else, and that there was now no ferryboat for two hundred miles below Denver; hence he had no choice but to take the upper or mountain route. So we crossed the Platte directly at Denver
                                                            Horace Greeley, June, 1859

The Cherokee Trail followed down Cherry Creek to the South Platte River. In 1849, the Cherokee traveled down the South Platte River to the mouth of the Cache la Poudre River. The Cherokee of 1850 crossed the South Platte River below the mouth of Cherry Creek [present-day Denver] and traveled north along the **foothills of the Rocky Mountains** to the Cache la Poudre River at Laporte. The South Platte River was easier to cross [less water] here than farther downstream, but the 1850 trail had to cross several major tributaries of the Platte, all running east from the Rocky Mountains. Much of the 1850 Cherokee Trail is closely followed by U. S. Highway 287.

The first major stream the trail encountered was **Clear Creek**, where mountain man Jim Baker ran a toll bridge in the early 1860s. A marker in Inspiration Point Park, 49th and Sheridan in Denver, reads:

ONE MILE NORTH OF THIS POINT **GOLD WAS DISCOVERED** ON JUNE 22, 1850, BY A PARTY OF CALIFORNIA-BOUND CHEROKEES. THE DISCOVERY WAS MADE BY LEWIS RALSTON, WHOSE NAME WAS GIVEN TO THE CREEK (A BRANCH OF CLEAR CREEK). REPORTS OF THE FIND BROUGHT THE PROSPECTING PARTIES OF 1858, WHOSE DISCOVERIES CAUSED THE PIKE'S PEAK GOLD RUSH OF 1859, WHICH RESULTED IN THE PERMANENT SETTLEMENT OF COLORADO.

The Cherokee Trail 1850 Branch continued north, crossing **Boulder Creek** east of Boulder, **St. Vrain Creek** at Longmont, **Little Thompson River** near Berthoud, and **Big Thompson River** four miles west of downtown Loveland, at Namaqua Park. A marker here reads:

NAMAQUA   HOME TRADING POST AND FORT OF MARIANO MODENA, EARLY TRAPPER, SCOUT, AND PIONEER. FIRST SETTLEMENT IN THE BIG THOMPSON VALLEY. STATION ON OVERLAND STAGE ROUTE TO CALIFORNIA IN 1862.

From 1862 to 1864, Ben Holladay's Overland Stage Line ascended the Cache la Poudre River to Laporte. In 1864, he changed the route to include Denver. His new route entered Denver via the Fort Morgan Cutoff, then crossed the South Platte River at Denver, following the Cherokee Trail 1850 Branch along the Foothills to Laporte.

The Cherokee Trail 1850 Branch crossed the Cache la Poudre River at Laporte. Here the trail reunited with the 1849 Branch, which had ascended the north side of the Cache la Poudre River.

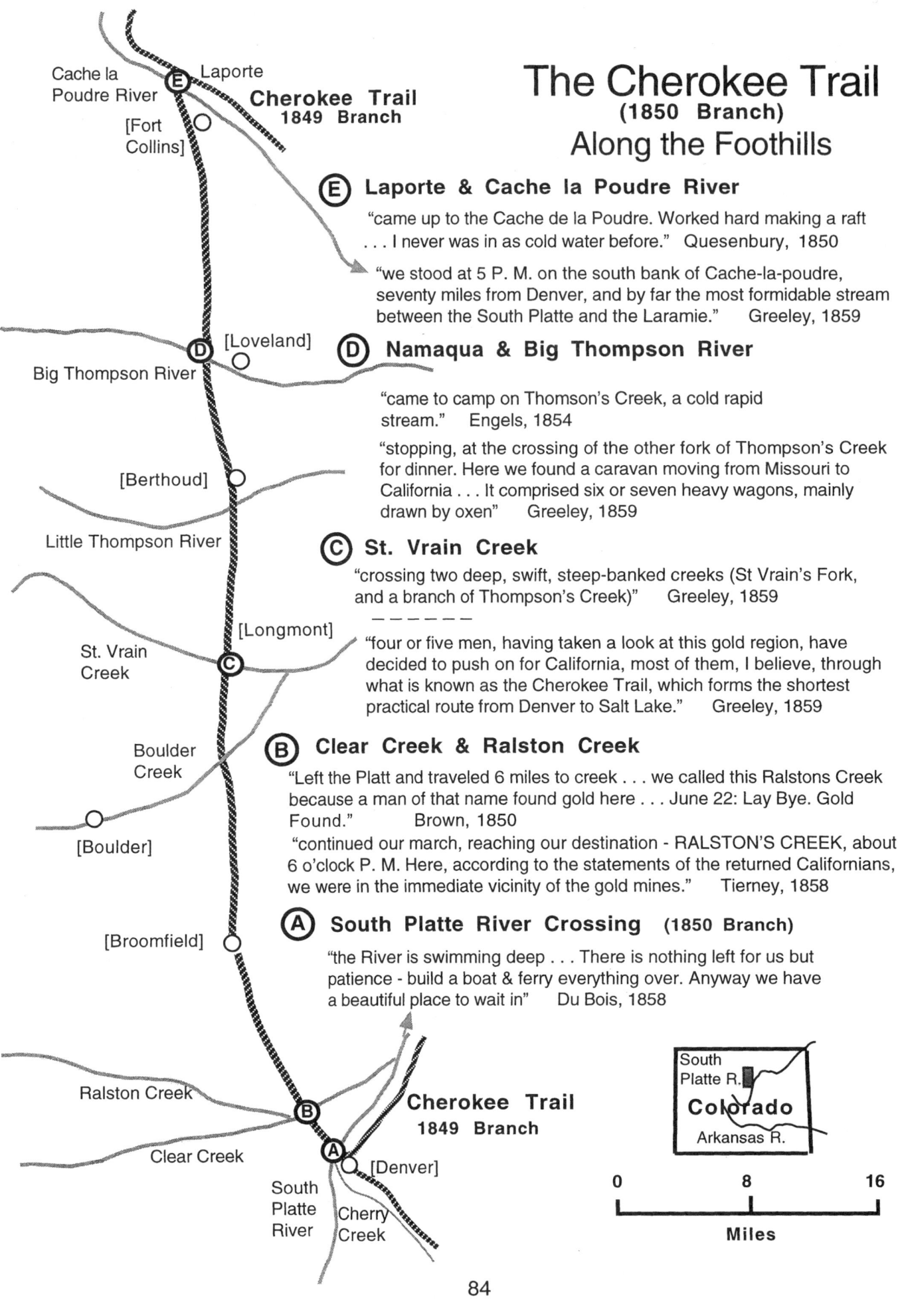

"Gold Was Discovered" marker in Inspiration Point Park in northwest Denver. Nearby is Clear Creek and Ralston Creek, where gold was found in 1850.

Pilings (foreground) of the early bridge across the Big Thompson River at Namaqua. Here the Cherokee Trail 1850 Branch crossed the river.

The Cherokee Trail Across the Laramie Mountains

The ascent of the hills (for they do not deserve the name of Mountains) was so gradual as to cause little fatigue in travelling over them   William Ashley, February, 1825

The **Laramie Mountains** extend from northern Larimer County, Colorado, north and northeast into western Laramie and eastern Albany Counties in Wyoming. The Laramie Mountains divide the watersheds of the North and South Forks of the Platte River. In the area of the Cherokee Trail, waters flow south to the Cache la Poudre River, then into the South Platte River. To the north, water runs into the Laramie River, then into the North Platte River. The mountains were called the "**Black Hills**" by many early travelers. The Cherokee Trail follows closely present-day U. S. Highway 287 from Laporte, Colorado, to Tie Siding, Wyoming.

The Cherokee Trail 1849 route, which had followed the Cache la Poudre River upstream from its mouth east of Greeley to Laporte, merged with the Cherokee Trail, 1850 route, which had followed the foothills north from Denver, to Laporte.

The combined trail continued up the **Cache la Poudre River** for three more miles to present-day Teds Place. Here the trail left the river and headed north to cross the Laramie Mountains. Today's U. S. Highway 287 travels through "Hook And Moore Glade" for six miles, from a point one mile north of Teds Place to Owl Canyon. The Cherokee Trail ran one mile to the west, west of the hills seen from U. S. 287.

From Livermore north to Virginia Dale, the Cherokee Trail and U. S. Highway 287 vary no more than one mile. The highway makes a large cut through Grayback Ridge, two miles northwest of Livermore. The trail rounded the west end of the ridge.

Steamboat Rock, six miles due north of Livermore was a major landmark for travelers on the trail. It is two miles east of the Cherokee Trail and U. S. Highway 287. One branch of the later Overland Stage Line traveled due north from Laporte and stayed well east of the Cherokee Trail until they united at a point west of Steamboat Rock.

The Cherokee Trail - Overland Trail then followed up Dale Creek, passing the **Virginia Dale Stage Station**.

A marker on U. S. Highway 287, one mile south of the stage station reads:

THREE-QUARTERS OF A MILE NORTHWEST FROM THIS POINT IS THE ORIGINAL **VIRGINIA DALE** FAMOUS STAGE STATION ON THE OVERLAND ROUTE TO CALIFORNIA, 1862-1867. ESTABLISHED BY JOSEPH A. (JACK) SLADE AND NAMED FOR HIS WIFE, VIRGINIA. LOCATED ON CHEROKEE TRAIL OF 1849. FAVORITE CAMP GROUND FOR EMIGRANTS. VICE PRESIDENT COLFAX AND PARTY WERE DETAINED HERE BY INDIAN RAIDS IN 1865. ROBERT J. SPOTSWOOD REPLACED SLADE.

U. S. Highway 287 then turns northwest to miss Virginia Dale. The Cherokee Trail enters Wyoming one and a half miles east of U. S. 287.

The Cherokee Trail summit of the Laramie Mountains is three miles southeast of Tie Siding, Wyoming.

The Cherokee Trail
Across the Laramie Mountains

Ⓒ Laramie Mountains

"as I advanced toward the summit . . . they assumed quite an altered character: The ascent of the hills (for they do not deserve the name of Mountains) was so gradual as to cause little fatigue in travelling over them"   Ashley, 1825

"The road we are travelling now is surrounded by hills piled on hills, with mountains in the background"   Smith, 1839

"met 3 trains from Arkansas Going to California with sheep and cattle . . . camped in the black hills"   Hundley, 1856

Ⓑ Virginia Dale

"At midnight we drew up at Virginia Dale Station, the residence and headquarters of Mr. J. A. Slade, one of the division agents of the Overland Stage Line. Nature, with her artistic pencil, has been most extravegant with her limnings. Even in the dim starlight, its beauties were most striking and apparent."   Bliss, 1862

"Virginia Dale station, in a lovely little valley imprisoned by towering mountains. One of these precipitous walls is known as Lover's Leap."   Richardson, 1865

"A night at Virginia Dale. This is a most beautiful ampitheatre, surrounded by mountains, with Dale Creek running through the center; and is near the boundary line between Colorado and Dakota."   Seymour, 1866

Ⓐ Steamboat Rock

"jutting out into the plain, resembled most perfectly a steamboat, wanting only the chimneys to render the image complete; the hull, the water line, the bow sprit, the wheel house, the cabin with its green blinds, the texas and the hen coop were all there. This I named Steamboat Rock"   Patterson, 1859

"'Steamboat Butte,' which from a distance presents to view all the characteristics of a steamboat, with upper cabin, chimneys, pilot-house etc."   Seymour, 1866

○ Owl Canyon

"travelled along a kind of *vallon* bounded on the right by red buttes and precipices, while on the left a high rolling country extended a range of the Black Hills, beyond which rose the great mountains around Long's Peak"   Frémont, 1843

"Followed up the river a mile or so when the trail turned to the right, up a valley of red bluffs on the right and high steeping hills to the left . . . camped on the right in a gorge [Owl Canyon] made by a small branch passing through the red bluffs"   Quesenbury, 1850

"Traveled up north Bank of the Cashe La Poudra River 3 miles, when we left the River and turned north into a Pass through the hills"   Brown, 1850

"Our passage across the first range of mountains which was exceedingly difficult and dangerous, employed us three days"   Ashley, 1825

"traveled . . . along the river, which for this distance of six miles, runs directly through a spur of the main range . . . it was a mountain valley of the narrowest kind - almost a chasm"   Frémont, 1843

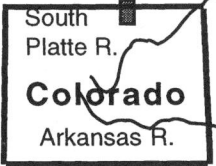

Cherokee Trail (1850 Branch)

Cherokee Trail (1849 Branch)

87

Swale of the Cherokee-Overland Trail near Bonner Spring, north of Teds Place.
U.S. Highway 287 passes through Owl Canyon at upper right.

Ruts of the Overland Trail below Grayback Ridge, northwest of Livermore.
U.S. 287 cuts through the ridge, while the trail rounded its western tip.

Steamboat Rock and Tug Rock, trail landmarks east of the Cherokee Trail and U.S. Highway 287, midway between Livermore and Virginia Dale.

From the summit of the Laramie Mountains, U.S. Highway 287 descends to the Laramie Plains and Tie Siding, Wyoming. The trail rounded the hill to the right.

It Almost Happened
First Transcontinental Railroad Through Greeley and Fort Collins?

The general route of the Cherokee Trail up the Cache la Poudre River and over the Laramie Mountains (Black Hills) was surveyed, and then seriously considered for the route of the Union Pacific Railroad, the first transcontinental railroad.

Excerpts of a November 23, 1866 letter from J. L. Williams, Government Director of the Union Pacific Railroad, to O. H. Browning, Secretary of the Interior:

> Grouping the ten routes thus briefly described into two classes, five of them cross the Snowy range and five the Black Hills range. Of those in the Snowy range examinations indicate the Berthoud Pass, designated No. 4, as having most of the elements of a feasible line. Contrasting the Berthoud line with the two available lines over the Black Hills, either Lodge Pole or Crow Creek line, over Evans Pass, designated as Route No. 7, or the Cache la Poudre line No. 6, the comparison is greatly against the Berthoud
>
> the broad and smooth plain of the Platte Valley opens favorable approaches through its several tributaries to any mountain crossing that may be selected. The point of crossing the mountain is, therefore, the problem first to be solved. In the wide range of these surveys, continued now through three years, ten distinct points of crossing have been examined.

A February 28, 1866 letter from Williams to James Harlan, Secretary of the Interior, gave more information on the Cache la Poudre survey line:

> (2) Cache la Poudre route, 218 miles. - Diverging at mouth of Lodge Pole Creek, this line follows up South Platte and the Cache la Poudre Creek to base of mountains at Laporte, thence bearing northwest along and near Dale Creek . . . the Cache la Poudre line leads to a depression in the mountain (Antelope Pass) 353 feet lower than the summit over which the Lodge Pole line passes . . . On the other hand this route [Cache la Poudre] must be charged with the obvious disadvantage of 32 miles additional length . . . A commercial view of the question might find compensation in the nearer approach of the Cache la Poudre line to the existing mining operations of Colorado, so near indeed that a branch road to Denver would probably be constructed when that new State shall have acquired the needful strength.

The Union Pacific chose to build its mainline up Lodgepole and Crow Creeks. This route passes through Julesburg, in extreme northeastern Colorado.

In 1910, the Denver Laramie & Northwestern Railroad started construction of a roadbed along Fish Creek, northwest of Virginia Dale. The railroad was never completed over the Laramie Mountains, but segments of a roadbed and a tunnel remain today.

The Cherokee-Overland Trail over the Laramie Mountains was a proposed route for the Union Pacific Transcontinental Railroad.

Overland Trail marker on U.S. Highway 287 at the Colorado-Wyoming state line. The combined Cherokee-Overland Trail is one mile east.

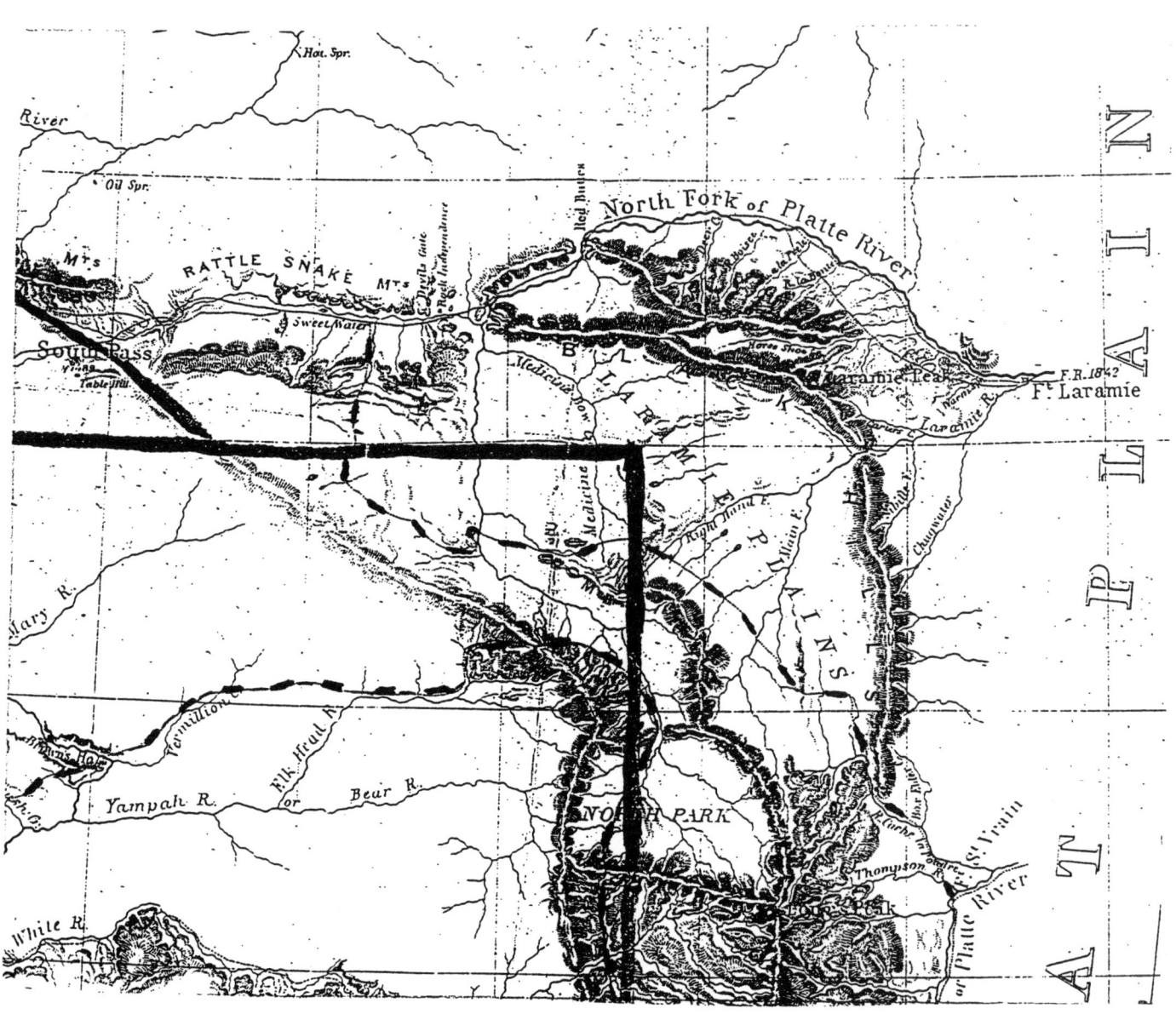

1848 map drawn by Charles Preuss, showing John C Frémont's route from Fort St. Vrain to the North Platte River in 1843, and his eastbound route through Browns Hole and North Park in 1844. The map appeared in the 1848 U. S. Senate Documents, Serial set 511. His route has been highlighted by the author.

III.
The Cherokee Trail
In Wyoming

The Cherokee Trail in Wyoming

After crossing the Laramie Mountains at the Colorado-Wyoming border, the Cherokee Trail entered the Laramie Plains. Near present-day Tie Siding, Wyoming, the trail branched into two distinct branches:
> - The **Cherokee Trail North Branch** was traveled by the 1849 California-bound gold seekers led by Lewis Evans, and included Cherokee Indians.
> - The **Cherokee Trail South Branch** was used in 1850 by several parties of gold seekers, including John Lowery Brown, Cherokee.

The Cherokee Trail North Branch

The Cherokee Trail North Branch ran northwest across the **Laramie Plains** to pass north of the **Medicine Bow Mountain Range**. This segment of the trail was used by William Ashley in 1825, John C. Frémont in 1843, and starting in 1862, by Ben Holladay's Overland Stage Line. Holladay's route became known as The Overland Trail. In the Laramie Plains, the trail crossed Laramie River, Little Laramie River and Cooper Creek, all popular camping sites and stage stations on the Overland Stage Line. The trail then entered hilly country and crossed Rock Creek at present-day Arlington.

Five miles northwest of Arlington the Cherokee Trail turned southwest to follow down Pass Creek <u>south</u> of **Elk Mountain**, the northern-most mountain of the Medicine Bow Range. The Overland Trail passed <u>north</u> of Elk Mountain.

The Cherokee Trail crossed the **North Platte River** near present-day Pick Bridge, eight miles northwest of Saratoga. This crossing was later the site of a ferry run by a man named Bennett, and is five miles upstream from Johnson Island, the crossing point of the Overland Trail.

The Overland Trail led southwest to cross the Continental Divide at Bridger Pass, then continued west passing south of the Great Divide Basin, to Bitter Creek. The Cherokee Trail crossed the Overland Trail west of the North Platte River, then turned north, following present-day Wyoming Highway 71 for 12 miles, to Rawlins.

From the South Platte River in Colorado to the Rawlins area, the Cherokee of 1849 had followed the same basic route as John C. Frémont had traveled in 1843. Frémont continued north to the Sweetwater River and west over South Pass. The Cherokee, wanting to hit the Green River as soon as possible, turned west to cross the **Great Divide Basin**, keeping north of the tract taken by today's Interstate 80.

The Cherokee Trail (still the north branch) reached Bitter Creek at **Point of Rocks**, 25 miles east northeast of Rock Springs. From Point of Rocks the Cherokee Trail <u>and</u> the Overland Trail continued down Bitter Creek to Rock Springs.

At Rock Springs, the Cherokee Trail turned north, up **Killpecker Creek**, to round the north end of White Mountain. The trail turned west to cross the Green River approximately 18 miles northwest of the town of **Green River** and 10 miles southeast of the Oregon-California Trail crossing of the Green River. Heading southwest, the Cherokee of 1849 merged with the **Oregon-California Trail** five miles northeast of present-day Granger. The Cherokee followed this established trail to **Fort Bridger**.

The Cherokee of 1849 continued west on the Hastings Cutoff.

The Cherokee Trail South Branch

From the southeast corner of the Laramie Plains, near Tie Siding, the Cherokee Trail South Branch left the 1849 Cherokee-Evans route and turned west to cross the southern end of the **Laramie Plains**. The trail passed **Sportsman Lake** at the northern tip of Boulder Ridge, then passed north of **Chimney Rock**, landmark on the Colorado-Wyoming border. The trail crossed the **Laramie River** near the historic Boswell Ranch, seven miles south of Woods Landing. The Cherokee Trail South Branch then entered the **Medicine Bow Mountain Range**, closely following present-day Forest Service Road 526, to the Mountain Home area on Wyoming Highway 230. The trail returned to present-day Colorado to cross the northern edge of **North Park** before turning northwest to cross the North Platte River above the entrance to Northgate Canyon.

The trail reentered Wyoming, running along the east base of the **Sierra Madre Mountains**, west of Wyoming Highway 230. Crossing **Encampment River** at the town of Riverside, the trail then passed north of the Sierra Madre Mountain Range, crossing the Continental Divide at "**Twin Groves**," 20 miles west southwest of Saratoga. The route followed by the 1850 Cherokee then proceeded west, passing **Five Buttes**, 15 miles north of Savery; crossed **Muddy Creek** at a point 14 miles north of Baggs, on Wyoming Highway 789; rounded North Flat Top Mountain, then headed south to Cherokee Rim, within two miles of the **Little Snake River**.

The Cherokee then proceeded west along Powder Rim to Lower Powder Spring, called "**Sulphur Spring**" by early travelers. Continuing west, the trail followed the upper end of **Vermillion Creek**, crossing Wyoming Highway 430 about 45 miles southeast of Rock Springs. The trail passed the **Malinda Armstrong grave** on Trout Creek, west of U. S. Highway 191, 20 miles south of Rock Springs. The trail continued west, between Sage Creek and Currant Creek, to cross the **Green River** at the mouth of **Currant Creek**. This is near Buckboard Crossing in the Flaming Gorge National Recreation Area. Continuing almost due west, the trail crossed **Smiths Fork** eight miles before arriving at **Fort Bridger** on Blacks Fork. Here the Cherokee Trail South Branch reached the Oregon-California Trail and the Hastings Cutoff.

The Cherokee of 1850 followed the Hastings Cutoff into Utah and Nevada, then followed the Carson Branch of the California Trail to the goldfields.

In Wyoming, the Cherokee of 1850 followed, as far west as Twin Groves, the old "pack trail" (no wagons) to **Fort Crockett** and Browns Hole. West of Twin Groves, this pack trail descended Savery Creek to the Little Snake River at present-day Savery, Wyoming. Located here is Jim Baker's cabin and grave. To the west was the small outpost, **Fraeb's Fort**, built by Henry Fraeb. The pack trail followed down the Little Snake River to Powder Wash, passing through present-day Baggs, Wyoming. After passing Lower Powder Spring, the trail descended Shell Creek and Vermillion Creek to Fort Crockett, in Browns Hole in northwestern Colorado. Much of this trail west of Baggs was part of the later "Outlaw Trail," made famous by Butch Cassidy (Robert LeRoy Parker) and the Sundance Kid (Henry Longabaugh) in the 1890s and early 1900s. From Fort Crockett, a trail continued northwest to Fort Bridger, ascending the Green River and Henrys Fork.

The Cherokee Trail
Wyoming's North Branch

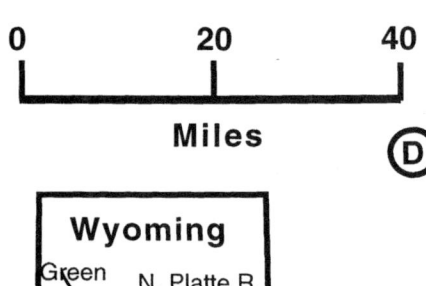

(D) Great Divide Basin

"the Evan's road must have passed over the plateau of table country & divide north of our track, & Bridger says it is very poorly grassed and watered"   Carrington, 1850

"struck for the head of 'Bitter creek,' passing over an undulating and elevated country [Great Divide Basin] for sixty-five miles throughout which we found occasional ponds of water, but saw no running Streams. This elevated plateau divides the waters of the Atlantic from those that flow into the Pacific . . . we followed Evans' road . . . there are several ponds of water near the western border, with good grass near. From thence to the next water the distance is fifteen miles. This is a small spring branch that runs into Bitter creek, and at the head of it had sufficient water for the largest government trains."   Marcy, 1858

"The crossing of the continental divide by the Union Pacific is thus by way of an open prairie of comparative low elevation, about 7000 feet, instead of a mountain range. The work of building the road there was unexpectedly light, and it almost seems that nature made this great opening in the Rocky Mountains expressly for the passage of a transcontinental railway."   Dodge, 1870

(G) Green River

"When we got to the Green River we rested 3 days . . . started for the road [Oregon Trail] which was 8 miles off but to save distance we traveled twelve miles before we reacheth it"   Pyeatt, 1850

(E) Point of Rocks

"At the Bend 'S' we leave the Evans track altogether which takes a more Northerly & worse route - Up a branch"   Gunnison, 1850

(F) Bitter Creek

"struck upon 'Evans' trail, which descending the creek on the right bank for about a mile turns off to the right, following up the valley of a branch [Killpecker Creek] coming into Bitter Cr from the N."   Stansbury, 1850

"Evan's road (made with 47 wagons in /49) on right bank of Creek . . . off up the creek on Evans road"   Carrington, 1850

"Bitter creek is enclosed upon both sides by very elevated bluffs that are cut up into numerous canons and arroyas rendering it almost impractical to pass with wagons except directly upon the north bank where the road already runs."   Marcy, 1858

"Crossed at one-quarter of a mile from camp Bitter creek, after preparing the banks and paving the ford with stone from the hills. At the crossing struck into the Evans road, which proved to be very good. and mostly over level country."   Bryan, 1858

The Cherokee Trail
Wyoming's North Branch

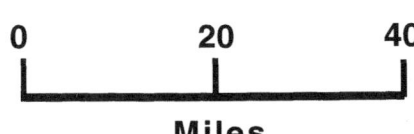

Ⓑ Elk Mountain

"entered the pass of the Medicine *Butte*, through which led a broad trail . . . The Medicine *Butte* is isolated by a small tributary of the North fork of the Platte"   Frémont, 1843

"arrived at the bank of a small stream putting out of the pass between the Medicine Bow Butte & the main range South thro which Fremont passed in 18 [blank] & afterward Evans team of 47 wagons"   Stansbury, 1850

"a march of three miles brought us to the point where the road north of the Medicine Bow butte leaves the Cherokee road."   Bryan, 1858

"South side the Medicine Bow butte is the best road over the Cherokee trail."   Marcy, 1858

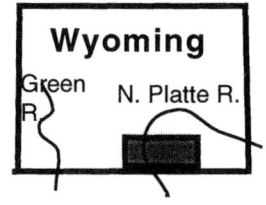

Ⓐ Laramie Plains

"The Laramie Plains are bounded north and east by the Black Hills . . . and west by the Medicine Bow Mountains . . . The Laramie river traces its way through the whole extent"   Sage, 1842

"To-day marched along the Cherokee road. This road is over the return route of Captain Stansbury . . . Camped at the end of fourteen miles on Cooper's creek"   Bryan, 1858

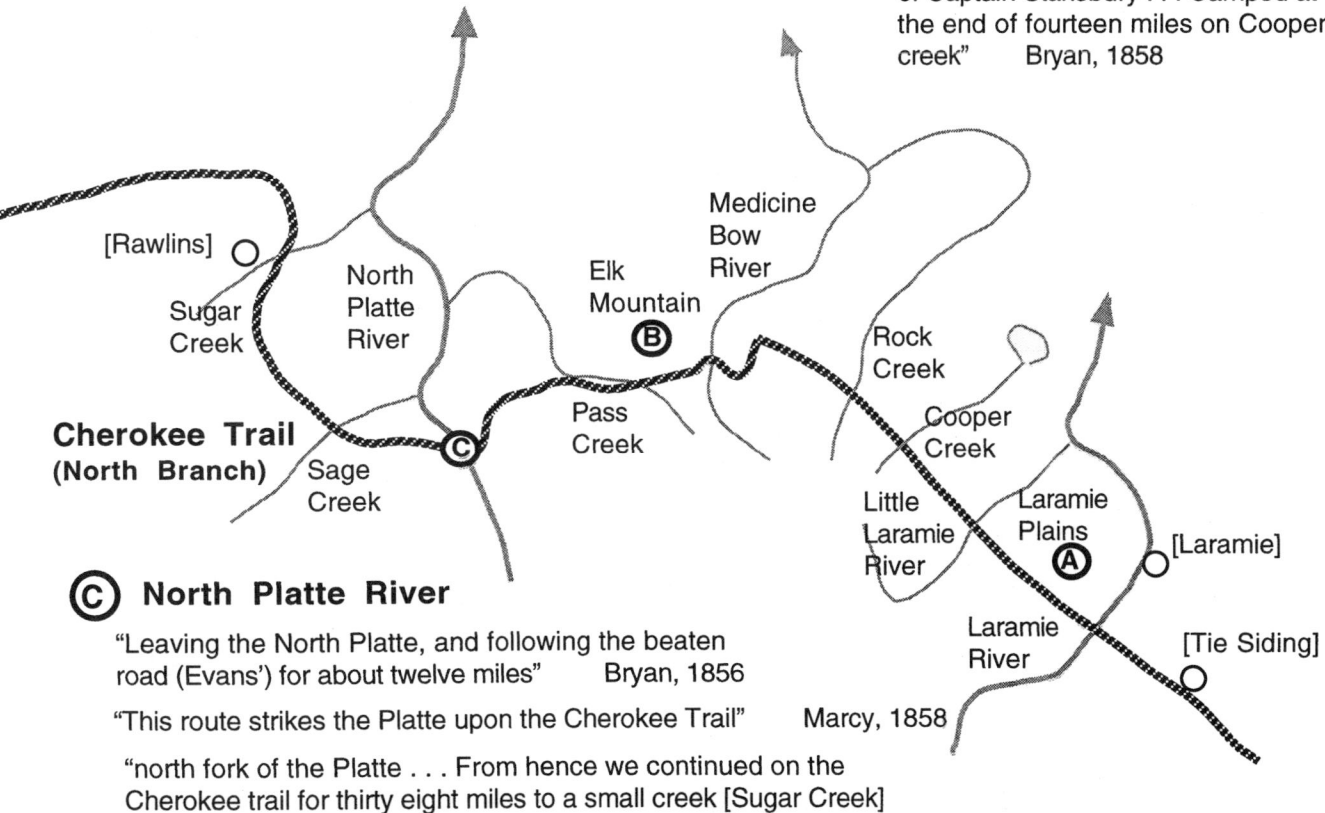

Ⓒ North Platte River

"Leaving the North Platte, and following the beaten road (Evans') for about twelve miles"   Bryan, 1856

"This route strikes the Platte upon the Cherokee Trail"   Marcy, 1858

"north fork of the Platte . . . From hence we continued on the Cherokee trail for thirty eight miles to a small creek [Sugar Creek] which runs into the Platte. Here we left the road to the right and struck for the head of 'Bitter Creek'"   Marcy, 1858

The Cherokee Trail and the Overland Trail ran northwest across the Laramie Plains, to round the north end of the Medicine Bow Mountains.

Grave of Carl Oscrosse, near Sage Creek, west of the North Platte River crossing. Here the Cherokee Trail turned northwest to present-day Rawlins.

The Cherokee Trail North Branch reached Bitter Creek at Point of Rocks, east of Rock Springs. This is the site of the Point of Rocks station on the Overland Trail.

After crossing the Green River, the Cherokee Trail North Branch merged with the established Oregon-California Trail five miles north of Granger, Wyoming.

The Cherokee Trail
North Branch (1849 - Evans Route)
Elk Mountain - Pass Creek

0   3   6
Miles

← Direction of travel

① Chronological order

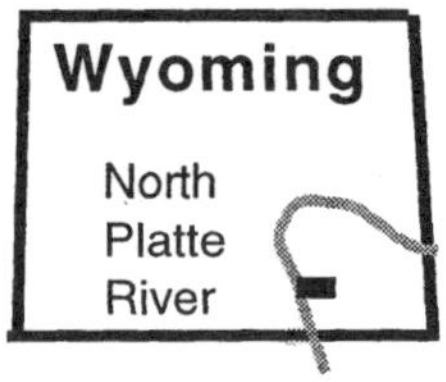

Wyoming
North Platte River

② "arrived at the bank of a small stream putting out of the pass between the Medicine Bow Butte & the main range South thro which Fremont passed in 18 [blank] & afterward Evans team of 47 wagons. As Fremont had represented this pass as very rough . . . I determined to examine the route farther north. We nooned upon this little stream which we gave the name of Pass Creek."   Stansbury, 1850

④ "we had determined to examine the north side of Medicine-Bon butte, to avoid, if possible, the canon of Pass creek on the south side . . . Captain Stansbury had already reported that a practicle route existed to the north of the butte, but as it had never been attempted with wagons, we hesitated somewhat"   Bryan, 1856

⑤ "the road forked, one, Bryant's, going to the north of Medicine Bow Bute, and the other to the south of it; we took the northern"   Loring, 1858

"South side the Medicine Bow butte is the best road over the Cherokee trail."   Marcy, 1858

⑥ "a march of three miles brought us to the point where the road north or the Medicine Bow butte leaves the Cherokee road."   Bryan, 1858

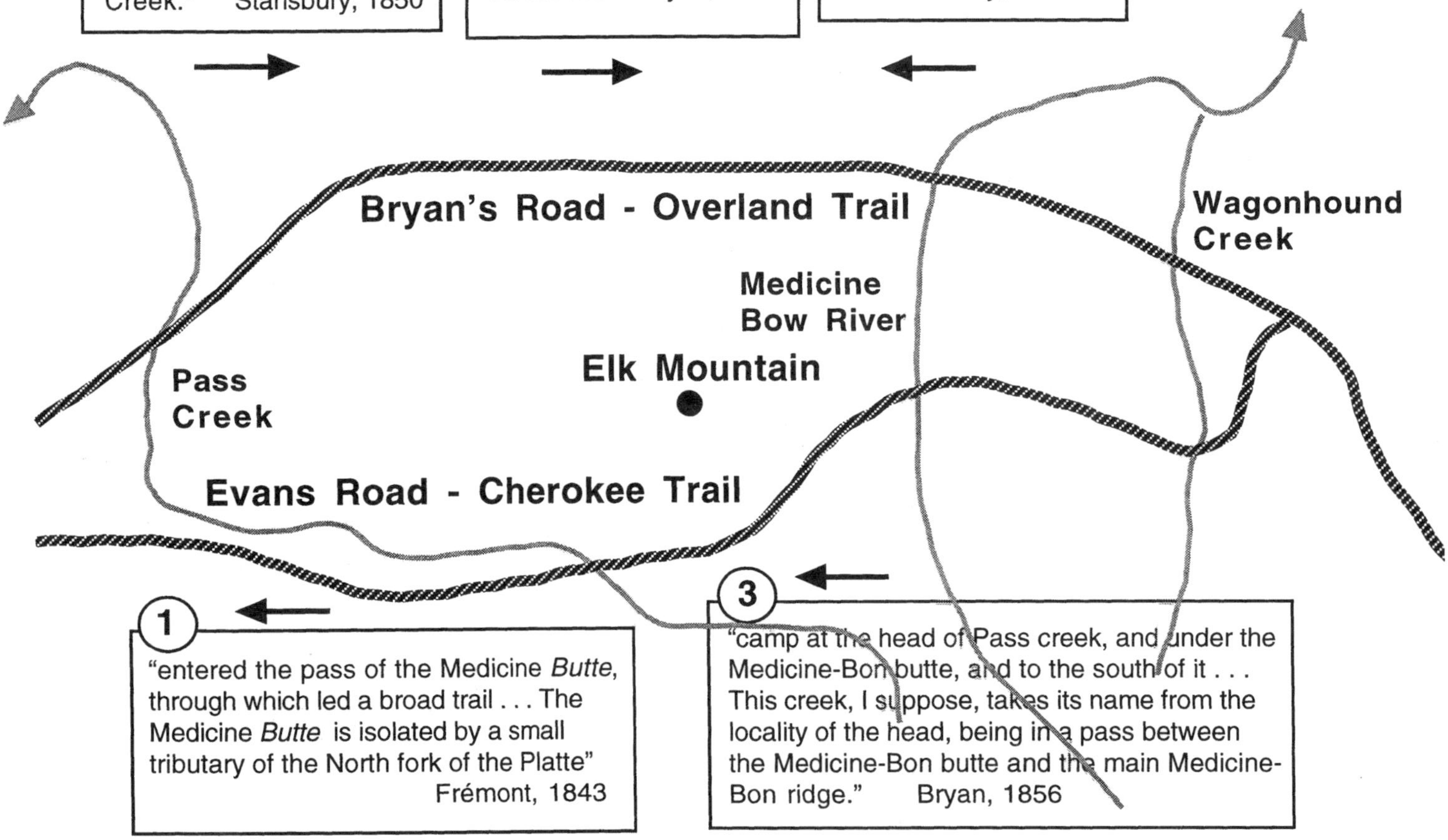

Bryan's Road - Overland Trail

Wagonhound Creek

Medicine Bow River

Pass Creek

Elk Mountain ●

Evans Road - Cherokee Trail

① "entered the pass of the Medicine *Butte*, through which led a broad trail . . . The Medicine *Butte* is isolated by a small tributary of the North fork of the Platte"   Frémont, 1843

③ "camp at the head of Pass creek, and under the Medicine-Bon butte, and to the south of it . . . This creek, I suppose, takes its name from the locality of the head, being in a pass between the Medicine-Bon butte and the main Medicine-Bon ridge."   Bryan, 1856

The Cherokee Trail North Branch followed down Pass Creek, south of Elk Mountain. The later Overland Trail passed north of Elk Mountain.

Pass Creek as it emerges from the canyon between Elk Mountain and Coad Mountain. Ashley in 1825 and Frémont in 1843 followed down the creek.

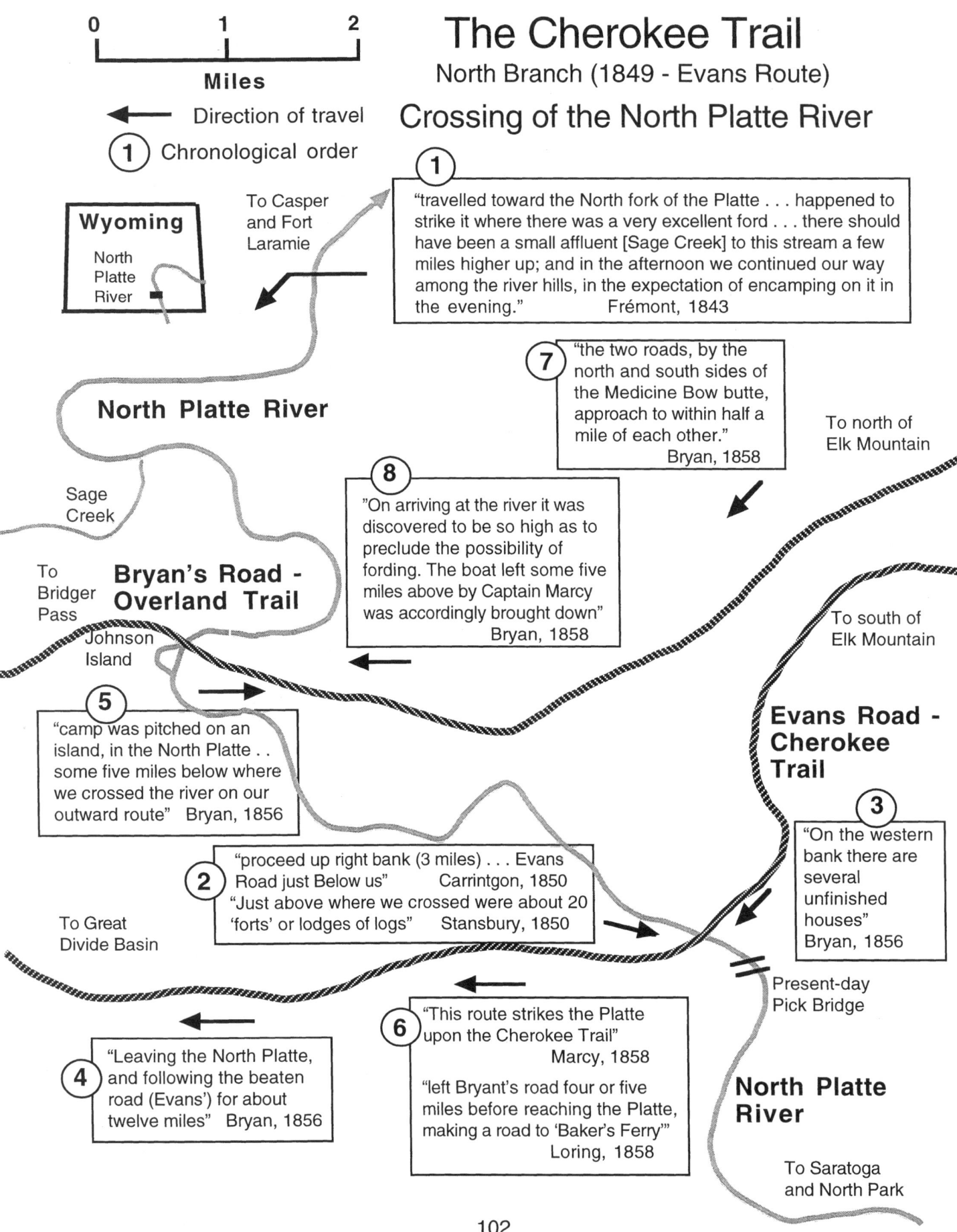

The Cherokee Trail North Branch crossed the North Platte River north of present day Pick Bridge. The Sierra Madre Mountains can be seen to the south.

Eroded ruts of the trail west of the North Platte River crossing. Photo looking east across the river to the Medicine Bow Mountains.

The Continental Divide

The Rocky Mountains are placed as a barrier of safety to keep people from crossing thru country the abode of wild beasts, where human beings would never thrive.
                              Unknown Senator, 1830

The Rocky Mountains <u>did</u> offer a major barrier for western migration. The key to crossing the Rocky Mountains is the relatively low crossings of the Continental Divide in south central Wyoming. The Cherokee Trail made the long northerly trip up the Colorado Front Range to take advantage of these relatively easy Continental Divide crossings.

South Pass was the well-known pass used by the Oregon-California Trail and the Pony Express.

> The passage through these mountains is in a valley, so gradual in the ascent and descent, that I should not have known that we were passing them, had it not been that as we advanced the atmosphere gradually became cooler   Samuel Parker, 1835

The **Great Divide Basin** is located just southeast of South Pass. It is a large (roughly 40 mile by 90 mile) plateau area with no outlet for its waters. This basin was crossed by the Cherokee Trail North Branch (1849 Lewis Evans branch).
Albert Carrington, with the Howard Stansbury expedition of 1850, stated while east of Bridger Pass:

> The Evans' road must have passed over the plateau of table country & divide north of our track, & Bridger says it is very poorly grassed and watered

Randolph B. Marcy traveled much of the Great Basin-Cherokee Trail North Branch in 1858 and stated:

> struck for the head of "Bitter Creek," passing over an undulating and elevated district of country for sixty-five miles throughout which we found occasional ponds of water, but saw no running streams.
> This elevated plateau divides the waters of the Atlantic from those that flow into the Pacific.

The Great Divide Basin today is a major transportation crossing of the Continental Divide. It is the route of the Union Pacific mainline, the first transcontinental railroad.

> The crossing of the continental divide by the Union Pacific is thus by way of an open prairie of comparative low elevation, about 7000 feet,

instead of a mountain range. The work of building the road there was unexpectedly light, and it almost seems that nature made this great opening in the Rocky Mountains expressly for the passage of a transcontinental railway.
    Grenville Dodge, Chief Engineer Union Pacific Railway, 1866-1870.

The Great Divide Basin was also the route of the Lincoln Highway, the first coast-to-coast auto road. This highway evolved into U. S. Highway 30 and then Interstate 80.

Bridger Pass is located at the southeast corner of the Great Divide Basin. This pass was used by west-to-east bound Howard Stansbury expedition in 1850; Jim Bridger, guide. The pass was improved for wagon travel by Lt. Francis T. Bryan in 1857 and 1858. He was establishing a shorter and quicker route to the Mormon settlements in Utah.

John Bartleson traveled from Fort Bridger to Fort Laramie via Bitter Creek and Bridger Pass in December of 1857, approximating Stansbury's route. On Muddy Creek, on the west side of Bridger Pass, Bartleson stated:

> It would require a great deal of work here to make this canon passable . . . we also found here the wagon trail of Mr. Bryan, which is very plainly to be seen; we then took this trail, which we found to be a very good road; we travelled this to the summit of the dividing ridge . . . turned the dividing ridge, which is so level that it is hardly perceivable; we still follow the wagon trail, which is very good. I think this pass is better than the south pass.

In 1862, Ben Holladay moved his Overland Stage Line route <u>to</u> Bridger Pass route <u>from</u> the South Pass-Oregon Trail route. This move was prompted by Indian troubles on the Sweetwater River but the move benefited Holladay, for it shortened the route and came closer to Denver and the Colorado goldfield business.

Twin Groves is the present-day name for the Cherokee Trail South Branch Continental Divide crossing area. It is located at the north end of the Sierra Madre Mountain Range, 18 miles southeast of Bridger Pass.

The pass was used by traders in traveling to and from the forts on the South Platte River and Fort Davy Crockett in Browns Park in northwestern Colorado.

John C. Frémont used this pass in returning east from California in 1844:

> Leaving St. Vrain's fork [Savery Creek], we took our way directly towards the summit of the dividing ridge. . . . reached the summit towards midday, at an elevation of 8,000 feet. With joy and exultation we saw ourselves once more on the top of the Rocky Mountains . . . we saw spread out before us the valley of the Platte, with the pass of the Medicine Butte [Elk Mountain] beyond.

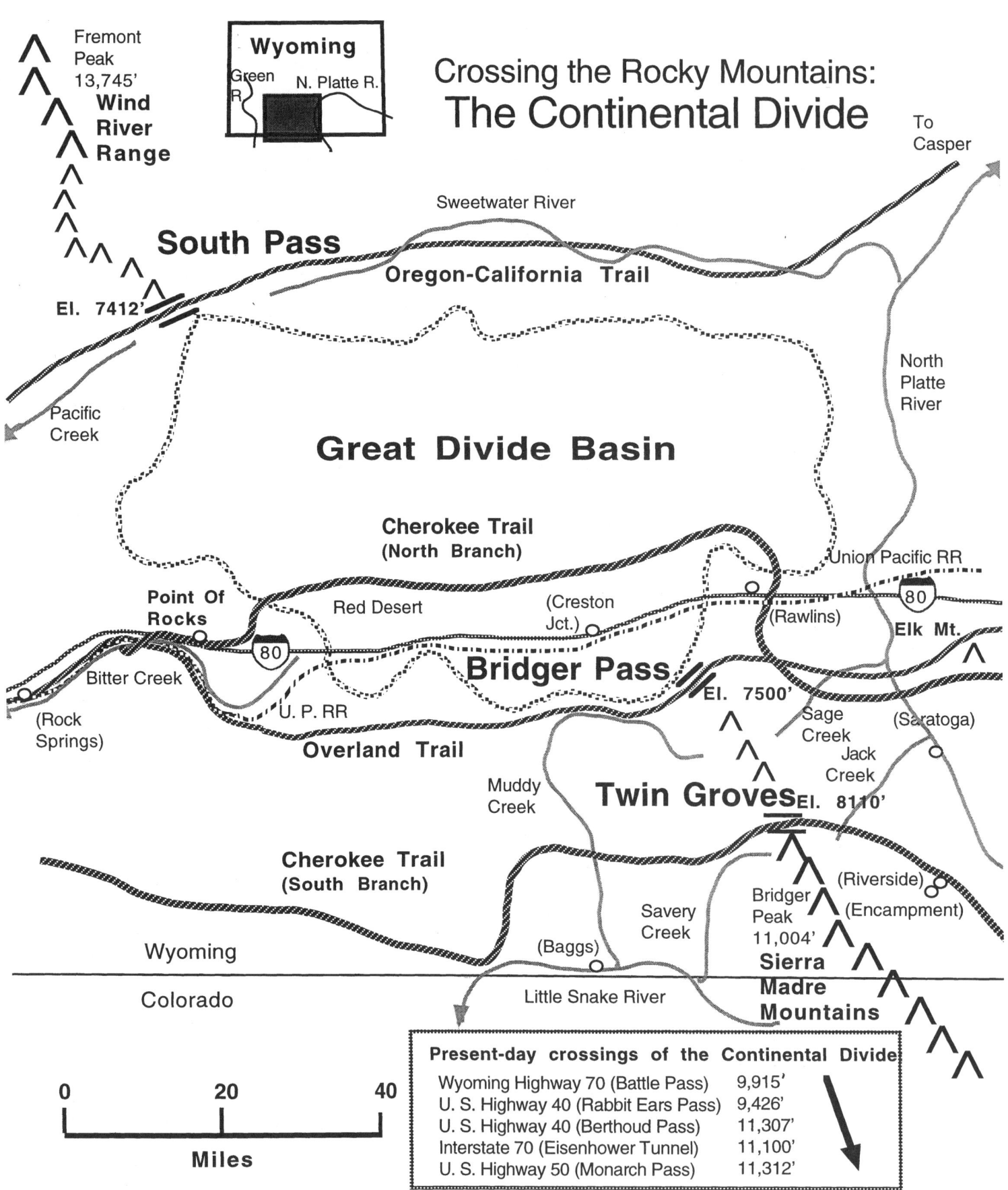

The Cherokee Trail North Branch crossed the Continental Divide via the Great Divide Basin, as did the first transcontinental "auto trail," the Lincoln Highway.

The Cherokee Trail South Branch crossed the Continental Divide at Twin Groves, southwest of Saratoga. The "two-track" passed between the two groves.

Trail to Interstate
Bitter Creek: Wyoming's Transportation Corridor
(Point of Rocks to the Green River)

The valley of Bitter Creek, from Point of Rocks to the Green River, has evolved into a major "transportation corridor."

South Pass, to the north, had served for many years as the primary trail across southern Wyoming, this being the route of the Oregon-California Trail. But 1849 saw the first wagons travel down Bitter Creek; and the start of a shift of Wyoming's main trail south from South Pass.

The Cherokee Trail North Branch, 1849

The 1849 California-bound Cherokee-Lewis Evans party, with wagons, had followed the 1843 route taken by John C. Frémont from the South Platte River in Colorado north to the Rawlins area. The Cherokee then turned west to cross the Great Divide Basin. They then followed down Deadman Wash-Tenmile Gulch to hit Bitter Creek at Point of Rocks. They descended Bitter Creek to present-day Rock Springs, where they turned north to follow up Killpecker Creek and around the north end of White Mountain, to the Green River.

The Stansbury Expedition, 1850

> Before leaving Salt Lake Valley, it had been determined not to return by the beaten track, but to endeavour to ascertain the practicality of some more direct route than that now travelled to the waters of the Atlantic. If it should prove to be practical to carry a road across the north fork of the Platte, near the Medicine Bow Butte, and, skirting the southern limits of the Laramie Plains, to cross the Black Hills in the vicinity of the heads of Lodge-pole Creek, and to descend that stream to its junction with the South Fork of the Platte, nearly a straight line would thus be accomplished from Fort Bridger, and the detour through the South Pass and the valley of the Sweetwater, as well as the ruggedness of the Black Hills, upon that line, be entirely avoided.
>
> Howard Stansbury, September 5, 1850, at Fort Bridger.

Much of this described route had been taken by the Cherokee of 1849. Much of this route would later be used by the Overland Stage Line, the Union Pacific Railroad, the Lincoln Highway and present-day Interstate 80. Stansbury's "Medicine Bow Butte" is present-day Elk Mountain.

Loring & Marcy, 1858

Col. William Loring and Capt. Randolph Marcy were moving mules and supplies from Fort Union, New Mexico to the Fort Bridger, Wyoming area. This expedition was launched to put down the "Mormon Rebellion" of 1857-1858. They had followed the Cherokee Trail from Pueblo, Colorado, north to the Rawlins area, then west across the Great Divide Basin to Bitter Creek.

> we followed Evans' road . . . there are several ponds of water near the western border, with good grass near. From thence to the next water the distance is fifteen miles. This is a small spring branch that runs into Bitter creek, and at the head of it had sufficient water for the largest government trains. . . . Our route strikes Bitter creek at the mouth of this creek, eight miles from its source, thence down the right bank of Bitter creek . . . Bitter creek is enclosed upon both sides by very elevated bluffs that are cut up into numerous canons and arroyas rendering it almost impractical to pass with wagons except directly upon the north bank where the road already runs.   Randolph B. Marcy, 1858

From the west edge of the Great Divide Basin, the Cherokee Trail had followed down Deadman Wash. Loring and Marcy cut more southwest, following down Tenmile Draw.

Bryan, 1858

Lt. Francis T. Bryan traveled to the Bridger Pass area in 1856, 1857 and 1858. His mission was to prepare a road for later military expeditions, a route that would be quicker and shorter than the South Pass route. In 1858 he crossed Bridger Pass and continued west to Fort Bridger. His notes on Bitter Creek include:

> July 21. - Marched to-day only nine miles . . . At about one mile from camp passed the mouth of the northeast branch [Tenmile Draw] and the sulphur springs. . . . The mouth of this branch offers the last good camp until Green river is reached. . . .
> July 22. - Crossed at one-quarter of a mile from camp Bitter creek, after preparing the banks and paving the ford with stone from the hills. At the crossing struck into the Evans road, which proved to be very good, and mostly over very level country. . . . The country for the last three days has been remarkably desolate and destitute of grass.

Overland Stage Line, 1862

Ben Holladay, in 1862, moved the route of his Overland Stage Line from the South Pass and Oregon-California Trail route south to the Bridger Pass-Bitter Creek route, closely following the routes of Stansbury and Bryan. Stage stations were established along Bitter Creek at Point of Rocks, Salt Wells, Rock Springs and Green River.

Union Pacific Railroad Survey, 1866

Grenville M. Dodge, Chief Engineer for the Union Pacific Railroad, recorded the following while searching for a railroad route across the Great Divide Basin and Red Desert in 1866:

> Following the Cherokee trail, we soon got entangled among the cliffs and precipices at the head of the middle fork of Bitter creek, and

worked our way as best as we could into Bitter creek valley, striking it at Point of Rocks. This examination satisfied us that to obtain a practicable line into Bitter creek valley . . . we must turn out of Red basin further east, and before encountering the rough, impassable country bordering the heads of the middle [Tenmile Draw] and north [Deadman Wash] forks of Bitter creek.

Union Pacific Railroad, 1868

The Union Pacific Railroad built its line down Bitter Creek, crossing the creek several times.

Lincoln Highway, 1913

The Lincoln Highway, the first coast-to-coast auto road, followed closely the route of the Union Pacific Railroad across Wyoming. The 1941 Work Projects Administration's (WPA) Wyoming Highway Guide said:

> An old concrete Lincoln Highway marker (R), 144.2 m., recalls the early days of the first transcontinental highway. On December 13, 1913, a string of bonfires nearly 450 miles long, lighted the route across southern Wyoming, heralding the opening of the pioneer transcontinental route.

U. S. Mail route, 1920

The 1941 WPA Wyoming Highway Guide described the first transcontinental air mail route:

> Since September 8, 1920, daily transcontinental mail service has been maintained across Wyoming through the Cheyenne airport. At first this mail route followed very closely the line of the Union Pacific Railroad. Later, with rapid development of radio, the building of larger and better airplanes, and the establishment of beacon lights, the airway across Wyoming was laid out with regular airports at Cheyenne, Laramie, Parco [now Sinclair], Rawlins, and Rock Springs, with intermediate landing fields and radio-beam stations at Medicine Bow, Cherokee, Rock Springs, Le Roy, Knight, and Bitter Creek.

U. S. Highway 30, 1926

In 1926, the Federal Government implemented a numbering system for major highways. East-West highways received even number designations. In Wyoming, U. S. Highway 30 was assigned to the Lincoln Highway segment across Wyoming, as far west as Granger.

Interstate 80

Today, Interstate 80 crosses the Great Divide Basin and follows down Bitter Creek from Point of Rocks to Green River.

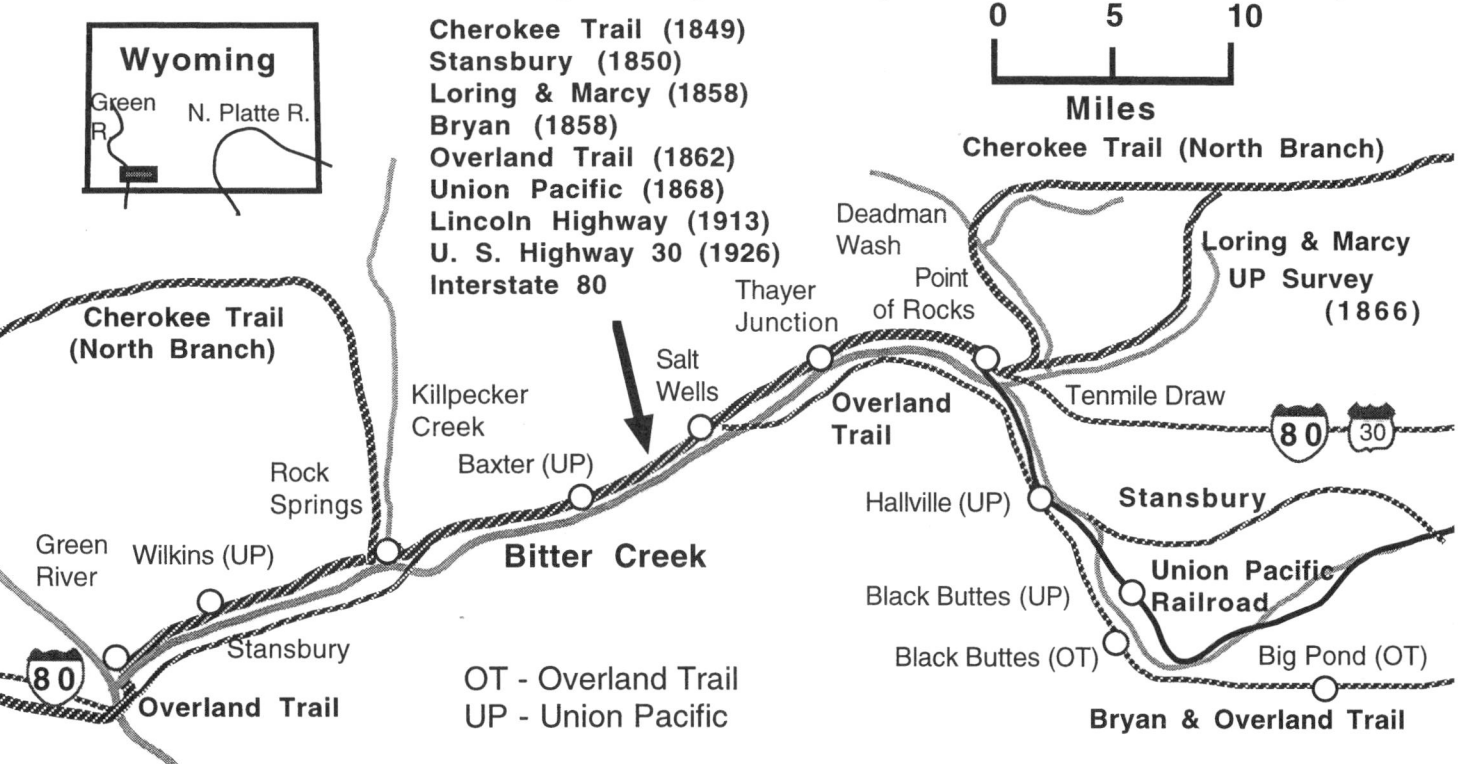

Bitter Creek, the Union Pacific Railroad, and Interstate 80 all pass between the stage station buildings and Point of Rocks (upper left).

Stops along Bitter Creek

Station-Stop	Overland Stage Line-Wells Fargo	Union Pacific Railroad (From *The Pacific Tourist*, 1884)	Lincoln Highway (From *A Complete Official Road Guide of the Lincoln Highway*, 1924)
Point of Rocks	Rock Point	"formerly the point of departure and the outfitting place for the Sweetwater Gold District, South Pass City, Atlantic City . . . Wells & Fargo Overland Express had a station here, and their old adobe buildings, rapidly going into decay, may still be seen across the creek"	"Pop. 50 . . . Gas, oil, store, meals, U. P. Railroad, express company, telephone company. Free camp."
Thayer		"simply a side track, 812 miles from Omaha . . . The moving trains will give the tourist an ever-changing view of the grand and beautiful scenery of this valley."	"Thayer Junction Pop. 20 . . . No tourist accommodations. One small store, U. P. Railroad, express company, telephone company. Drinking and radiator water, gas, oil."
Salt Wells	Salt Wells	"It is a telegraph station, and in the construction period of the road, was a place where considerable timber, wood, etc., was delivered."	
Baxter		"A side track where passenger trains do not stop. The valley narrows in this vicinity, and the rugged rocks with their ragged edges, if possible become more interesting to the observer"	
Rock Springs	Rock Spring	"This is the great coal station on the line of the Union Pacific Road. The company not only furnishes the finest lignite coal to be found, for its own use, but supplies the market at every point along its entire line."	"Pop. 6,456. . . . Three hotels, 6 garages. Local speed limit, 15 miles per hour. One railroad crossing at grade, protected. Three banks, U. P. Railroad, 80 general business places . . . Free camp grounds"
Wilkins		"A side track for passing trains between Rock Springs and Green River"	
Green River	Green River	"This is a regular eating station, breakfast, and supper, and is now one of the best kept hostelries on the road. . . . Being the end of a division, Green River has a large roundhouse with fifteen stalls . . . The old adobe town, remains of which are still visible, was on the bottom-land directly in front of the gorge"	"Pop. 2,140. . . . Four hotels, garages, auto supplies, tires, repair shop . . . U. P. and Oregon Short Line R. R.'s. . . . Good free camp ground . . . During the early part of the last century about 1825 and during the period Green River was the Rendezvous of early trappers, fur traders and explorers"

The Overland Trail and the Union Pacific Railroad followed Bitter Creek, which curves to the south at Point of Rocks. The Cherokee Trail joined the creek here.

The Overland Trail, the U.P. Railroad and the Lincoln Highway crossed Green River at the town of Green River. The Cherokee Trail crossed 18 miles north.

The Cherokee Trail
Wyoming's South Branch

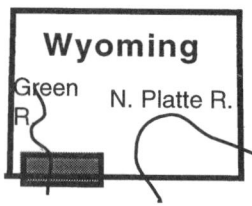

Ⓛ Fort Bridger

"came to Bridgers Ft. . . . at this place the Trace from Independence to Salt Lake passes"   Brown, 1850

"Forgot to mention that we passed Bridger's Fort yesterday morning. It is a poor concern and looked more like a picketed horse lot than a human habitation"   Quesenbury, 1850

Ⓙ Green River

"Green River is about [blank] yards wide, with numerous islands upon which Good Grass Grows into which we drove our horses and mules . . . The country along the Banks of the River is very rugged, looks Dreary & Desolate, with high Bold Bluffs on the west Bank"   Brown, 1850

"struck what was later called 'The Cherokee Trail.' It was the Jones route of 1850, leaving the North Platte River, crossing the desert and coming down to the Green River crossing below the outlet of Currant Creek."   Patterson, 1920

Ⓖ Lower Powder Spring

"we encamped on some Sulphur Springs"   Smith, 1839

"came to Sulphur Springs. Not fit for man or Beast to drink"   Brown, 1850

"Camped on 223 M. C. on small sulphur spring . . . An old road runs west . . . Suppose it to be the old Cherokee Trail"   Richards, 1873

Ⓘ Armstrong Grave

"turned out to encamp, at a spot not far from water. Here Malinda died and was laid by her loving friends in a lonely grave . . . IN MEMORY OF MALINDA ARMSTRONG Died Aug. 16 1852"   Patterson, 1920

Ⓚ Henrys Fork

"Encamped at the entrance of a small creek on the West Side [of the Green River] . . . I have made marks indicative of my intentions to Randavouze here & in consequence of which have given the name of Randavouze Creek [Henrys Fork]"   Ashley, 1825

Ⓗ Fort Crockett

"reached Fort Crockett . . The fort itself is the worst thing of its kind that we have seen on our journey . . . it is also known to the trappers as Fort Misery"   Wislizenus, 1839

"we descended to 'Brown's hole' . . . our encampment, which was opposite to the remains of an old fort on the left bank of the river"   Frémont, 1844

Ⓕ Little Snake River

"Tonight we put our horses in an old horsepen we found at our camping place, which is on Snake River, a tributary of the Colorado of the West"   Smith, 1839

"We struck a small stream known as St. Vrains fork [Savery Creek], down which we journeyed to its junction with Little Bear river [Little Snake River], an affluent of Green river"   Shortess, 1839

"reached the Yampah, or Little Snake . . . this stream heads in the New Park Mountains"   Sage, 1842

The Cherokee Trail
Wyoming's South Branch

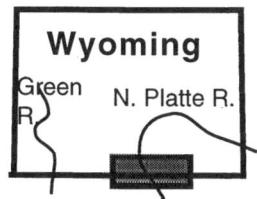

D Twin Groves & Continental Divide

"we had a very rough road to travel over, and at evening encamped on a ridge called 'the Divide'. It divides the waters of the Atlantic from the Pacific."   Smith, 1839

"Leaving St. Vrains fork, [Savery Creek] we took our way directly toward the summit of the dividing ridge . . . elevaton of 8,100 feet"
    Frémont, 1844

C North Park & North Platte River

"entered a very large valley, called the Park, at the entrance of which we crossed the north fork of the river Platte"   Smith, 1839

"On reaching the Platte we were ushered into a large and circular valley, known as the New Park . . . the river makes its exit from this place [North Park] by a forced passage through narrow defiles, between the Medicine Bow and New Park Mountains, forming a canyon several miles in length"   Sage, 1842

"the valley narrowed as we ascended, and presently degenerated into a gorge through which the river passed as through a gate. We entered it, and found ourselves in the New Park"   Frémont, 1844

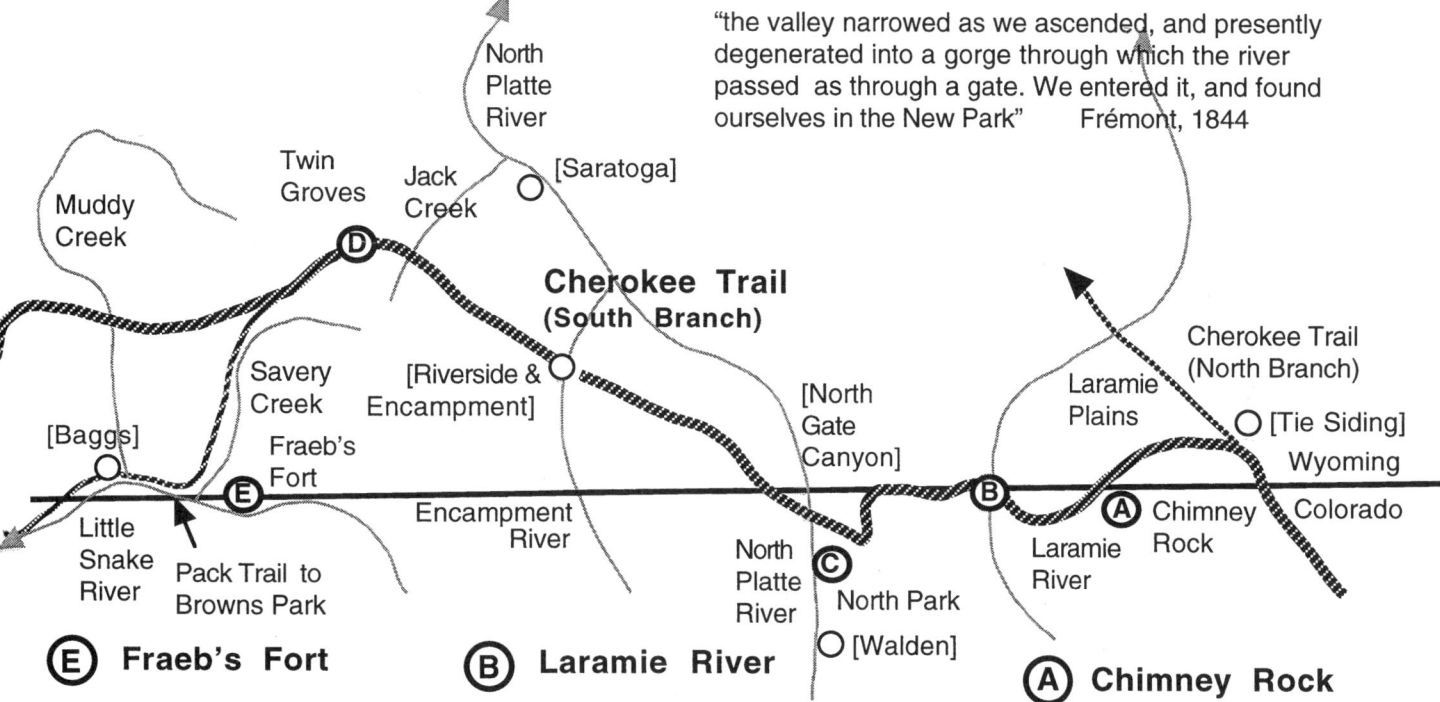

E Fraeb's Fort

"passed a fort, formerly occupied by a company of trappers under the command of Frapp, near which himself and four other whites were killed"   Sage, 1842

"encamped a little below a branch of the river, called St. Vrains fork [Savery Creek]. A few miles above was a fort at which Frapp's party has been defeated two years since"   Frémont, 1844

B Laramie River

"Crossed Larrima River. Struck into the hills Pine better cottonwood timber . . . very hard pulling for the Mules"   Brown, 1850

"Our course along the Cherokee Trail was about southwest from the Big Laramie River, over ridge after ridge and after traveling twenty five miles we entered North Park"   Hayden, 1868

"The old Cherokee Indian trail to California, passes over the Big Laramie River here at Cummins, & goes through one of those primitive forests to the North Park of Colorado."   Mills, 1881

A Chimney Rock

"In this plain there is a very large rock, composed of red sand stone & resembling a chimney. It is located on a fork [Sand Creek] of the Laramie, called Chimney Rock"   Smith, 1839

Sheep at Sportsman Lake, west of Tie Siding. The Cherokee Trail South Branch passed the lake as it cut across the south edge of the Laramie Plains.

Now-abandoned Wyoming-Colorado Scenic Railroad and The Cherokee Trail descended Lawrence and Pinkham Creeks to North Park. (photo by Jim Jones)

The Cherokee Trail South Branch passed Five Buttes, west of the Continental Divide crossing at Twin Groves. Photo taken from the top of one of the buttes.

The trail ran along the top of Cherokee Rim (left), just north of the Little Snake River. The location is on the Colorado-Wyoming border, west of Baggs, Wyoming.

The Cherokee Trail South Branch passed Lower Powder Spring, west of Baggs. From the spring, a pack trail ran southwest to Browns Park.

Grave of Malinda Armstrong, who died here on August 16, 1852, while traveling east from California. She was 18 years old.

Fort Bridger

Fort Bridger was built by Jim Bridger and Louis Vasquez in 1843. It was established specifically for the wagon trains of the Oregon-bound emigrants. In 1846, the Hastings Cutoff was established. This trail led west of Fort Bridger to Salt Lake City, and extended west to join the California Trail in Nevada. The California gold rush of 1849 increased the traffic through Fort Bridger. It was at Fort Bridger that the Cherokee Trail South Branch joined the Oregon-California Trail.

William Quesenbury, member of an 1850 Cherokee party stated:

> Forgot to mention that we passed Bridger's Fort yesterday morning. It is a poor concern and looked more like a picketed horse lot than a human habitation.

Fort Bridger was bought by the Mormon Church in 1855, for $8,000. The fort was reconstructed and served as a Mormon emigrant supply center.

In 1859, the fort became a U. S. Army post. The fort was used as a stop for the Pony Express and the Overland Stage Line, but was bypassed by the Union Pacific Railroad. The U. S. Army closed the fort in 1890.

Today, the fort is a state historic site, providing living-history demonstrations during the summer months. Many of the U. S. Army era buildings remain. A replica of the log trading post has been constructed.

An archaeological dig next to the museum building at Fort Bridger is revealing the site of the 1843 trading post, established by Jim Bridger and Louis Vasquez.

West of Fort Bridger

The Cherokee Trail North Branch joined the Oregon-California Trail 35 miles northeast of Fort Bridger. The Cherokee Trail South Branch joined this trail at Fort Bridger.

From Fort Bridger the Oregon-California Trail led northwest to Fort Hall, Idaho and the Snake River. Fifty miles southwest of Fort Hall, the California Trail branched southwest to the Humboldt River in Nevada. The Oregon Trail continued northwest to Oregon.

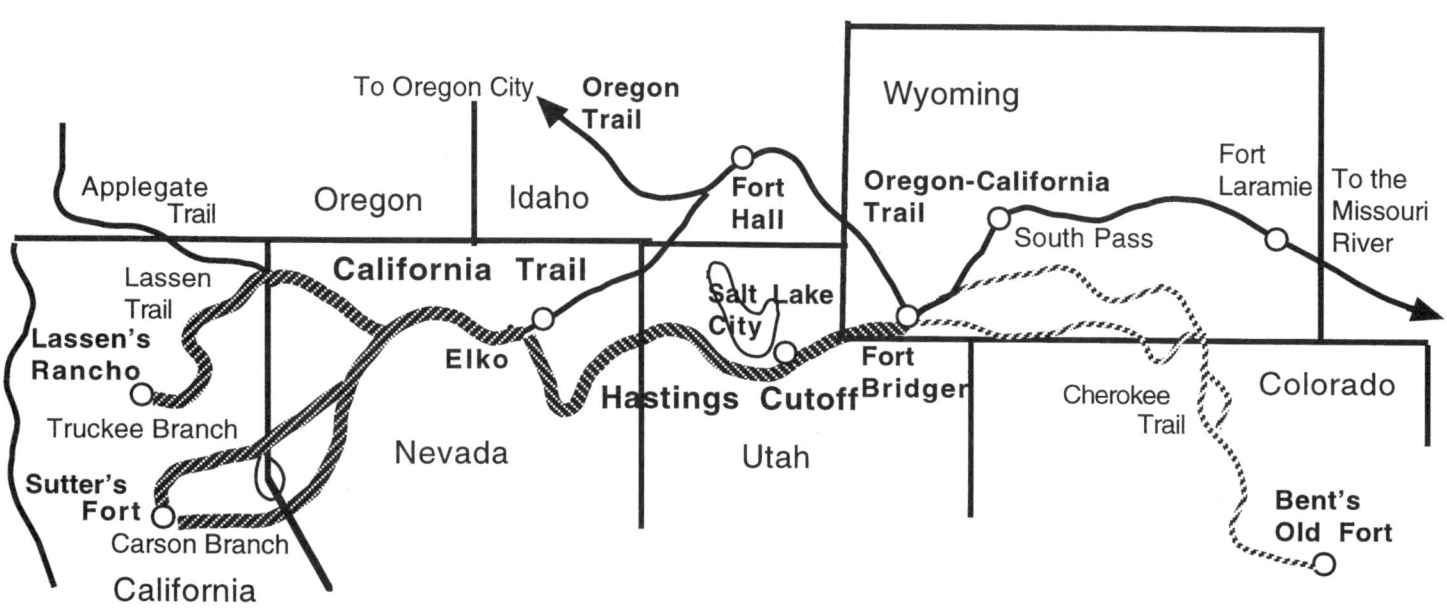

From Fort Bridger, the Cherokee of 1849 and 1850 took the Mormon Trail west-southwest to Salt Lake City. This trail was also called the Hastings Cutoff. The trail was named for Landsford Hastings, who with Jim Bridger, began promoting this route west in 1846. This was the road taken by the ill-fated Donner Party in 1846. From Salt Lake City, the Hastings Cutoff passed south of the Great Salt Lake, then crossed the Great Salt Lake Desert. After rounding the southern tip of the Ruby Mountains in Nevada, the Hastings Cutoff joined the California Trail west of present-day Elko, Nevada. The California Trail continued west along the Humboldt River.

The Cherokee of 1849 and 1850 took three different routes into California.

West of present-day Winnemucca, Nevada, the Applegate-Lassen Trail led to Lassen's Rancho on the Sacramento River northwest of present-day Chico.

The Truckee Branch of the California Trail passed through present-day Reno, then north of Lake Tahoe to Sacramento. This branch of the trail was also known as the Donner Trail, named for the Donner Party, which was caught in a snowstorm on the east side of the Sierra Nevada summit.

The third branch taken by the Cherokee was the Carson Branch, which passed south of Lake Tahoe, to Placerville (called Hangtown in the early days) and Sacramento.

The Hastings Cutoff west of Fort Bridger descended Echo Canyon, Utah, to the Weber River. This is also the route of the Union Pacific Railroad and Interstate 80.

After crossing the Great Salt Lake Desert, the Hastings Cutoff reached Donner Spring, at the base of Pilot Peak, on the Utah-Nevada state line.

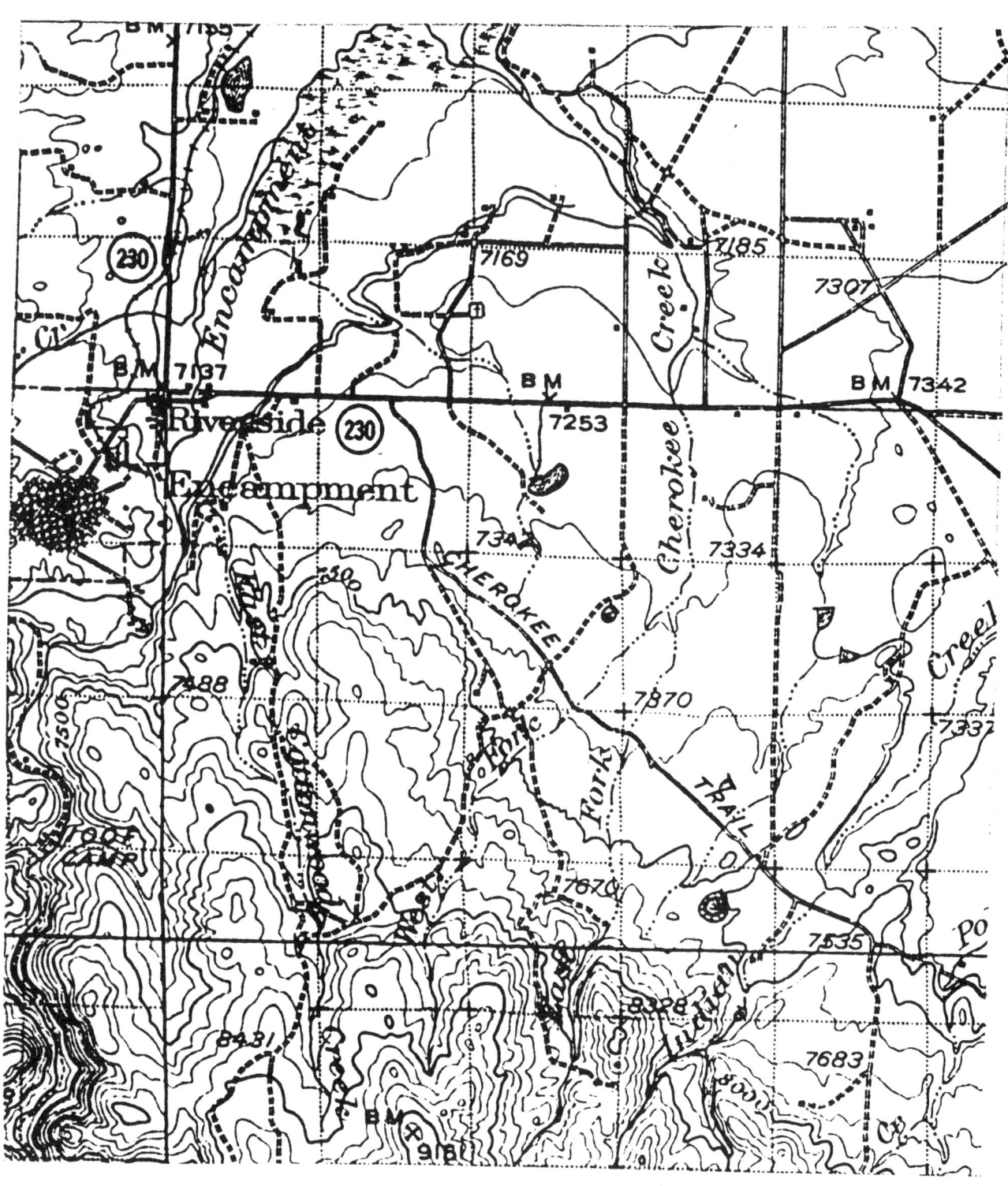

United States Geological Survey 1:125,000 scale map of the Riverside and Encampment, Wyoming, area. Map edition of 1939, reprinted in 1949.

IV.
The Cherokee Trail
Later Uses

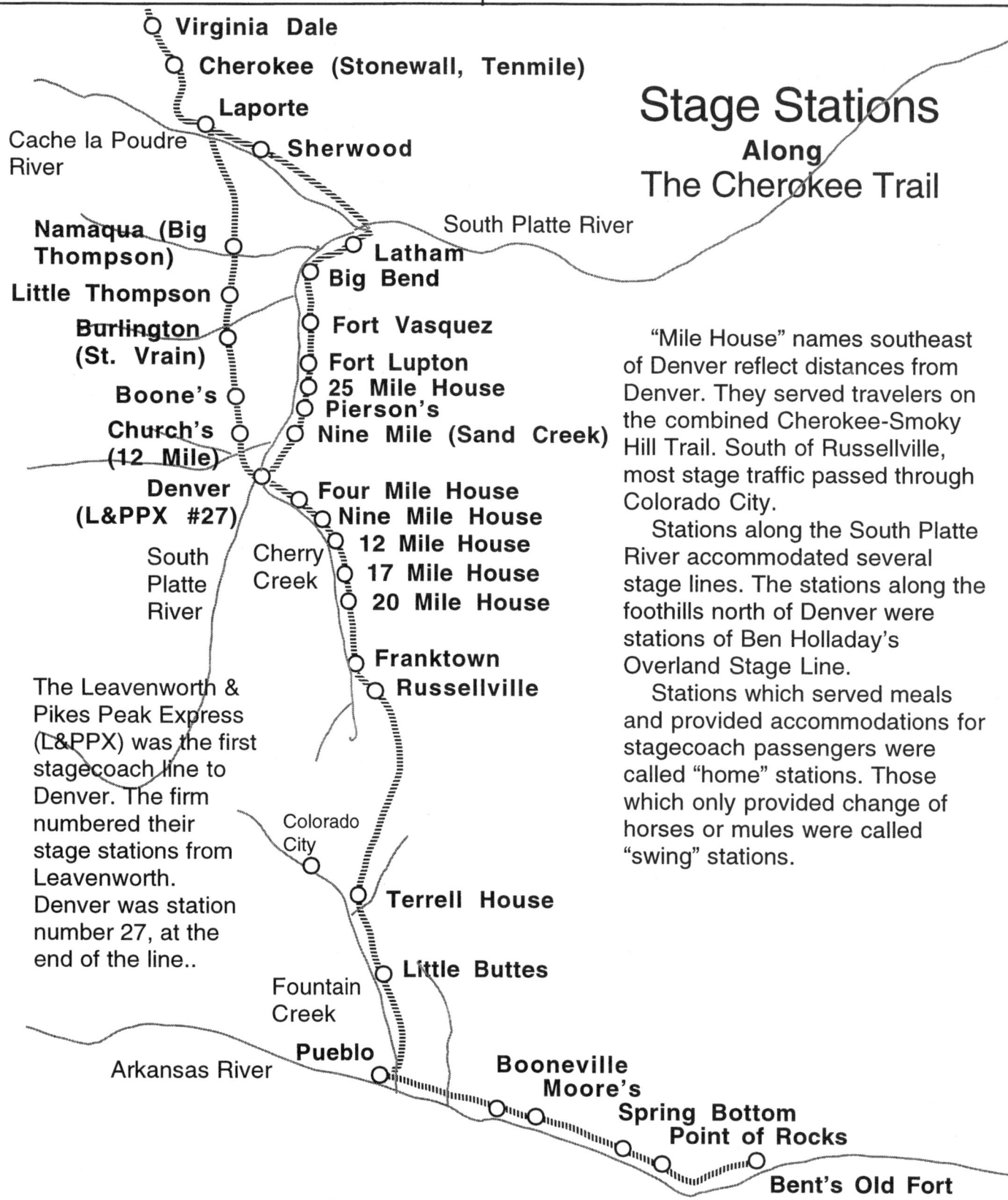

The Cherokee stage station on the Overland Trail was the setting of the Louis L'Amour fictional book *The Cherokee Trail*. Steamboat Rock in the background.

The Virginia Dale stage station was named for the wife of Jack Slade, an employee of Ben Holladay's Overland Stage Line. Dale means "valley."

The Decline of the Cherokee Trail

The era of the **railroads** put an end to the use of the Cherokee Trail as a major long-distance travel route. Travel by train (passengers, mail and freight) was quicker and more convenient. Because of the cost, many people still traveled by wagon, but they often followed the railroad for safety, mail and supplies. The long-distance mail and most freight went by railroad.

Railroads that closely followed the Cherokee Trail.

1868: The **Union Pacific** completed its tracks across Wyoming as far west as Evanston. The route from the Laramie area to the Fort Bridger area followed in many places the Cherokee Trail North Branch.

1870: The **Denver Pacific** completed its Cheyenne to Denver tracks. The route followed the Cherokee Trail 1849 Branch from Greeley to Denver.

The **Kansas Pacific** reached Denver from Kansas City. Although it did not follow any part of the Cherokee Trail, it provided easy access to Denver from the Missouri River, cutting down the traffic along the Arkansas River-Cherokee Trail south of Denver.

1871: The **Denver & Rio Grande** reached Colorado Springs from Denver. Although the route did not follow the Cherokee Trail, it traversed the Arkansas-Platte Divide.

1872: The **Denver & Rio Grande** reached Pueblo from Colorado Springs, providing a railroad from the Arkansas River to the South Platte River along Colorado's Front Range.

1875: The **Atchison Topeka & Santa Fe** completed construction of its line up the Arkansas River as far west as Rocky Ford, west of Bent's Old Fort.

1876: The **Atchison Topeka & Santa Fe** completed its tracks up the Arkansas River to Pueblo.

1877: The **Colorado Central** completed tracks from the Cheyenne area south to Longmont. The line from Fort Collins to Longmont closely followed the Cherokee Trail 1850 Branch.

1881: The **Denver Utah & Pacific** and the **Denver Longmont & Northwestern** complete a line from Denver to Longmont. This closely followed the Cherokee Trail 1850 Branch.

1882: The **Denver & New Orleans** completed its line from Denver to Pueblo. This railroad closely followed the Cherokee Trail up Cherry Creek to Parker, and from the Falcon area south to Pueblo. (The first standard gauge railroad over the Arkansas-Platte Divide).

The **Greeley Salt Lake & Pacific** ran from Greeley to Fort Collins, closely following the Cache la Poudre-Cherokee Trail 1849 Branch.

Settlements and Homesteads

After the Colorado gold rush of 1859, permanent settlements were established along the Cherokee Trail. With settlements, came homesteads, sawmills, military camps and the like. This "taming of the west" was accelerated with the coming of the railroads, which provided easier travel west.

Most early settlements and homesteads were established close to trails and waterways, for they needed, as did the trail traveler, water, wood and grass.

The long-distance Cherokee Trail was now used for more short-distance, local traffic: settlement to settlement, homestead to settlement, homestead to the railroad, etc. The traveler traversing the Cherokee Trail from Bent's Old Fort to Fort Bridger would now traverse the following named roads:

"Pueblo and Fort Lyon Road"
"Road from Colorado [City] to Pueblo"
"Jimmy Camp Road"
"Cherry Creek Road to Denver"
"Road to Camp Collins"
"Laramie Road"
"Tie road from North Park"
"Road from Saratoga to North Park"
"Road from Saratoga across the Continental Divide"

Abandoned homestead along the Cherokee Trail South Branch in Wyoming. Few roads and no railroad followed this rather isolated section of the trail.

Decline of the Jimmy Camp Road

The Cherokee Trail between Fountain Creek and Cherry Creek was also known as the Jimmy Camp Road. Before the Colorado gold rush of 1859, there were no settlements between present-day Pueblo and present-day Denver. The only real attractions in this region were Pikes Peak and the springs at present-day Manitou Springs, both well west of the Cherokee Trail.

Northbound travelers who chose to visit these sites followed up Fountain Creek, but usually returned east to the Jimmy Camp area before continuing north. This was especially true for travelers with wagons, for the Jimmy Camp Road was the only pre-1859 wagon road across the Arkansas-Platte Divide.

Augustus Voorhees stated in July of 1858:

[July] 8. Drove twelve miles. We left the Cherokee trail to the right and followed the creek [Fountain] to the foot of the mountain [Pikes Peak] . . .
9. . . . We climbed up the mountain all day, found some hard climbing and large rocks. . . .
10. . . . The mountain was covered with hail. We got to the top at three o'clock, but it was so cloudy we could not see the country beyond
12. We broke up camp and struck east for the old road. We got to what is called Jims Camp. There is a fine spring and lots of pine wood there. It is on the Cherokee trail, to Calaforny.

With the establishment of Denver in 1858 and Colorado City in 1859, the favored trail across the Arkansas-Platte Divide shifted west to the Monument Creek-Plum Creek route, west of the Jimmy Camp Road-Cherokee Trail. This "west branch of the Trappers Trail" was taken by Albert Richardson in October of 1859:

. . . reached Colorado City, founded a few weeks before, and containing fifteen or twenty log-cabins. . . .
A morning visit to the curious Fontaine qui Bouille (fountains which boil,) two miles from Colorado City, at the head of the creek I had followed up since leaving the Arkansas. . . .
. . . The railroad will make the springs a popular summer resort. The vicinity combines more objects of interest and grandeur than any other spot on the continent: Pike's Peak, the great South Park, the Garden of the Gods and the Fontaine qui Bouille

Richardson's prediction of a railroad and a resort came true. In 1871, the Denver & Rio Grande Railroad completed it's line south of Denver to Colorado Springs. Colorado City is now part of the western section of Colorado Springs, one and a half miles east of Manitou Springs. This Plum Creek-Monument Creek route also developed into the main automobile road across the Arkansas-Platte Divide, U. S. Highway 85, predecessor of Interstate 25.

With the establishment of Colorado City, now part of Colorado Springs, much of the trail traffic along the Front Range moved west from the Cherokee Trail.

Palmer Lake was the crossing point of the Arkansas-Platte Divide by the Denver & Rio Grande Railroad and the early "auto trail" route along the Front Range.

Colorado Territorial Post Offices Along The Cherokee Trail

Wyoming | Nebraska

- Virginia Dale (1868)
- Laporte (1862)
- Namaqua (1868)
- Big Thompson (1862)
- Little Thompson (1875)
- Burlington (1862)
- Ralston's (1863)
- Denver City (1860)
- Cherokee City (1862)
- Latham (1863)
- Evans (1870)
- St. Vrain (1859)
- Fort Lupton (1861)
- Hughes (1871)
- Cherry Creek (1869)
- Pine Grove (1870)
- Frankstown (1862)
- Russellville (1862)
- Elbert (1875)
- Easton (1872)
- Fountain (1864)
- Wood Valley (1862)
- Pueblo (1860)
- Booneville (1863)
- Hayne's Ranch (1861)
- Bent's Fort (1863)

Colorado Territory was created in 1861 and was divided into 17 counties. Several communities along the Cherokee Trail evolved into seats of local government.

County	County Seat
Arapahoe	**Denver**
Boulder	Boulder
Clear Creek	Idaho
Costilla	San Miguel
Douglas	**Frankstown**
El Paso	Colorado [City]
Fremont	Canon City
Gilpin	Central City
Guadalupe	Guadalupe
Huerfano	Autubes
Jefferson	Golden City
Lake	Oro City
Larimer	**Laporte**
Park	Tarryall City
Pueblo	**Pueblo**
Summit	Parkville
Weld	**St. Vrain**

Namaqua - present-day Loveland
Litttle Thompson - present-day Berthoud
Burlington - present-day Longmont
Hughes - present-day Brighton
Pine Grove - present-day Parker
Frankstown - 's' later removed
Elbert - moved to Denver & New Orleans Railroad in 1882
Easton - name changed to Eastonville

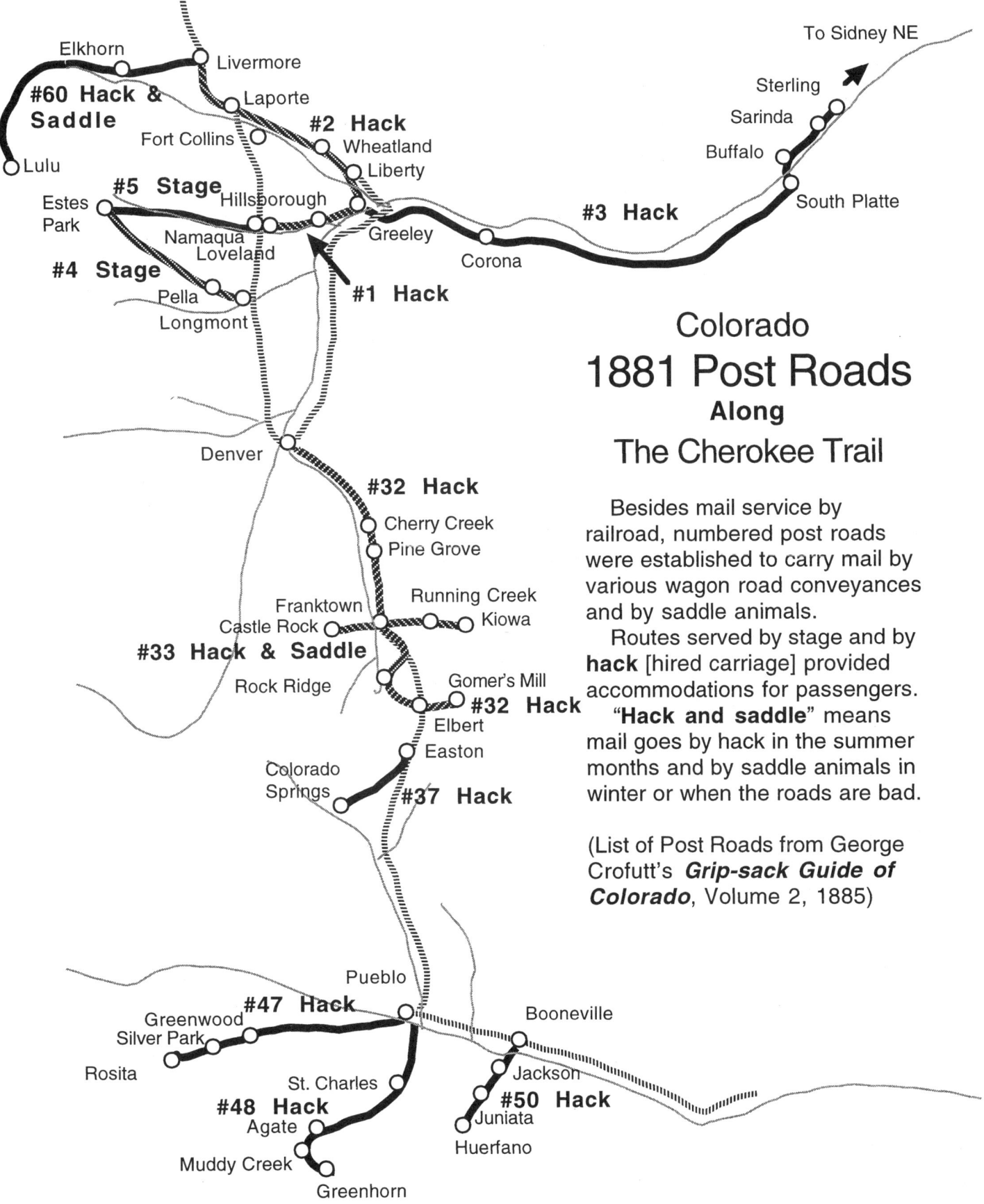

Later Transportation Systems Along the Cherokee Trail

The Cherokee Trail was the major north-south **wagon trail** along the Colorado Front Range. Its route was dictated by the waterways and terrain of the region.

Starting in the early 1870s, **railroads** were built along the Front Range. Their routes followed early wagon roads, for they also needed water and gentle terrain.

Many wagon roads developed into major automobile roads. Some of these major routes were termed "**Auto Trails**." They carried descriptive names and were promoted by towns and businesses along the route.

In 1926, the U. S. Government established a numbering system for **Federal Highways**: odd numbers for north-south roads, even numbers for east-west routes.

Along the Arkansas River   The Cherokee Trail followed the north side of the river.
- **Railroads**: The Atchison Topeka & Santa Fe Railroad completed a line up the Arkansas River to Rocky Ford in 1875, then on to Pueblo in 1876. This route followed the south side of the Arkansas River.
- **Auto Trails:** Following the south side of the river were the Albert Pike Highway, National Old Trails Road and the Dallas-Canadian-Denver Highway (one road, multiple names). East of Pueblo, the Bee Line Road ran north of the Arkansas River to the Crowley area.
- **Highways:** U. S. Highway 50 follows the auto trail route on the south side of the Arkansas River. Colorado Highway 96 follows the north side to Crowley.

Along Fountain Creek   The Cherokee Trail followed the east side of the creek between Pueblo and the town of Fountain.
- **Railroads**: In 1872, the Denver & Rio Grande Railroad built west of Fountain Creek from Fountain to Pueblo. In 1882 the Denver & New Orleans built their line east of Fountain Creek from Fountain to Pueblo. In 1887 the Atchison Topeka & Santa Fe followed closely the Rio Grande route.
- **Auto Trails:** Along the west side of Fountain Creek ran the Albert Pike Highway, Colorado to Gulf Highway, Dallas-Canadian-Denver Highway, National Park-to-Park Highway, Buffalo Highway and the Glacier to Gulf Highway (one road, multiple names).
- **Highways:** U. S. Highway 85, later joined by U. S. 87, followed the auto trail route. This route, with minor variations, became Interstate 25.

Across the Arkansas-Platte Divide   The Cherokee Trail followed up Jimmy Camp Creek, then over the divide to Cherry Creek.
- **Railroads**: No railroad followed the Cherokee Trail across the divide. The Denver & Rio Grande ran well west of the trail, along Monument and East Plum Creek. The Denver & New Orleans ran slightly east of the Cherokee Trail passing through (new) Elbert and Falcon.
- **Auto Trails:** No named auto trail followed the Cherokee Trail. The roads listed along Fountain Creek ran west along Fountain and Plum Creeks.
- **Highways:** U. S. 85 & 87 and Interstate 25 ran west of the trail.

Along Cherry Creek   The Cherokee Trail followed the east side of the creek from Franktown to Denver.
- **Railroads**: In 1881, the Denver & New Orleans built its tracks from Denver south to Parker, then southeast to Elizabeth.
- **Auto Trails:** No named road ran along Cherry Creek.
- **Highways:** Today, Colorado Highway 83 follows the Cherokee Trail south as far as Franktown. The highway used to pass through Russellville. Interstate 25 was originally planned to follow Highway 83.

Along the South Platte River   The Cherokee Trail 1849 route followed the east side of the river from Denver to the Greeley area.
- **Railroads**: In 1870, the Denver Pacific followed closely the Cherokee Trail from Greeley to Denver. This was the first railroad into Denver, linking it with Cheyenne and the Union Pacific Transcontinental Railroad.
- **Auto Trails:** The Denver-Black Hills Highway and an early branch of the Lincoln Highway followed the South Platte River to Denver.
- **Highways:** U. S. Highway 85 follows the river from Denver to Greeley.

Along the Cache la Poudre River   The Cherokee Trail followed up the north side of the river to Laporte.
- **Railroads**: In 1882, the Greeley Salt Lake & Pacific built from Greeley to Fort Collins.
- **Auto Trails:** No named road ran along the Cache la Poudre.
- **Highways:** No federal or major state road runs along the Cache la Poudre between Greeley and Fort Collins.

Along the Foothills   The Cherokee Trail 1850 Branch ran from Denver, along the foothills, to Laporte.
- **Railroads**: In 1877, the Colorado Central built from Longmont to Fort Collins. In 1881, the Denver Utah & Pacific and the Denver Longmont & Northwestern built from Denver to Longmont.
- **Auto Trails:** The Rocky Mountain Highway, Buffalo Highway, Powder River Trail and an early branch of the Lincoln Highway ran from Denver to Fort Collins (one road, multiple names).
- **Highways:** In 1926 U. S. Highway 285 followed the route of the auto trail. The number was changed to U. S. 87, then U. S. 287.

Across the Laramie Mountains   The Cherokee Trail ran from Laporte north and northwest to the Laramie Plains in Wyoming.
- **Railroads**: No railroads ran across the Laramie Mountains, but the route was considered for the Union Pacific transcontinental route.
- **Auto Trails:** The Rocky Mountain Highway closely followed the route of the Cherokee Trail.
- **Highways:** In 1926, U. S. 285 replaces the auto trail, the number later changed to U. S. 287.

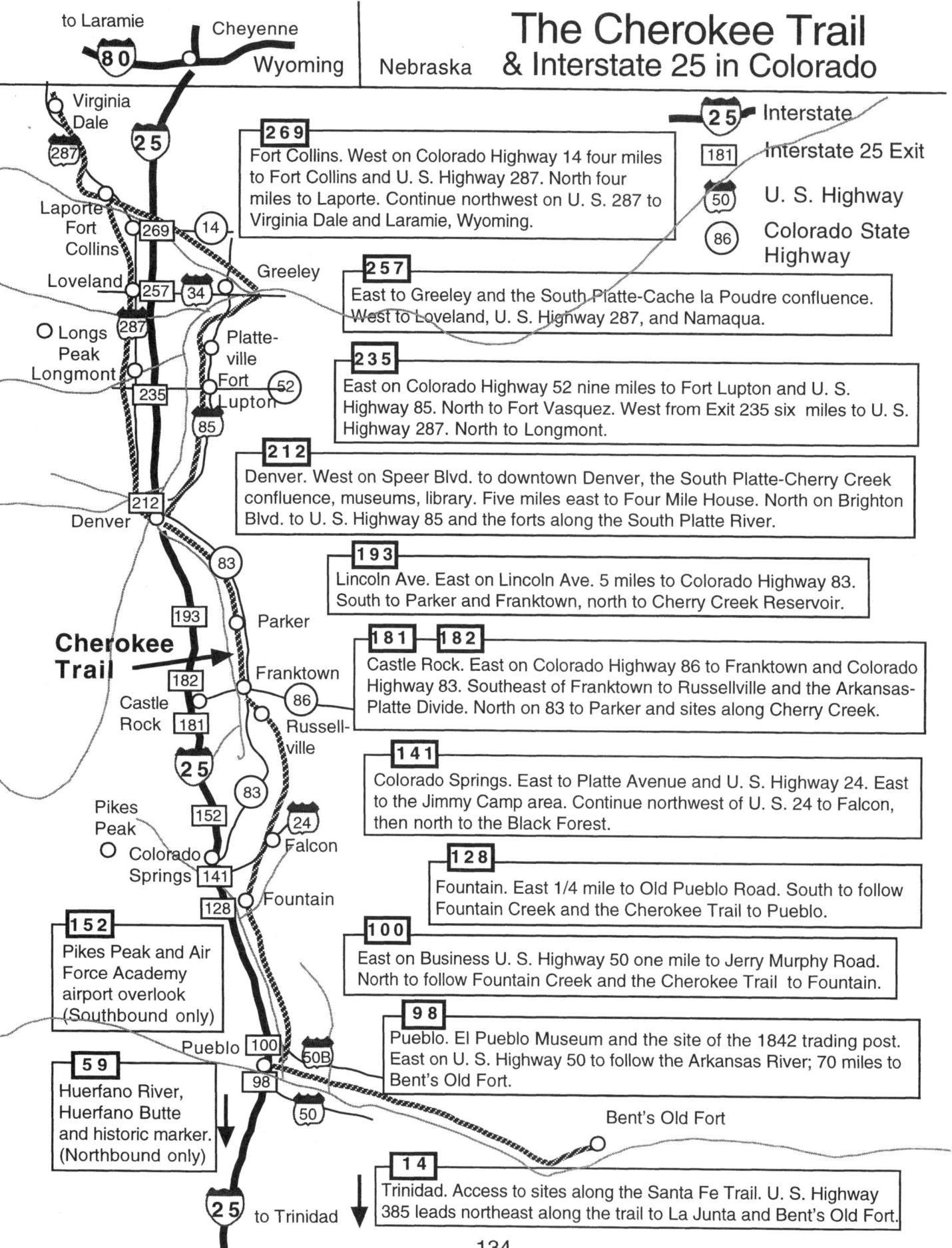

Pikes Peak from the Air Force Academy overlook at Interstate 25 Milepost 152 (southbound only). The peak was a major landmark on the Cherokee Trail.

Old gas station on E. Harmony Road in Fort Collins, two miles west of I-25 Exit 265. Longs Peak, Cherokee Trail landmark, in the background.

The Cherokee Trail
(North Branch) & Interstate 80 in Wyoming

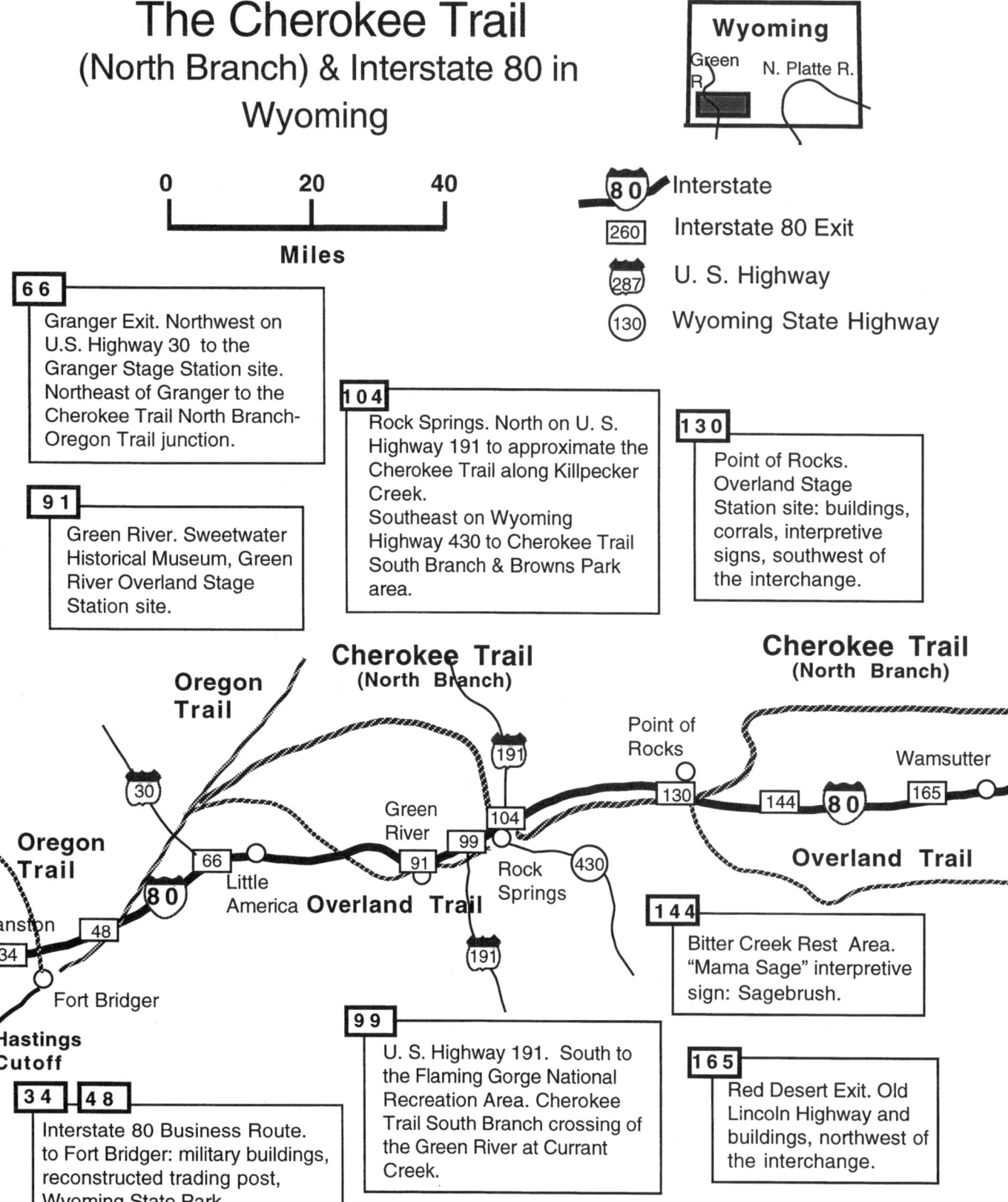

66 Granger Exit. Northwest on U.S. Highway 30 to the Granger Stage Station site. Northeast of Granger to the Cherokee Trail North Branch-Oregon Trail junction.

91 Green River. Sweetwater Historical Museum, Green River Overland Stage Station site.

104 Rock Springs. North on U.S. Highway 191 to approximate the Cherokee Trail along Killpecker Creek. Southeast on Wyoming Highway 430 to Cherokee Trail South Branch & Browns Park area.

130 Point of Rocks. Overland Stage Station site: buildings, corrals, interpretive signs, southwest of the interchange.

144 Bitter Creek Rest Area. "Mama Sage" interpretive sign: Sagebrush.

165 Red Desert Exit. Old Lincoln Highway and buildings, northwest of the interchange.

34 48 Interstate 80 Business Route. to Fort Bridger: military buildings, reconstructed trading post, Wyoming State Park. Oregon Trail-Cherokee Trail South Branch junction.

99 U.S. Highway 191. South to the Flaming Gorge National Recreation Area. Cherokee Trail South Branch crossing of the Green River at Currant Creek.

The Cherokee Trail
(North Branch) & Interstate 80 in Wyoming

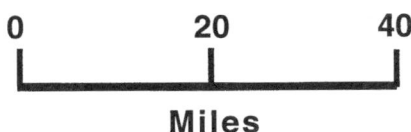

184
Lincoln Highway memorial, first coast-to-coast highway. Southwest of the interchange, adjacent to a stretch of the old highway.

187
Creston Junction. South on Wyoming 789 for 16 miles to the Overland Trail and marker; 37 miles to the Cherokee Trail South Branch; 51 miles to Baggs.

267
Wagonhound Rest Area. Cherokee Trail marker on the frontage road 1/2 mile west of rest area. Good view of Elk Mountain to the west.

272
Rock Creek crossing. Overland Stage station site.

297
West on Wyoming 12 for 4 miles to the Little Laramie Crossing.

215
Rawlins. South on Wyoming 71 to follow the Cherokee Trail. 10 miles to Sheep Mountain; 15 miles to The Bridger Pass Road and the Overland Trail.

228
Fort Steele 2 miles north. Union Pacific and Lincoln Highway crossing of the North Platte River.

235
Walcott Junction. South on Wyoming 130 for 9 miles to the Overland Trail crossing and marker; south 20 miles to Saratoga; south 38 miles to Encampment and Riverside and the Cherokee Trail South Branch. Continue south to North Park in Colorado.

260
Town of Elk Mountain. Southwest on the Pass Creek Road to follow the trail south of Elk Mountain. West on Rattlesnake Road to follow the Overland Trail north of Elk Mountain.

313
South on U.S. 287 to Tie Siding and the Cherokee Trail in Colorado.

311
Southwest on Wyoming 230 for 7 miles to Overland Trail Marker; to Woods Landing and North Park. West on Wyoming 130 for 7 miles to Overland Trail marker; to Snowy Range Pass.

137

The Cherokee Trail North Branch and the later Overland Trail crossed Rock Creek near present-day Arlington, Interstate 80 Exit 272.

The Cherokee Trail crossed Wagonhound Creek near the Wagonhound rest area, I-80 Exit 267. The trail passed south of Elk Mountain, seen in the background.

Abandoned building in the town of Red Desert, Interstate 80 Exit 165. The original town was a station on the transcontinental Union Pacific Railroad.

The Union Pacific Railroad descends Bitter Creek, paralleling Interstate 80, from Point of Rocks, I-80 Exit 130, west to Green River, Exit 91.

198 REPORT OF THE

Itinerary of a march from New Mexico to Camp Scott, Utah Territory, made by Captain R. B. Marcy, 5th infantry, in 1858, commencing at the point where the road from Fort Leavenworth enters the Raton mountains and terminating at the confluence of Black's and Ham's Forks of Green river, upon the South Pass road to Salt Lake City.

Date.	Hour.	Measured distances.		Bearings.	Remarks.
		Camp to camp.	Total.		
1858.		Miles.	Miles.		
Mar. 23	6 a. m.	5.25	5.25	N. 25° W.	
				N. 25° W.	
				N. 25° W.	
				N. 25° W.	
				N. 25° W.	
				N. 30° W.	
24	12¼ p. m.	10.13	15.38	N. 30° W.	
	6½ a. m.			N. 30° W.	
				N. 30° W.	Good grass, wood, and water are found upon all these streams, which are tributaries of the Arkansas. They take their rise in the eastern slopes of the mountains, and are fed from springs.
				N. 35° W.	
				N. 35° W.	
				N. 35° W.	
25	12¼ p. m.	10.10	33.73	N. 30° W.	
	6½ a. m.			N. 30° W.	
				N. 30° W.	
				N. 20° W.	
26	10½ a. m.	11.25	44.98	N. 25° W.	
	6½ a. m.			N. 30° W.	
				N. 25° W.	
27	9½ a. m.	10	54.98	N. 25° W.	
	6½ a. m.			N. 30° W.	
				N. 30° W.	
				N. 20° W.	
				N. 20° W.	
28	12½ p. m.	16	70.98	N. 20° W.	Good crossing.
				N. 35° W.	
				N. 35° W.	
29 to 31	12 m.	12.50	83.48	N. 35° W.	Good ford at the crossing of the Arkansas; water twelve inches deep; rocky bed. Old Pueblo is not occupied.
	6 a. m.			N. 25° W.	
				N. 25° W.	
				N. 25° W.	
				N. 25° W.	
				N. 25° W.	
Ap'l 1	11½ p. m.	13.50	96.98	N. 25° W.	The *Cherokee trail*, noted, extends from the Cherokee nation to California, and has been travelled for several years by emigrants.
	6 a. m.			N. 25° W.	
				N. 25° W.	
				N. 25° W.	Good grass, wood, and water at all points along the valley of Fontaine qui Bouille creek.
				N. 25° W.	
2 to 5	1¾ p. m.	17	113.98	N. 25° W.	The mineral spring is 2¼ miles to the left of our road, upon an Indian trail that leads in the nets. It is believed to contain a large per centage of soda, and is very pleasant to the taste, resembling Congress water.
				N. 25° W.	
6 to 28	6 a. m.	7	120.98	N. 25° W.	
				N. 25° W.	
				N. 20° E.	
				N. 20° E.	
				N. 20° E.	

A page from Randolph B. Marcy's 1858 itinerary. His report was printed in the 1858-1859 U. S. Senate Executive Documents, Serial set 975.

V.
The Cherokee Trail
References and Resources

General Land Office Surveyor Notes and Plats

The Homestead Act was passed in 1862. The **General Land Office** (GLO) sent surveyors out to **survey the public lands** prior to the homesteading of a region.

The surveyor kept notebooks, the written record of his survey. He recorded natural features, such as rivers and creeks, hills, bluffs, forested areas and quality of the soil. He also noted man-made features such as farm fields, villages, cabins, roads and trails.

These "**surveyor notes**" are excellent primary sources of trail information, for the surveyor recorded exactly what he saw, the trail and the direction of the trail. He usually named the trail, but often noted nothing more than "wagon road" or "road."

The initial survey was conducted only along township boundaries. Next a surveyor walked the section lines within the township.

Township maps were drawn later, from the surveyor notes, by someone other than the surveyor. These GLO "**land plats**" involved the marking of only known points along the township and section lines, then "connecting the dots" to show creeks, roads and trails.

The land plat of the township boundary survey is called the "Exterior Lines" plat, and shows much less detail than the "township" plat drawn from the section line survey. Even with the greater detail of a township plat, the surveyor walked only the section lines, therefore the location of a noted trail will be accurate only where it intersects a section line.

The surveyor's unit of measurement is the "chain."
 1 chain = 66 feet
 80 chains = 1 mile
 1 section = 1 mile square = 640 acres
 1 township = 36 square miles.

Surveyor notes and land plats are available at the following Bureau of Land Management (**BLM**) offices. They are stored on microfiche, but hard copies can be obtained for a fee.

Colorado survey notes and plats:
 2850 Youngfield St.
 Lakewood, Colorado 80215
 (303) 236-2100

Wyoming survey notes and plats:
 5353 Yellowstone Road
 Cheyenne, Wyoming 82003
 (307) 775-6256

On the following page, the township surveyed by D. C. Oakes in 1881 shows Township 12 North, Range 100 West, in present-day Moffat County, Colorado. The page of surveyor notes (inset) shows the notes the surveyor recorded for the one mile, south to north line, between sections 16 and 17. A stone was set at 1/2 mile (quarter section marker) and at the north section corner. A gulch and the Cherokee Trail were noted, as well as a summary of the land and soil conditions.

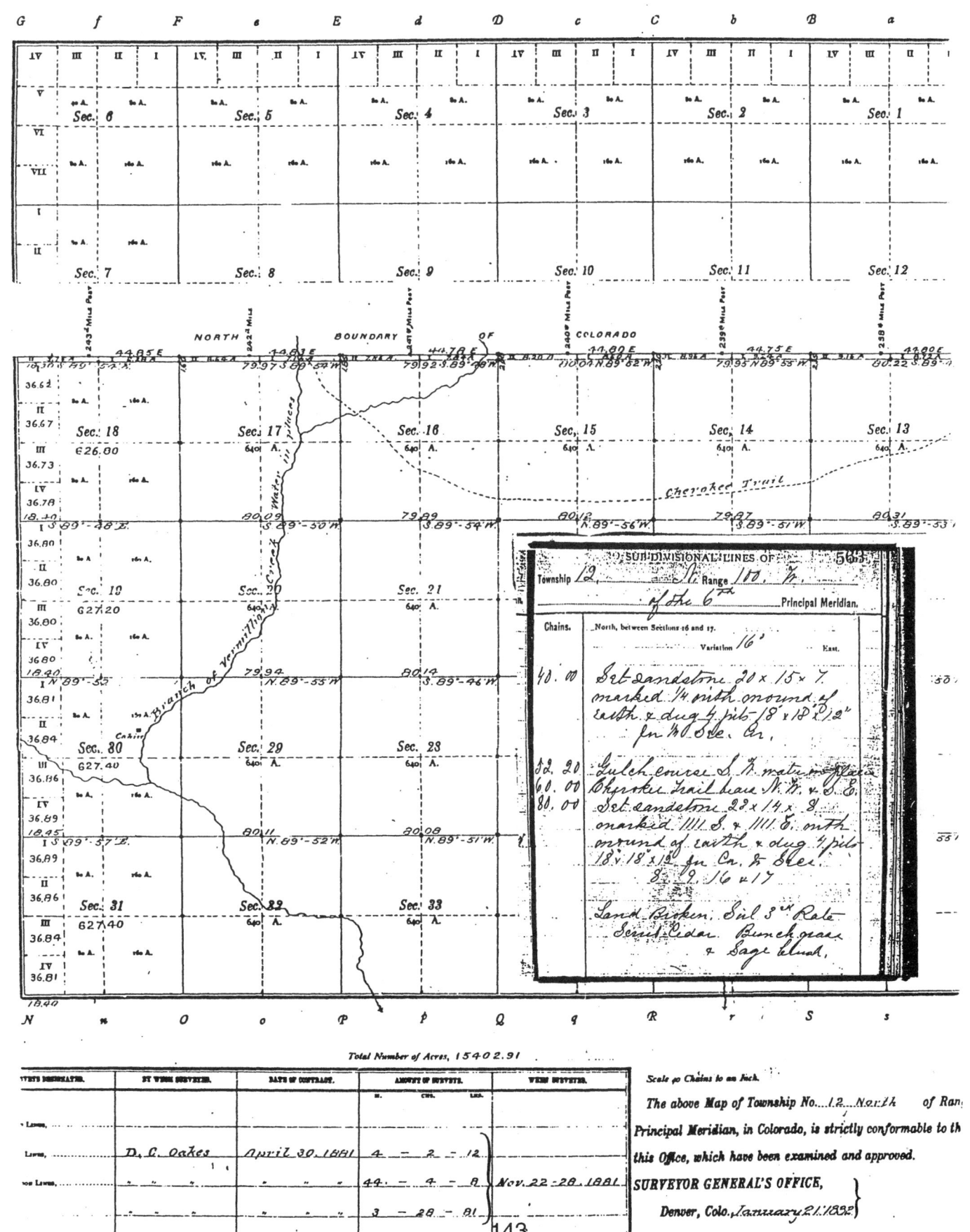

Trail terminology: <u>Depression</u> - A shallow dip in the surface. Often faint and difficult to see. Compaction of the soil can cause a change in the vegetation.

<u>Swale</u> - Deeper and more obvious than a depression. Sloping sides. Wagons normally traveled directly up or down steep hills, avoiding tilting of the wagons.

Rut - A deep depression, has steep sides and no center mound. Erosion can alter a trail trace, causing irregular sides and bottom.

Wagons often traveled side by side, resulting in several parallel traces. Snow, vegetation differences and a sharp sun angle often make trails more visible.

Sites, Activities, Museums and Historical Societies

Colorado

Along The Arkansas River

Bent's Old Fort National Historic Site. East of La Junta. Reconstructed trading post. Tours and interpretive programs. (719) 384-2596.

Otero Museum. La Junta. Local history, transportation history: the trails and the Santa Fe Railroad.

El Pueblo Museum. Pueblo. A Colorado Historical Society facility. History of southern Colorado, the trapping and trading era. On the grounds is the site of the original trading post, with some archaeological excavations. 324 W. 1st St., 81003. (719) 583-0453.

Pueblo County Historical Society Museum. Pueblo. Vail Hotel (National Register of Historic Places). Local history. The Edward Broadhead Library and the Pueblo County Historical Society. 217 S. Grand, 81003.

Across The Arkansas-Platte Divide

Pioneer Museum. Colorado Springs. History of the Pikes Peak region. Located in the 1903 El Paso County Courthouse, 215 S. Tejon St., 80903. (719) 578-6650. Located in the basement is the library of the Starsmore Center for Local History.

Old Colorado City History Center and Historical Society. Colorado City and Manitou Springs history. 1 South 24th St., Colorado Springs, 80904. (719) 636-1225.

Jimmy Camp Creek Park. Colorado Springs. Proposed city park and hiking trails.

Black Forest Regional Park. El Paso County Park, intersection of Shoup and Milan Roads. Two-mile hiking trail through an undeveloped, natural area.

Elbert County Historical Society. Kiowa. Museum, local and Smoky Hill Trail history. P.O Box 43, 80117.

Along Cherry Creek

Franktown Museum. Franktown. Local history. Historic Frankstown, Inc., P.O. Box 5887, 80116.

Castlewood Canyon State Park. Four miles south of Franktown. Hiking trails, historic Castlewood Dam. P.O. Box 504, Franktown, 80116. (303) 688-5242.

Douglas Public Library District. Castle Rock. "Local History Collection": History of Douglas County, the Cherry Creek Valley and the Divide. 961 S. Plum Creek Blvd., 80104-2788. (303) 814-0795.

Pikes Peak Grange. Franktown. National Register of Historic Places.

Parker Area Historical Society. Parker. Local history. Custodian for the 20 Mile House-Pine Grove Post Office. P.O. Box 604, 80134.

Cherry Creek Greenway. Hiking, biking and horse trail follows Cherry Creek from Castlewood Canyon to Cherry Creek Reservoir.

Cherry Creek Reservoir State Park. Aurora. Hiking, nature study, special events. 4201 S. Parker Road, 80014. (303) 690-1166.

Melvin Schoolhouse Museum-Library. Aurora. Two-room school house, Smoky Hill Trail history. Cherry Creek Valley Historical Society. Mailing address: 16100 E. Smoky Hill Road, 80015.

Aurora History Museum. Aurora. Local history, living history, historic properties and research library. 15001 E. Alameda Dr., 80012. (303) 739-6665.

Cherry Creek Bikeway. Denver. Hiking and biking path along Cherry Creek from Cherry Creek Reservoir to Confluence Park on the South Platte River.

Four Mile House Historic Park. Denver. Four Mile House, National Register of Historic Places. Living history, special events. 715 S. Forest St., 80222. (303) 399-1859.

Denver Public Library. Extensive collection of western history books, maps, manuscripts, photographs and newspapers in the Western History Department. 10 West 14th Ave. Pkwy, 80204. (303) 640-6291.

Colorado Historical Society and Museum. Denver. Permanent and changing exhibits on the history of Colorado. Special events. Western history books, manuscripts and photographs in the Stephen Hart Library. 1300 Broadway, 80203. (303) 866-3682.

Colorado State Archives. Denver. Official state repository for public records. Census records, land records, maps, military records, newspapers and photographs. 1313 Sherman St., 80203. (303) 866-2358.

Along the South Platte River

South Platte River Trail. Hiking and biking trail along the South Platte River from Confluence Park north into Adams County.

Adams County Museum. Brighton. History and cultures of Adams County. 9601 Henderson Road, 80601. (303) 658-7103.

Fort Lupton Museum. Fort Lupton. History of southern Weld County. 453 First Street, 80621. (303) 857-1634.

South Platte Valley Historical Society. Fort Lupton. Involved in the reconstruction of Fort Lupton. P. O. Box 633, 80621.

Fort Vasquez Museum. Platteville. Reconstructed fort. Visitor center and museum on the history of the fur trade. 13412 U.S. Highway 85, P. O. Box 728, 80651. (970) 785-2832.

Platteville Prairie Museum. Platteville. Local and Fort St. Vrain history.

Along the Cache la Poudre River

City of Greeley Museum. Greeley. Museum of the cultural history of the high plains. Historic buildings have been relocated to Centennial Village. 919 7th Ave., 80631. (970) 350-9220.

Along the Foothills
Loveland Museum and Gallery. Loveland. Local history of Loveland and the Big Thompson Valley. Exhibit on Mariano Medina, mountain man. Fifth and Lincoln, 80537. (970) 962-2410.

Fort Collins Museum. Fort Colliins. History of Fort Collins and Laramie County. Large collection of Folsom points. Cabin of Antoine Janis, early settler. 200 Mathews St., 80521. (970) 221-6738.

Wyoming

Wyoming State Archives. Cheyenne. Official state repository for public records. Microfilmed and original records from 1867. Barrett Building, 2301 Central, 82002. (307) 777-7826.

Wyoming State Museum. Cheyenne. Wyoming and Western memorabilia. Barrett Building, 24th and Central, 82002. (307) 777-7014.

American Heritage Center. Laramie. Research center: manuscripts, diaries, maps and photographs. Serves as the University of Wyoming archives. 2111 Willett Drive, 82071. 1-800-445-5303.

Saratoga Museum. Saratoga. Housed in a 1915 Union Pacific railroad depot. History of the North Platte Valley. 104 Constitution Ave., P. O. Box 1131, 82331. (307) 326-5511.

Carbon County Museum. Rawlins. Artifacts, newspapers and photographs of early Carbon County. 9th and Walnut, P.O. Box 52, 82301. (307) 324-9611.

Grand Encampment Museum. Encampment. Several furnished, historic buildings including a stage station and U. S. Forest Service guard station. Artifacts, maps and photographs of the Encampment-Riverside area. P. O. Box 395, 82325. (307) 327-5308.

Little Snake River Museum. Savery. Located in the old Savery School. Artifacts of the Little Snake River Valley. Major attraction is the Jim Baker Cabin, built in 1873. Savery, 82332. (307) 383-7262.

Sweetwater County Historical Museum. Green River. Artifacts, photographs and research material of Sweetwater County. 80 West Flaming Gorge Way, 82935. (307) 875-2611 ext. 263.

Flaming Gorge National Recreation Area. South of Green River and Rock Springs. Water sports, camping and hiking. P.O. Box 279, Manila, Utah, 84046. (801) 784-3445.

Fort Bridger State Historic Site. Fort Bridger. Reconstruction of Jim Bridger's trading post. Ruins and preserved buildings of the 1858-1890 Army post. Museum. Special activities. P.O. Box 35, 82933. (307) 782-3842.

Bibliography: Journals Quotes

Allyn, Joseph Pratt. *West by Southwest*, ed. David K. Strate. Dodge City: Kansas Heritage Center, 1984.

Ashley, William H. *The West of William H. Ashley*, ed. Dale L. Morgan. Denver: The Old West Publishing Company, 1964.

Barclay, Alexander. *The Adventures of Alexander Barclay Mountain Man*, ed. George Hammond. Denver: Old West Publishing Company, 1976.

Barney, Libeus. *Letters of the Pikes Peak Gold Rush*. Talisman Press, 1959.

Bartleson, John. *Letters to the Secretary of War*. U. S. Congress, 35th Cong. 2nd sess., Serial set 975, 1858-1859.

Beckwith, E. G. "Report of Explorations For a Route For the Pacific Railroad," U. S. House of Representatives, 33th Cong. 2nd Sess., Ex. Doc. 91. Serial Set 792, 1855.

Bell, John R. *The Journal of Captain John R. Bell*. Glendale: The Arthur H. Clark Company, 1957.

Berthoud, E. L. Map in *Kansas in Maps*. By Robert W. Baughman. Topeka: Kansas State Historical Society, 1961.

Bliss, Edward. "Denver to Salt Lake by Overland Stage in 1862." *Colorado Magazine*, Vol. 8, No. 5 (1931). Denver: The State Historical Society of Colorado.

Brown, John. *Autobiography of Pioneer John Brown 1820 - 1896*. Salt Lake City: John Zimmerman Brown, 1941.

Brown, John Lowery. "The Journal of John Lowery Brown, of the Cherokee Nation en Route to California in 1850," ed. Muriel Wright. *Chronicles of Oklahoma,* Vol. 12(June, 1934). Oklahoma City: Oklahoma Historical Society.

Bryan, Francis T. *Report of Lieut. F. T. Bryan Concerning His Operations in locating a Practical Road Between Ft. Riley to Bridger's Pass 1856*. U. S. Senate, 35th Cong. 1st sess. Serial set 920, 1858.

Carrington, Albert. In *Exploring the Great Salt Lake,* ed. Brigham D. Madsen. Salt Lake City: University of Utah Press, 1989.

Cooke, Philip St. George. *Scenes and Adventures in the Army*. Philadelphia: Lindsay & Blakiston, 1859.

Dodge, Grenville M. *How We Built the Union Pacific Railway*. Denver: Sage Books, reprint, 1965.

DuBois, John Van Deusen. *Campaigns in the West, 1856-1861*, ed. George P. Hammond. Tucson: Arizona Pioneers Historical Society, 1949.

Durley, Jeff. "Diary." Denver Public Library, Western History Dept. Manuscript #RBV21.

Engels, William H. "Diary of a Cattle Drive." *Flashback,* Vol. 21 No. 1(February, 1971), Fayetteville. Arkansas: Washington County Historical Society.

Evans, Hugh. "Journal of a Dragoon Campaign in 1835." *Mississippi Valley Historical Review*, Vol. 14(September, 1927).

Farnham, Thomas J. "Travels in the Great Western Prairies, etc., May 21 - October 16, 1839," ed. Reuben Gold Thwaites. *Early Western Travels, 1848-1846.* Vol. XXVIII. Cleveland: The Arthur H. Clark Company, 1906.

Field, Matt. *Matt Field on the Santa Fe Trail*, ed. John E. Sunder. Norman: University of Oklahoma Press, 1960.

Fitch, Julian. *Report*, in "Fort Wallace and its Relation to the Frontier," by Mrs. Frank C. Montgomery. Kansas State Historical Society, Vol. 17(1926-1928).

Franklin, William. *March to South Pass: Lieutenant William B. Franklin's Journal of the Kearny Expedition of 1845*, ed. Frank Schubert. Washington: U. S. Government Printing Office, 1979.

Frémont, John C. *Report of The Exploring Expedition to the Rocky Mountains in the Year 1842 and to Oregon and California in the Years 1843-1844.* Washington D. C, 1845.

Gass, A. M. "Overland Routes to the Goldfields, 1859", ed. LeRoy R. Hafen. *Southwest Historical Series* Vol. XI. Philadelphia: Porcupine Press, 1974.

Greeley, Horace. *An Overland Journey from New York to San Francisco in the Summer of 1859.* New York: Alfred A. Knopf, reprint, 1964.

Gunnison, John Williams. In *Exploring the Great Salt Lake,* ed. Brigham D. Madsen. Salt Lake City: University of Utah Press, 1989.

Hartley, William. "Map of the Recently Discovered Gold Regions in Western Kansas and Nebraska." St. Louis: Wm. Hartley & Co., 1858.

Hayden, Ferdinand V. "Preliminary Report of the U. S. Geological Survey of Wyoming." U. S. House of Rep., 42nd Cong. 2nd sess., Serial set 1520, 1871-1872.

Hundley, Ellen. "From Utah to Texas in 1856," ed. Kenneth L. Holmes, *Covered Wagon Women,* Vol 7. Glendale: The Arthur H. Clark Company, 1988.

Kingsbury, Lt. Gaines. Report of the Expedition of Dragoons, under Colonel Henry Dodge in 1835. U. S. Congress. 24th Cong. 1st sess., ASP021, 1836.

Loring, William W. *Letters to the Secretary of War.* U. S. Congress. 35th Cong. 2nd sess., Serial set 975, 1858-1859.

Marcy, Randolph B. *Letters to the Secretary of War.* U. S. Congress. 35th Cong. 2nd sess., Serial set 975, 1858-1859.

---------- *The Prairie Traveler. A Handbook for Overland Expeditions.* New York: Harper & Brothers, 1859.

Melvin, Jane. "The Twelve Mile House." *The Colorado Magazine.* Vol. 12, No. 5(September, 1935). Denver: The State Historical Society of Colorado.

Mills, Robert. "Adventures of an Englishman in Cummins City." *Annals of Wyoming,* Vol. 60, No.2(Fall, 1988). Cheyenne: Wyoming State Archives.

Mitchell, John. in "The Cherokee Trail," by Jack E. and Patricia K. A. Fletcher. *The Overland Journal* , Vol.13 No. 2(Summer, 1995). Independence: Oregon-California Trails Association.

Parker, Samuel. *Journal of an Exploring Tour Beyond the Rocky Mountains.* Ithaca, New York: Mack, Andrus & Woodruff, 1842.

Parkman, Francis. *The Oregon Trail.* Garden City, New York: International Collectors Library, 1945.

Parsons, William B. "Pikes Peak Guidebooks of 1859," ed. LeRoy R. Hafen, *Southwest Historical Series*, Vol. 9. Philadelphia: Porcupine Press, 1974.

Patterson, E. H. N. "Overland Routes to the Goldfields, 1859," ed. LeRoy R. Hafen. *Southwest Historical Series,* Vol. XI. Philadelphia: Porcupine Press, 1974.

Peck, R. M. "Relations with the Indians of the Plains, 1857-1861." ed LeRoy R. Hafen and Ann W. Hafen. *Far West and Rockies Series*, Vol. 9. Glendale: The Arthur H. Clark Company, 1959.

Pike, Zebulon Montgomery. *Exploratory Travels through the Western Territories of North America.* Denver: W. H. Lawrence & Co., reprint, 1889.

Post, Charles. "Overland Routes to the Goldfields, 1859," ed. LeRoy R. Hafen. *Southwest Historical Series,* Vol. XI. Philadelphia: Porcupine Press, 1974.

Powell, Philander. "The Diary of Philander Powell." *Flashback,* Vol. 37 No. 3(August, 1987). Fayetteville, Arkansas: Washington County Historical Society.

Pyeatt, John Rankin. "Some Pyeatt Letters," *Flashback,* Vol. 29 No. 1(February, 1979), Fayetteville, Arkansas: Washington County Historical Society.

Quesenbury, William. "Diary to California." *Flashback,* Vol. 3 No. 2(May, 1973). Fayetteville, Arkansas: Washington County Historical Society.

Richards, William. A. "Diary Kept by W. A. Richards in Summer of 1873," *Annals of Wyoming.* Vol. 8 No. 1(July, 1931). Cheyenne: Wyoming State Archives.

Richardson, Albert D. *Beyond the Mississippi: From the Great River to the Great Ocean.* Hartford: American Publishing Company, 1867.

Root, Frank A. *The Overland Stage to California.* Glorieta, New Mexico: The Rio Grande Press, Inc., 1970.

Sage, Rufus B. "Scenes in the Rocky Mountains and in Oregon, California, New Mexico, Texas and the Grand Prairies," reprint: ed LeRoy R. Hafen and Ann W. Hafen. *Far West and Rockies Series*, Vol. 4 & 5. Glendale: The Arthur H. Clark Company, 1956.

Seymour, Silas. *Incidents of a Trip Through the Great Platte Valley.* New York: D. Van Nostrand, 1867.

Shortess, Robert. "To the Rockies and Oregon 1839-1842," ed. LeRoy R. Hafen and Ann W. Hafen. *Far West and Rockies Series,* Vol 3. Glendale: The Arthur H. Clark Company, 1955.

Smith, E. Willard. "To the Rockies and Oregon 1839-1842," ed. LeRoy R. Hafen and Ann W. Hafen. *Far West and Rockies Series,* Vol 3. Glendale: The Arthur H. Clark Company, 1955.

Stansbury, Howard. *Exploring the Great Salt Lake,* ed. Brigham D. Madsen. Salt Lake City: University of Utah Press, 1989.

Steele, John. "Extracts from the Journal of John Steele," *Utah Historical Review*, Vol. 6 No. 1(January, 1933). Salt Lake City: Utah State Historical Society.

Tierney, Luke. "Pikes Peak Guidebooks of 1859," ed. LeRoy R. Hafen, *Southwest Historical Series*, Vol. 9. Philadelphia: Porcupine Press, 1974.

Villard, Henry. "To the Pike's Peak Country in 1859 and Cannibalism on the Smoky Hill Route." *The Colorado Magazine.* Vol 8, No. 6(November, 1931). Denver: The State Historical Society of Colorado.

Voorhees, Augustus. "Pikes Peak Guidebooks of 1859," ed. LeRoy R. Hafen, *Southwest Historical Series*, Vol. 9. Philadelphia: Porcupine Press, 1974.

Willing, George M. "A Journey to the Pike's Peak Gold Mines," *Mississippi Valley Historical Review.* Vol. 14 No. 3 (December, 1927).

Wislizenus, Frederick A. *A Journey to the Rocky Mountains, 1839.* Glorieta, New Mexico: The Rio Grande Press, Inc, reprint, 1969.

Williams, J. L. *Reports of Government Directors Union Pacific Railroad Company.* U. S. Senate, 47th Cong. 1st sess. Serial set 2336, 1886.

Secondary Sources

Barry, Louise. *The Beginning of the West*. Topeka: Kansas State Historical Society, 1972.

Brigham, Lillian Rice. *Colorado Travelore*. Denver: The Peerless Printing Co., 1939.

Crofutt, Geo. A. *Grip-Sack Guide to Colorado*, Vol. II. Omaha: The Overland Publishing Co, 1885. Reprint, CUBAR, 1966.

Erb, Louise Bruning, Ann Bruning Brown and Gilberta Bruning Hughes. *The Bridger Pass Overland Trail 1862-1869*. Littleton, Colorado: ERBGEM Publishing Co.,1989.

Fletcher, Jack E. and Patricia K. A. "The Cherokee Trail." *The Overland Journal*, Vol. 13 No. 2(Summer, 1995). Independence: Oregon-California Trails Association.

Forman, Grant. *Marcy & the Gold Seekers*. Norman: University of Oklahoma Press, 1939.

Franzwa, Gregory M. *The Santa Fe Trail Revisited*. St Louis: The Patrice Press, 1989.

Goetzmann, William H. *Army Exploration in the American West 1803-1863*. New Haven: Yale University Press, 1959.

Gowens, Fred R. and Eugene E. Campbell. *Fort Bridger*. Provo, Utah: Brigham Young University Press, 1975.

Hafen, LeRoy R. *The Overland Mail 1849-1869*. Cleveland: The Arthur H. Clark Company, 1926.

--------- *Colorado and its People*, Vol. I. New York: Lewis Historical Publishing Co., Inc, 1948.

Howbert, Irving. *Memories of a Lifetime in the Pike's Peak Region*. New York: G. P. Putnam's Sons, 1925.

Jessen, Kenneth. *Railroads of Northern Colorado*. Boulder: Pruett Publishing Company, 1982.

Jones, Clyde W. "What Happened at Russellville." *The Denver Westerners Roundup*, Vol. 50 No. 5(September-October, 1994). Denver: The Denver Westerners.

Jones, James R. "Jim." *Denver & New Orleans, In the Shadow of the Rockies*. Denver: Sundance Publications, Ltd., 1997.

Lavender, David. *Bent's Fort*. Garden City, New York: Doubleday & Company, 1954.

Lee, Wayne C. and Howard C. Raynesford. Trails of the Smoky Hill. Caldwell, Idaho: Caxton Printers, Ltd., 1980.

Lincoln Highway Association. *A Complete Official Guide of the Lincoln Highway*. Tucson: The Patrice Press, reprint, 1993.

Long, Margaret. *The Smoky Hill Trail*. Denver: The W. H. Kistler Publishing Company, 1947.

Mathews, Carl. *Early Days Around the Divide*. St. Louis: Sign Book Co.,1969.

Mattes, Merrill. *The Great Platte River Road*. Lincoln: The Nebraska Historical Society, 1969.

Moody, Ralph. *The Old Trails West*. New York: Thomas Y. Crowell Company, 1963.

Morison, Jack L. "Early Colorado Auto Trails." *The Denver Westerners Roundup*, Vol. 47 No. 1(January-February, 1991). Denver: The Denver Westerners.

Patterson, Mary. "The Story of a Pioneer." *Quarterly Bulletin*, Vol. 1 No. 1 & 2(August 15, 1923). Cheyenne: State of Wyoming Historical Department.

Scott, Glenn R. *Historic Trail Maps of the Pueblo 1 x 2 Quadrangle*. Denver: U. S. Geological Survey, 1975.

--------- *Historic Trail Map of the Greater Denver Area*. Denver: U. S. Geological Survey, 1976.

Scott, Glenn R. and Carol Rein Shwayder. *Historic Trail Map of the Greeley 1 x 2 Quadrangle*. Denver: U. S. Geological Survey, 1993.

The Pacific Tourist, ed. Frederick E. Shearer. New York: Crown Publishers, Inc., reprint, 1970.

Ubanek, Mae. *Wyoming Place Names*. Missoula: Montana Press Publishing Company, 1988.

von Ahlefeldt, Judy. *Thunder, Sun and Snow - The History of Colorado's Black Forest*. Colorado Springs: Century One Press, 1979.

West of Fort Bridger, ed. Roderic J. Korns and Dale L. Morgan, revised and updated by Will Bagley and Harold Schindler. Logan: Utah State University Press, 1994.

Wilkins, Tivis E. *Colorado Railroads*. Boulder: Tivis Wilkins, 1974.

Writers Program of the Public Work Projects Administration. *Wyoming - A Guide to its History, Highways, and People*. Lincoln: University of Nebraska Press, 1941. Bison Book reprint, 1981.

Cherokee Trail marker near the Interstate 80 Wagonhound rest area, between Laramie and Rawlins, Wyoming.

Index

Air Force Academy, Colo., 134, 135
Alabama, 3
Albert Pike Highway, 132
Alexander, Thomas (grave), 23, 55
Allyn, Joseph Pratt, 45
Applegate-Lassen Trail, 120
Archer, Col. James, 72
Arkansas, 15, 18, 19, 23, 32, 36, 39, 65, 87
Arkansas River, 4, 5, 10, 12, 14, 17, 19, 22, 24, 25, 27, 28, 29, 32, 34, 35, 42, 43, 44, 45, 48, 49, 51, 53, 69, 81, 132, 134
Arkansas-Platte Divide, Colo., 4, 6, 14, 15, 19, 20, 22, 25, 27, 42, 43, 51, 53, 54, 55, 56, 58, 63, 69, 82, 128, 129, 132, 134
Arlington, Wyo., 9, 94, 138
Armstrong, Malinda (grave), 8, 28, 95, 114, 118
Ashley, William H., 4, 8, 27, 86, 87, 94, 101, 114
Atchison Topeka & Santa Fe Railroad, 34, 126, 132
Auraria, Colo., 22, 23, 55

Badito, Colo., 48
Baggs, Wyo., 9, 18, 26, 30, 95, 117, 118, 137
Baker, Jim, 83, 95
Baker's Ferry, Wyo., 102
Banning-Lewis Ranch, Colo., 25
Barclay, Alexander, 45
Barney, Libeus, 52
Bartleson, John, 105
Baxter, Colo., 44
Baxter, Wyo., 112
Beale, Edward, 48
Bear Creek, Wyo., 82
Becknell, William, 3, 27, 34
Beckwith, E. G., 28, 36
Bee Line Road, 132
Bell, John R., 70
Bent, William, 44

Bent & St. Vrain Company, 5, 36, 44, 77
Bent's New Fort, Colo., 28, 36
Bent's Old Fort, Colo., 3, 5, 6, 7, 12, 13, 19, 22, 24, 27, 28, 32, 34, 36, 37, 44, 45, 52, 74, 124, 126, 130, 134
Berthoud, Colo., 83
Berthoud Pass, Colo., 90
Big Bend station, Colo., 124
Big Thompson River, Colo., 7, 17, 42, 83, 84, 85
Big Thompson station, Colo., 124, 130
Bijou Creek, Colo., 11
Bitter Creek, Wyo., 8, 16, 17, 24, 94, 96, 97, 99, 104, 105, 108, 109, 110, 111, 113, 136
Black Forest (The Pineries), Colo., 4, 7, 10, 25, 53, 54, 55, 60, 61, 62, 68, 134
"Black Hills." *See* Laramie Mountains
Black Squirrel Creek, Colo., 4, 7, 20, 39, 42, 53, 55, 58, 60, 61, 62
Blackfoot Cave, Colo., 7, 54, 55
Blacks Fork, Wyo., 8, 95
Bliss, Edward, 29, 87
Bonner Spring, Colo., 88
Boone's station, Colo., 124
Booneville, Colo., 124, 130, 131
Boswell Ranch, Wyo., 26, 95
Boulder, Colo., 83
Boulder Creek, Colo., 42, 83
Boulder Ridge, Wyo., 95
Bridge to Nowhere, Colo., 68
Bridger, Jim, 8, 16, 28, 96, 104, 105, 119, 120
Bridger Pass, Wyo., 16, 17, 24, 26, 28, 94, 104, 105, 106, 109, 137
Brighton, Colo., 130
Brighton Blvd., Colo., 25, 72, 74, 134
Brown, John, 13, 28, 39, 45
Brown, John Lowery, 17, 18, 28, 29, 70, 79, 84, 87, 94, 114, 115
Browns Hole (Park), Colo., 6, 8, 11, 12, 18, 27, 92, 95, 105, 114, 118, 136
Brush Corral, Colo., 53, 55, 60
Bryan, Francis T., 28, 29, 30, 96, 97, 100, 102, 105, 109, 111

Bryan's Crossing (Johnson Island), Wyo., 21, 24, 26
Bryan's Road, Wyo., 100, 102
Buffalo Highway, 132, 133
Burlington (St. Vrain) station (Longmont), Colo., 124, 130
Burns, Wyo., 82
Butterfield, David, 29, 63, 69
Butterfield Overland Despatch (BOD), 63, 69

Cache la Poudre River, Colo., 4, 5, 6, 7, 13, 14, 15, 16, 19, 20, 22, 24, 25, 28, 29, 42, 43, 64, 69, 74, 75, 78, 79, 80, 82, 83, 84, 86, 87, 90, 133, 134
California, 3, 10, 15, 17, 18, 21, 22, 23, 26, 28, 32, 34, 39, 84, 95, 105, 118, 119
California Ranch, Colo., 63
California Trail, 95, 119, 120. *See also* Oregon-California Trail
Camp Collins, Colo., 127
Caney, Kans., 32
Carrington, Albert, 28, 96, 102, 104
Carson, Kit, 11, 74, 75
Castle Rock, Colo., 11, 134
Castle Rocks, Wyo., 82
Central Overland California & Pikes Peak Express Company, 23
Cherokee City Post Office, Colo., 24, 130
Cherokee Indians, 3, 28, 30, 33
Cherokee Peak, Wyo., 21
Cherokee Rim, Wyo., 95, 117
Cherokee (Stonewall, Tenmile) station, Colo., 124
Cherry Creek, Colo., 4, 7, 10, 14, 15, 17, 18, 19, 21, 22, 23, 25, 30, 42, 43, 53, 54, 55, 63, 65, 70, 71, 128, 133, 134
Cherry Creek Post Office, Colo., 130, 131
Cherry Creek Reservoir State Park, Colo., 22, 67, 69, 134

Cheyenne, Wyo., 24, 29, 82, 110, 126, 133
Cheyenne Indians, 19, 39
Chico, Calif., 120
Chico Creek, Colo., 7, 17, 44, 45, 46
Chico Creek Cutoff, Colo., 17, 44, 45, 46, 49, 50
Chimney Rock, Colo., 9, 95, 115
Choteau, Auguste Pierre, 32
Church's (12 Mile) station, Colo., 124
Cimarron Cutoff, 34
Cimarron River, 34
Clear Creek, Colo., 7, 25, 42, 83, 84, 85
Coad Mountain, Wyo., 101
Colorado Central Railroad, 126, 133
Colorado City, Colo., 29, 127, 128, 129
Colorado Highway 83: 63, 68, 133, 134
Colorado Springs, Colo., 4, 25, 49, 53, 68, 126
Colorado to Gulf Highway, 132
Continental Divide, 18, 24, 26, 81, 94, 95, 96, 104, 105, 106, 107, 115, 127
Coody's Bluff, Okla., 32
Cooke, Philip St. George, 13, 28, 42, 65, 76
Cooper Creek, Wyo., 94, 97
Crow Creek, Colo., 5, 13, 82, 90
Currant Creek, Wyo., 26, 95, 114, 136

Dale Creek, 42, 86, 87, 90
Dallas-Canadian-Denver Highway, 132
Daugherty, Jimmy, 7, 10, 53, 55
Denver, Colo., 4, 7, 17, 20, 21, 22, 23, 24, 25, 54, 63, 64, 68, 69, 74, 81, 83, 90, 105, 124, 126, 127, 130, 131, 134
Denver Laramie & Northwestern Railroad, 90
Denver Longmont & Northwestern Railroad, 126, 133
Denver & New Orleans (Colorado & Southern) Railroad, 29, 53, 60, 62, 72, 126, 130, 132, 133
Denver Pacific Railroad, 24, 29, 126, 133

Denver Post, 68
Denver & Rio Grande Railroad, 24, 29, 61, 126, 128, 129, 132
Denver Utah & Pacific Railroad, 126, 133
Denver-Black Hills Highway, 133
Devil's Gate, Wyo., 11
Dodge, Grenville M., 29, 96, 105, 109
Dodge, Henry, 4, 27, 44, 81
Donner emigrant party, 28, 120
Donner Spring, Ut., 121
Drake, Lester, 72
DuBois, John Van Deusen, 39, 45, 55, 70, 84
Durley, Jeff, 29, 79

Easton Post Office, Colo., 39, 53, 60, 130, 131
Eastonville (Easton) Colo., 53, 60, 61, 62, 130
El Dorado, Kans., 32
Elbert County, Colo., 25, 69, 72
Elbert Post Office, Colo., 130, 131
Elbert, Samuel, 72
Elizabeth, Colo., 133
Elk Mountain (Medicine Bow Butte), Wyo., 9, 12, 16, 18, 20, 24, 26, 28, 94, 97, 100, 101, 102, 105, 108, 137, 138
Elko, Nev., 120
Encampment, Wyo., 9, 26, 30, 122, 137
Encampment River, Wyo., 95
Engels, William H., 28, 55, 79, 84
Evans, Hugh, 27, 45
Evans, John, 72
Evans, Lewis, 15, 16, 17, 26, 28, 32, 94, 96, 97, 100, 108
Evans Post Office, Colo., 130
Evans Road (Trail), 16, 17, 20, 21, 32, 96, 100, 102. 104, 109
Evanston, Wyo., 29

Fagan, Charles Michael, 7, 20, 21, 22, 23, 25, 54, 55, 58, 59
Falcon, Colo., 25, 132, 134
Farnham, Thomas J., 27, 45

Field, Matt, 45
Fitch, Julian, 39
Five Buttes, Wyo., 95, 117
Flaming Gorge National Recreation Area, Wyo., 26, 95, 136
"Foothills" of Colorado, 42, 43, 64, 83, 84, 129, 133
Fort Bridger, Wyo., 3, 8, 16, 17, 18, 20, 21, 23, 24, 26, 28, 29, 39, 58, 94, 95, 105, 109, 114, 119, 120, 121, 136
Fort Collins, Colo., 7, 52, 78, 90, 126, 134, 135
Fort Crockett, Colo., 6, 8, 12, 27, 95, 105, 114
Fort Hall, Id., 27, 120
Fort Jackson, Colo., 5, 6, 7, 25, 27, 74, 76
Fort Kearny, Nebr., 22, 28
Fort Laramie, Wyo., 4, 10, 12, 13, 14, 15, 19, 22, 23, 27, 28, 36, 48, 82, 105
Fort Leavenworth, Kans., 19, 28
Fort Lupton, Colo., 5, 6, 7, 11, 13, 20, 25, 27, 74, 76, 124, 130, 134
Fort Lyon, Colo., 127
Fort Morgan, Colo., 24, 81
Fort Morgan Cutoff, Colo., 24, 29, 35, 69, 72, 81, 83
Fort Smith, Ark., 28
Fort St. Vrain, Colo., 5, 6, 7, 10, 11, 13, 14, 15, 20, 23, 25, 27, 39, 52, 70, 74, 75, 76, 77, 83, 92, 130
Fort Steele, Wyo., 137
Fort Union, N.M., 20, 23, 29, 30, 39, 58
Fort Vasquez, Colo., 5, 6, 7, 25, 27, 74, 75, 76, 77, 124, 134
Fountain, Colo., 25, 53, 130
Fountain City, Colo., 49, 50
Fountain Creek, Colo., 4, 5, 7, 10, 11, 13, 15, 17, 19, 21, 22, 23, 25, 42, 43, 44, 49, 50, 51, 55, 128, 132, 134
Four Mile House, Colo., 7, 25, 63, 64, 65, 67, 124, 134
Fowler, Jacob, 4, 27, 48, 49, 50

Fraeb, Henry, 5, 12, 95, 115
Fraeb's Fort, Wyo., 12, 95, 115
Franklin, William, 12, 28, 39, 40, 74, 76
Franktown, Colo., 4, 7, 25, 54, 63, 68, 124, 130, 131, 133, 134
Frémont, John C., 10, 16, 27, 28, 39, 50, 52, 74, 75, 76, 82, 87, 92, 94, 97, 100, 101, 102, 105, 108, 114, 115
Fremonts Fort, Colo., 11

Gantt, John, 7, 44, 45
Gantt's Fort, Colo., 7, 44, 45
Garden of the Gods, Colo., 128
Gardner, James Frank, 7, 63
Gass, A. M., 29, 50, 55
General Land Office (GLO), 30, 31, 39, 142, 143
Georgia, 3
Gilcrest, Colo., 25, 75
Gilpin, William, 29
Glacier to Gulf Highway, 132
Gomer, Phillip, 72
Goshen Hole, Wyo., 14, 82
Grand Saline, Okla., 32
Granger, Wyo., 8, 17, 99, 110, 136
Grayback Ridge, Colo., 86, 88
Great Divide Basin, Wyo., 9, 16, 20, 94, 96, 104, 106, 107, 108, 109
Great Salt Lake, Ut., 16, 120, 121
Greeley, Colo., 5, 7, 42, 52, 74, 75, 78, 80, 89, 90, 126, 131, 134
Greeley, Horace, 7, 23, 29, 39, 70, 79, 83, 84
Greeley Salt Lake & Pacific Railroad, 126, 133
Green River, Wyo., 8, 16, 26, 94, 95, 96, 99, 108, 113, 114
Green River (town), Wyo., 109, 112, 113, 136
Gunnison, John, 17, 28, 36, 48, 96

Harper, Joseph P., 60, 61
Hartley, William, 39
Hastings Cutoff, 3, 8, 26, 28, 94, 95, 119, 120, 121

Hastings, Landsford, 120
Hayden, Ferdinand, 18, 29, 115
Hayne's Ranch Post Office, Colo., 130
Henrys Fork, Wyo., 8, 27, 95, 114
Holladay, Ben, 24, 29, 69, 78, 81, 83, 94, 105, 109, 124, 125
"Hook & Moore Glade," Colo., 86
Horse Creek, Wyo., 82
Huerfano Butte, Colo., 134
Huerfano River, Colo., 48, 134
Hughes Post Office, Colo., 130
Humboldt River, Nev., 120
Hundley, Ellen, 18, 28, 55, 65, 87

Independence, Mo., 5
Independence Camp, Colo., 7, 49, 50
Inspiration Point Park, Colo., 83, 85
Interstate 25: 25, 49, 53, 58, 68, 128, 132, 133, 134, 135
Interstate 80: 26, 94, 105, 110, 111, 121, 136, 137, 138, 139

Jack Creek, Wyo., 9
James, Edwin, 14, 52
James Peak, Colo., 52
Jimmy Camp, Colo., 4, 7, 13, 21, 22, 23, 53, 55, 56, 60, 128, 134
Jimmy Camp Creek, Colo., 4, 7, 25, 42, 49, 53
Jimmy Camp Road (Trail), Colo., 4, 35, 39, 53, 55, 61, 127, 128
Johnson Island, Wyo. *See* Bryan's Crossing
Jones, John S., 72, 73
Julesburg, Colo., 24, 79, 81, 90

Kansas, 22, 32, 34, 44
Kansas Pacific Railroad, 34, 36, 60, 69, 72, 126
Kearny, Stephen Watts, 12, 40, 44, 82
Killpecker Creek, Wyo., 94, 96, 108, 136
Kingsbury, Lt. Gaines, 27, 45, 70
Kiowa Creek, Colo., 13, 53
Kit Carson, Colo., 34, 61

L'Amour, Louis, 3, 125
La Junta, Colo., 5, 7, 24, 34, 44
LaGrange, Wyo., 82
LaRamie, Jacques, 7, 9
Laporte, Colo., 7, 16, 17, 24, 25, 78, 79, 80, 81, 83, 84, 86, 90, 124, 130, 131, 134
Laramie, Wyo., 9, 26, 110, 127
Laramie Mountains ("Black Hills"), 6, 7, 16, 18, 25, 27, 42, 43, 78, 86, 87, 89, 90, 94, 97, 108, 133
Laramie Plains, Wyo., 11, 16, 17, 18, 20, 24, 26, 27, 78, 89, 94, 95, 97, 98, 108, 116
Laramie River, Wyo., 6, 18, 94, 95, 97, 115
Lassen's Rancho, Calif., 120
Latham, Colo., 24, 78, 79, 124, 130
Leavenworth, Kans., 52, 124
Leavenworth & Pikes Peak Express (L&PPX), 29, 72, 73, 124
Liberty, Colo., 131
Lincoln Highway, 26, 105, 107, 108, 110, 111, 112, 113, 133, 136, 137, 139
Little Buttes station, Colo., 124
Little Laramie River, Wyo., 94, 137
Little Snake River, 6, 9, 12, 95, 114, 117
Little Thompson River, Colo., 42, 83
Little Thompson station, Colo., 124, 130
Livermore, Colo., 86, 88, 89, 131
Lodgepole Creek, 24, 79, 81, 82, 90, 108
Long, Stephen, 4, 7, 14, 27, 42, 52, 74, 81
Longabaugh, Henry (Sundance Kid), 95
Longmont, Colo., 17, 25, 83, 126, 130, 131, 134
Longs Peak, Colo., 7, 77, 135
Loring, William W., 20, 22, 29, 54, 58, 100, 102, 108, 111
Louisiana Purchase, 27
Loveland, Colo., 17, 25, 83, 130, 131, 134

Lower Powder (Sulphur) Spring, Wyo., 6, 8, 18, 95, 114, 118
Lupton, Lancaster, 5, 7, 11, 27, 74, 76

Manitou Springs, Colo., 49, 128
Marcy, Randolph B., 3, 20, 21, 22, 29, 30, 39, 53, 54, 55, 58, 60, 65, 96, 97, 100, 102, 104, 108, 109, 111, 140
Mathews, Carl, 60
McPherson, Kans., 3, 32, 33
"Medicine Bow Butte," Wyo. See Elk Mountain
Medicine Bow Mountains, Wyo., 18, 26, 94, 95, 97, 98, 103, 115, 116
Melvin, Jane, 64, 65
Milk Fort, Colo., 7, 44, 45
Mills, Robert, 115
"Mississippi Saints," 13, 14, 28, 49, 82
Missouri, 23, 32, 36, 84
Mitchell, James, 17, 28
Modena, Mariano, 83
Monument Creek, Colo., 4, 11, 53, 128, 132
Moody, Ralph, 38
Moore's station, Colo., 124
Mormon Battalion, 44, 49
Mormon Campaign, 20, 108
Mormons, 13, 14, 28, 44, 49, 53, 82, 119
Mormontown, Colo., 7, 44, 45, 47, 49
Mountain Home, Wyo., 95
Muddy Creek, Wyo., 26, 95, 105

Namaqua (Loveland), Colo., 7, 17, 83, 84, 85, 124, 130, 131, 134
National Old Trails Road, 132
National Park-to-Park Highway, 132
Nebraska, 81
Neosho (Grand) River, Okla., 32
Nevada, 95, 119
New Mexico, 14, 22, 23
Nine Mile House, Colo., 63, 124
Nine Mile (Sand Creek) station, Colo., 124
North Carolina, 3

North Flat Top Mountain, Wyo., 95
North (New) Park, Colo., 6, 12, 18, 26, 27, 28, 36, 92, 95, 115, 127, 137
North Platte River, 3, 9, 12, 20, 21, 23, 24, 26, 28, 42, 48, 82, 86, 92, 94, 97, 98, 100, 102, 103, 115, 137
Northgate Canyon, 95, 115
Nowata, Okla., 32

Oakes, Daniel C., 72, 73, 142, 143
Oklahoma, 3, 32
Old Pueblo Road, Colo., 49, 134
Olney Springs, Colo., 24
Oregon, 120
Oregon Trail, 3, 35, 78, 96, 136. *See also* Oregon-California Trail
Oregon-California Trail, 3, 8, 10, 11, 17, 18, 19, 26, 28, 69, 81, 82, 94, 95, 99, 104, 105, 106, 108, 119, 120
Oscrosse, Carl (grave), Wyo., 98
Outlaw Trail, 95
Overland Stage Line, 3, 16, 24, 29, 74, 78, 79, 81, 83, 86, 87, 94, 105, 108, 109, 112, 119, 124, 125
Overland Trail, 8, 16, 17, 26, 35, 69, 79, 88, 91, 94, 98, 99, 100, 101, 102, 106, 111, 113, 125, 136, 137, 138
Overton Road, Colo., 25, 49
Ovid, Colo., 81
Owl Canyon, Colo., 86, 87, 88
Owl Creek, Colo., 42

Palmer Lake, Colo., 4, 129
Parker, Colo., 25, 29, 30, 63, 64, 66, 126, 130, 133, 134
Parker, James Sample, 64
Parker, Robert LeRoy (Butch Cassidy), 95
Parker, Samuel, 104
Parkman, Francis, 14, 15, 28, 45, 53, 55, 65, 75, 76
Parsons, William B., 22, 29, 39, 50
Pass Creek, Wyo., 9, 16, 94, 100, 101, 137
Patterson, E. H. N., 29, 87
Patterson, Mary, 114

Peck, Robert M., 19, 21, 28, 39, 44, 70, 76
Pick Bridge, Wyo., 26, 94, 103
Pierce, James H., 72
Pierson's station, Colo., 124
Pike, Zebulon, 4, 27, 52
Pikes Peak, Colo., 7, 14, 19, 21, 27, 44, 45, 49, 52, 56, 57, 74, 128, 134, 135
Pilot Peak, Nev., 121
Pine Grove Post Offce, Colo., 63, 66, 130, 131
Piney Creek, Colo., 22, 63, 69
Placerville, Calif., 120
Platteville, Colo., 24, 25, 74, 75
Plum Creek, Colo., 4, 11, 53, 128, 132
Point of Rocks, Colo., 4, 7, 14, 20, 21, 25, 54, 55, 57, 58
Point of Rocks, Wyo., 8, 17, 94, 96, 99, 108, 109, 110, 112, 113, 136
Point of Rocks station, Colo., 124
Pony Express, 81, 104, 119, 136
Post, Charles, 29, 39, 45, 50, 55
"Potato Hills," Colo., 44, 45, 46
Powder River Trail (auto road), 133
Powder Spring, Wyo. *See* Lower Powder Spring
Powder Wash, 95
Powell, Philander, 45
Preuss, Charles, 92
Pueblo, Colo., 4, 7, 10, 11, 12, 14, 15, 17, 19, 20, 23, 24, 25, 27, 28, 29, 44, 45, 47, 48, 49, 69, 70, 82, 108, 124, 126, 127, 130, 131, 132, 134
Pyeatt, John Rankin, 15, 16, 28, 70, 76, 78, 79, 96

Quesenbury, William, 28, 84, 87, 114, 119

Ralston Creek, Colo., 7, 17, 22, 25, 70, 83, 84, 85
Ralston, Lewis, 7, 83
Ralston's Post Office, Colo., 130
Randolph & Lock, 6
Raton Pass, N.M., 5, 34, 42, 44

Rawlins, Wyo., 9, 11, 16, 20, 21, 24, 26, 30, 94, 98, 108, 110, 137
Rawlins Peak, Wyo., 20
Raynesford, Howard, 69
Red Desert, Wyo., 17, 26, 109, 136, 139
Richard (Reshaw), John, 14, 15
Richards, William A., 18, 29, 114
Richardson, Albert D., 29, 39, 52, 87, 128
Rio Grande, 48
Riverside, Wyo., 9, 26, 30, 95, 122, 137
Riverside Cemetery, Colo., 72, 73, 74
Rock Creek, Wyo., 94, 137, 138
Rock Springs, Wyo., 8, 17, 94, 95, 99, 108, 109, 110, 112, 113, 136
Rocky Ford, Colo., 17, 126, 132
Rocky Mountain Highway, 133
Rocky Mountain News (Denver), 45
Rocky Mountains, 19, 20, 24, 42, 43, 44, 53, 81, 96, 104, 105
Root, Frank, 24, 39, 79
Running Creek, Colo., 4, 42, 53, 54, 72
Running Turkey Creek, Kans., 32, 33
Russell, William Green, 7, 29, 54
Russellville, Colo., 7, 11, 23, 25, 54, 55, 64, 124, 130, 134
Russellville (East Cherry Creek) Gulch, Colo., 23, 42, 54

Sacramento, Calif., 120
Sage Creek, Wyo., 98, 102
Sage, Rufus B., 6, 45, 49, 50, 53, 54, 55, 58, 65, 76, 97, 114, 115
Salina, Okla., 32
Salt Lake City, Ut., 22, 23, 84, 119, 120
Salt Wells, Wyo., 109, 112
San Luis Valley, 4, 27, 44, 48
Sangre de Cristo Pass, Colo., 4, 36, 44, 47, 48
Santa Fe, N.M., 32, 34, 36, 44
Santa Fe Trail, 3, 5, 19, 22, 24, 27, 32, 33, 34, 35, 36, 42, 44, 69, 134
Saratoga, Wyo., 26, 30, 94, 95, 107, 127, 137
Sarpy, Peter, 5
Savery, Wyo., 9, 95

Savery Creek, Wyo., 12, 95, 105, 115
Sedgewick, John, 19, 28
Seventeen Mile House, Colo., 7, 63, 124
Seymour, Silas, 29, 87
Sherwood station, Colo., 124
Shortess, Robert, 27, 114
Sierra Madre Mountains, Wyo., 9, 18, 26, 95, 103, 105
Simon, Ben, 17
Slade, Jack, 7, 86, 87, 125
Smith, E. Willard, 5, 6, 17, 27, 76, 87, 114, 115
Smiths Fork, Wyo., 8, 95
Smoky Hill Road, Colo., 22, 63, 69
Smoky Hill Trail, 22, 23, 25, 29, 34, 35, 63, 64, 65, 66, 67, 69, 124
South Park, Colo., 128
South Pass, Wyo., 3, 12, 23, 29, 78, 81, 94, 104, 106, 108, 109
South Platte River, Colo., 4, 5, 6, 7, 10, 13, 14, 15, 16, 17, 18, 19, 20, 21, 22, 23, 24, 25, 27, 42, 43, 48, 54, 63, 64, 69, 70, 71, 74, 76, 78, 79, 80, 81, 82, 83, 84, 86, 90, 105, 108, 133, 134
South Platte River Trail, 35, 69, 74, 81
"Spanish fort," Colo., 48
Spanish Peaks, Colo., 7, 44
Sportsman Lake, Wyo., 95, 115
Spotswood, Robert, 86
Spring Bottom station, Colo., 124
St. Vrain, Ceran, 7, 10, 36, 75
St. Vrain Creek, Colo., 7, 17, 42, 83, 84, 114
St. Vrain Post Office, Colo., 130
Stansbury, Howard, 16, 17, 28, 30, 96, 97, 100, 102, 105, 108, 111
Steamboat Rock, Colo., 7, 86, 87, 89, 125
Steele, John, 14, 28, 45, 55
Stonewall Creek, Colo., 42
Sublette, Andrew W., 27, 75, 77
Sugar Creek, Wyo., 9, 21, 94, 97
Sumner, Edwin, 19, 28, 82
Sweetwater River, Wyo., 94, 105, 108

Tahlequah, Okla., 32, 33
Taos, N.M., 4, 6, 10, 11, 15, 21, 27, 36, 39, 44, 48, 49, 82
Taos Trail, 4, 35, 44, 48, 49, 82. *See also* Trappers Trail
Teds Place, Colo., 25, 78, 86
Tennessee, 3
Terrell House station, Colo., 124
Texas, 23, 28
Thayer, Wyo., 112
The Buttes, Colo., 7, 49, 50, 51
Thompson, Phillip, 5, 7
Tie Siding, Wyo., 9, 26, 86, 89, 94, 95, 116, 137
Tierney, Luke, 21, 22, 29, 50, 55, 84
Timnath, Colo., 78
Trail of Tears, 3, 33
Trappers, 12, 19, 45, 49, 75
Trappers Trail, 4, 5, 10, 11, 13, 14, 19, 27, 28, 29, 35, 44, 48, 49, 53, 74, 82, 128. *See also* Taos Trail
Trinidad, Colo., 34, 134
Tug Rock, Colo., 89
Twelve Mile House, Colo., 7, 63, 64, 65, 124
Twenty Mile House (Pine Grove), Colo., 7, 63, 64, 65, 66, 124
Twenty-five Mile House, Colo., 124
Twin Groves, Wyo., 9, 18, 26, 27, 95, 105, 106, 107, 115, 117

U. S. Highway 24: 134
U. S. Highway 30: 105, 110, 111, 136
U. S. Highway 50: 132, 134
U. S. Highway 85: 68, 128, 132, 133, 134
U. S. Highway 87: 68, 132, 133
U. S. Highway 285: 133
U. S. Highway 287: 16, 17, 25, 26, 83, 86, 88, 89, 91, 133, 134, 137
Union Pacific Railroad, 24, 26, 29, 30, 81, 90, 91, 96, 104, 108, 109, 110, 111, 112, 113, 119, 121, 126, 133, 137, 139
Utah, 28, 29, 30, 95, 105

Van Wormer, Isaac P., 72
Vasquez, Louis, 5, 7, 27, 28, 75, 77, 119
Verdigris River, Okla., 32
Vermillion Creek, Wyo., 6, 8, 12, 95
Villard, Henry, 29, 39, 63, 65
Virginia Dale, Colo., 7, 86, 87, 88, 89, 90, 91, 124, 125, 130, 134
Voorhees, Augustus, 7, 21, 29, 30, 39, 50, 55, 128

Wagonhound Creek, Wyo., 100, 137, 138
Weir, Austin H., 60
Weir's Mill (CO), 53, 60, 61, 62
Wells Fargo, 29, 69, 112
West Bijou Creek, Colo., 11
West Kiowa Creek, Colo., 4, 42, 54, 57
Wheatland, Colo., 131
Wilkins, Wyo., 112
Williams, J. L., 90
Willing, George M., 22, 23, 29, 30, 39, 45, 50, 55, 65
Willow Creek, Wyo., 42
Windsor, Colo., 78
Wislizenus, Frederick A., 6, 27, 114
Wood Valley Post Office, Colo., 130
Woods Landing, Wyo., 26, 95, 116, 137
Woodward, Benjamin F., 72
Wyocolo, Wyo., 26

Yampa River, Colo., 12